W9-COL-056

ALSO BY

ALEXANDER MAKSIK

You Deserve Nothing
A Marker to Measure Drift
Shelter in Place

THE LONG CORNER

Alexander Maksik

THE LONG CORNER

Europa Editions
27 Union Square West, Suite 302
New York, NY 10003
www.europaeditions.com
info@europaeditions.com

This book is a work of fiction. Any references to historical events, real people, or real locales are used fictitiously.

First Publication 2022 by Europa Editions

Library of Congress Cataloging in Publication Data is available
ISBN 978-1-60945-751-8

Maksik, Alexander
The Long Corner

Art direction by Emanuele Ragnisco
instagram.com/emanueleragnisco

Cover design by Ginevra Rapisardi

Cover image: *The Dream* by Henri Rousseau 1910 (detail) / FineArt Alamy Stock Photo

Prepress by Grafica Punto Print – Rome

Printed in Canada

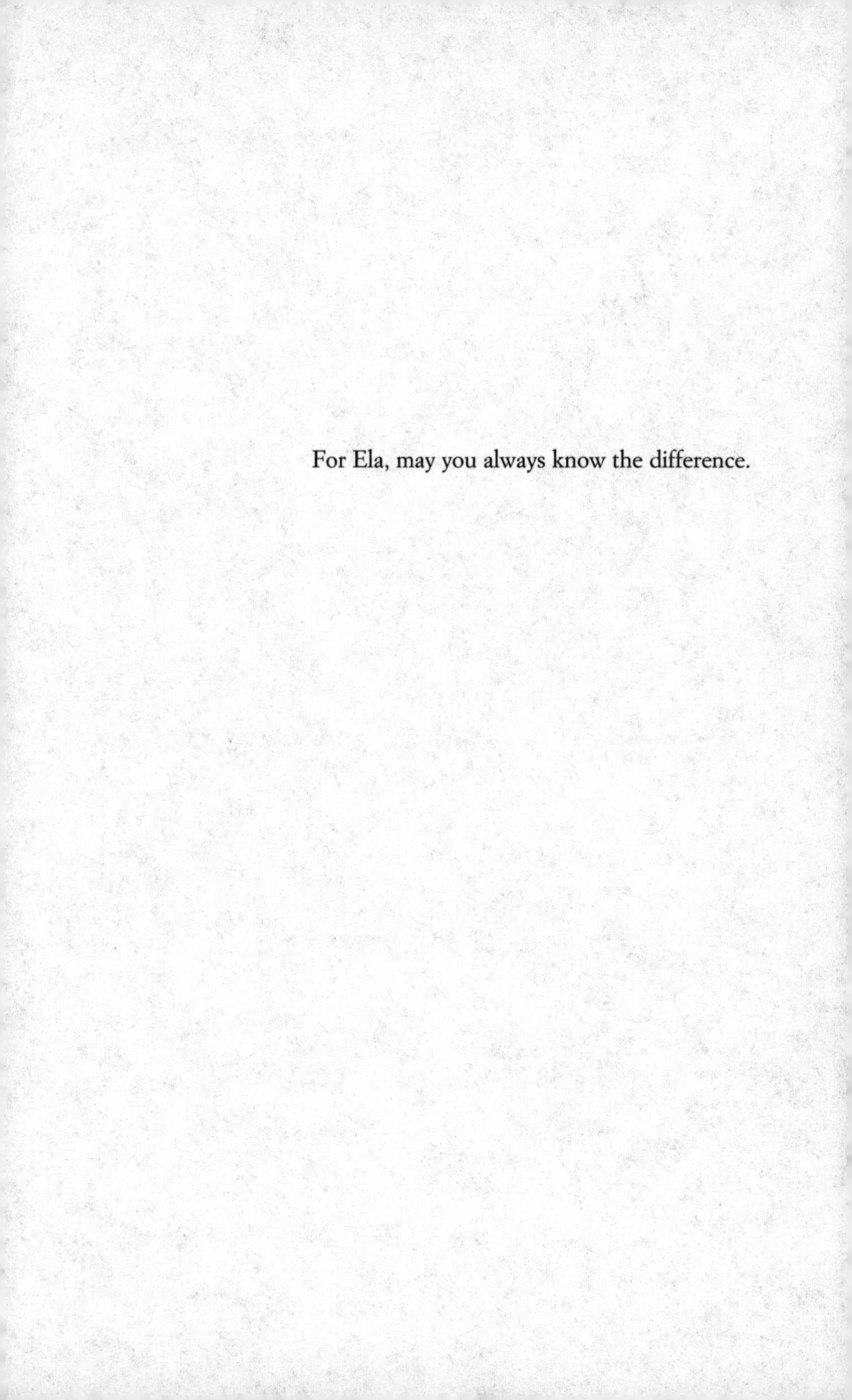

For Ela, may you always know the difference.

Part One

The art of any period tends to serve the ideological interests of the ruling class.

—John Berger, *Ways of Seeing*

1

Not long after Donald John Trump was elected president of the United States of America and all the fires he lit were just beginning to burn, Charity Joy Strickler dragged me to yet another concrete-floored room where I was expected to conduct myself in such a manner as would not embarrass her. In all ways, it was winter in New York City.

The room, which our jargon-drunk cohort referred to as a *space*, was an art gallery on West 24th Street. Though booze, not art, was the point that evening, I do remember the walls adorned with a great many skulls and crossbones repeated round and round in a variety of fluorescent pinks and yellows, blues and greens.

We were gathered there before those bright pirate flags to usher Manswood Bourbon into the American marketplace, a spirit which, to believe the promotional material, had been conceived and crafted by a famous film actor. It was Charity herself who had written those dark materials, Charity who had chaired the festivities and Charity who, at the very moment the ground began to shift beneath me, was addressing an attentive murder of pale people dressed in one version or another of the same old drab uniform.

The majority of our time together was spent at gatherings much like these and I can recall not a single event that wasn't in some way or another in service of our work. Hers was a two birds/one stone approach to living and from the moment we met there would be no distinction between our personal and professional lives. She was devoted to the twin gods of Efficiency and Usefulness, and little made her happier than a well-directed party that served to improve our lives.

Two weeks before the Manswood event, we'd stuffed ourselves into an underground bar accessed through a secret door in another bar. The former was all red velvet, waxed mustaches and old fashioned forty-dollar Old Fashioneds, while the latter was two-for-one Pabst Blue Ribbons in the can for hoi polloi. We were there to celebrate the birthday of either the CEO of a company that made hydrophobic yoga tights or the first anniversary of Mind GApp, an irritatingly slick meditation application for "sophisticated urbanites and restless globe roamers," in which Charity had invested not an insignificant amount of money.

Our days in those days bled into our nights. We traveled from home to work to space to home. All borders were dissolved. There was, as Charity liked to tell me, "Only life, only now," a phrase she'd learned from Mind GApp's disembodied Englishman.

And now here we were again this Manswood evening, Charity standing atop a block-stenciled crate in a tasteful black cocktail dress, recounting the bourbon's voyage from grain to bottle, while behind her dangled a blue neon sign:

Manswood
Bourbon is Life, Life is Bourbon

"These were the corn fields of his childhood," she was saying, "where he played hide and seek, where he dreamed of a better life, where he began his journey."

For Charity then, everything was a journey: our relationship, our careers, our diets, our bodies, ourselves. In her polished way, she was charming up there, speaking with the verve and conviction of a zealot, so easily balanced upon her barnwood bourbon box, recounting the twangy movie star's dream of a perfect potion, his exigent palate, the many years of tasting, the moment, at long last, when that amber elixir, the very color of his thick locks, flowed across those famously voluptuous lips.

"And now," she said, coming to climax, lofting the bottle high, "a dream has been realized which we are all here to celebrate. Once upon a time a little boy lay in a field of corn and dreamed of movies. And once upon a time a man lay in a field of corn and dreamed of that boy. And out of that dream came a bourbon unlike any other."

The audience stood stiller, fell quieter, not because of any interest in the details of her ridiculous origin story, but because maybe, just maybe, the man himself might materialize. Whether or not he did, I cannot say because it was then that I saw, leaning between two pink-skulled panels, a woman so golden, so vivid with life as to be utterly incongruous amongst all the dark-haloed eyes and hoary skin.

She was aflame with health, radiating both vigor and serenity, and her simple presence in that place seemed to me a direct condemnation of my very existence. For a moment, I thought she must have been a figment of my fraying mind, but now she was traveling toward me in a long dress, its fabric too thin, too bright and too blue for that grim season, in that terrible year, in our sad city. Her brown shoulders were bare, a white scarf looped around her neck, hair black, long and lustrous, troubling wide-set eyes undecided between greens and browns.

"Mr. Fields?"

I nodded.

"Mr. Fields, I'm Plume," she said. "The Coded Garden."

I shook my head.

She took a step forward and looked directly into my eyes. She smelled of orange blossoms and coconut oil.

"Mr. Fields, I wrote to you. I asked whether you would be open to learning more. Yes, you said. You said you would be, that I should send you information."

"So that I could learn more?"

"Yes."

"About a coded garden."

"*The* Coded Garden, yes."

"I'm sorry," I said, starting to laugh, "I really am sorry."

I looked around the room. I thought maybe it was a joke, but I knew no one who would have played it. Charity was too tedious for such inspiration, her imagination reserved for the shiny binaries of virulent capitalism and merciless self-improvement. And I didn't have any friends who had the verve for such a thing. Really, I didn't have any friends at all. Though I did know people. God, I knew so many people and not even one of them possessed the capacity for real trouble or true fun.

Now she offered me a variety of smile—kind, slightly pitying, totally devoid of irony—not readily available in New York City at the close of 2016.

"Mr. Fields, is there somewhere we might sit and talk for a moment, or do you need to be present for this?" She turned her hands out at the waist, raised her chin at the crowd, indicating the spectacle unfolding around us. For a moment she appeared to me like the world's most beautiful Christ.

I looked over at Charity, who in that instant had the side of her head mashed against that of a woman with frighteningly large eyes. The two of them were just then contorting their faces into bizarre expressions of false joy while engaging in the familiar ritual of self-portraiture.

"I do not need to be present for this," I said.

A few blocks away, at a quiet wine bar, she thanked me for my time.

"Truth be told, I'd have left that party with anyone who'd asked."

"How sad," she said.

Disconcerting, Plume. Sincerity blended with such beauty. Affectless affect. Spaced-out confidence, energetic eyes.

"Mr. Fields, I sent you several emails."

"So you said."

"About The Coded Garden."

"Right."

"And you don't remember?"

"I do not."

"Sebastian Light."

I shook my head. She sighed and looked away.

"I wrote to say that Sebastian Light greatly admired your profile of Ernst Frankel."

I nodded.

"The sculptor."

"I know who he is."

"Because you wrote the piece."

"Right, it would have been difficult to—"

She wasn't interested in my joke and seemed not at all amused by the absurdity of our dialogue.

"Did you not receive an award?"

"I did."

"Is it not a very prestigious award?"

"That was years ago."

"Well, in any case, in my letter I told you that Sebastian Light would very much like for you to come stay as his guest at The Coded Garden."

"It's a hotel?"

"It is not a hotel."

"What then?"

"None of what I'm telling you sounds familiar?"

"I'm sorry, no."

"But you are Solomon Fields?"

"Yes."

"And you wrote about Ernst Frankel, the sculptor?"

"Yes."

"And you don't remember our correspondence?"

I shook my head.

She sighed and looked out the window. "He told me it was like this in New York." She drew the meager scarf tighter around her throat. "'No one means anything here,' he said."

"Well that is certainly true."

She turned back and set her unsettling eyes on me. "Do you mean anything, Mr. Fields?"

We were entering another realm of the ludicrous and had she not been so beautiful, had I not been in such a tenuous state, had the ground in those days not been so unstable, I might have become annoyed, but this strange woman had arrived right on time, and I was very much enjoying our bizarre interlude, which, given the state of the nation, really seemed no stranger than anything else.

"Probably not," I said.

At last a waiter came by. I ordered a glass of wine. Plume ordered nothing. She looked like she lived on dew and sunlight.

"Mr. Fields, simply: Sebastian Light read your profile more than once. He found it beautiful. He was very impressed, very moved and he would like for you to come and stay."

"At The Coded Garden."

"Yes."

"Which is not a hotel."

"Correct."

"Will you remind me what it is?"

"A place for art. For beauty."

"An artist's colony?"

"If you like."

"I'm the furthest thing from a painter."

"Yes, that is, verbatim, what you wrote in your email."

"Forgive me. I receive so many emails, Plume. People want attention and they think I can provide it."

"Because you're a journalist."

"I'm not a journalist."

She raised her naked shoulders and shivered. "Well, you were once. I, too, was very moved by your profile. But whatever you are now, my forgiveness is irrelevant. What matters is that I am here. Sebastian Light has been preparing for a long time, but now he is ready, and he has sent me, quite literally, halfway around the world to have with you a single conversation. I am not here to speak with anyone else. I arrived yesterday and I will leave tomorrow."

"All to invite me to stay at an artist's colony."

She blinked twice.

"Because I once wrote twenty thousand words on a sculptor?"

"Yes. Will you accept his offer?"

"I know nothing about you, about this Light character. I don't know what a Coded Garden might be or do. I don't know, now that I think about it, even how you found me tonight. So, if you'd like to send some information, point me to a website, I'll be happy to look, but I have a job here, a fiancée, a—"

"The person on the box?"

"Yes," I said, laughing. "The person on the box."

She pressed her lips together, squinted as if she'd just tasted something rotten and then went on, "As I told you in my email, there is no website. He is very much against technology, but I can assure you that The Coded Garden is exquisitely beautiful and, in so many senses, so far away from here. You will be made very comfortable. You will be treated well. You may stay for as long or as short a time as you like. Sebastian Light wants only for you to witness what he has made."

"What has he made?"

She sighed. "Do you always require so much information before you make a decision?"

"Yes."

"Is that because you're a journalist?"

"I'm not a journalist."

"What are you then?"

I looked away from her to find the waiter bringing two glasses of water and my wine.

"Listen," Plume said. "I am here for one reason, to tell you that Sebastian Light would like for you to write about him. I would like to return with good news."

"So, you want more than for me to witness what he has made."

"Is writing not a kind of witnessing, Mr. Fields?"

I laughed, but her placid expression didn't change.

"I don't write that kind of thing anymore. I'm sorry."

"What kind of thing do you write?"

"Advertising."

"Well," she said, "He'll be disappointed."

She slid a black business card across the table. It was embossed in gold letters.

"You may send me an email. Or call."

She stood up, I left a twenty on the table and followed her. Outside on the street in that sharp-hipped, razor-jawed neighborhood, I was unnerved by her soft beauty.

"You should get back to your party, Mr. Fields. To your person on the box. To your *life*."

She leaned forward and gently pressed her lips to my neck. Then she left me standing in the dim light of the wine bar vestibule watching her descend 10th Avenue. It was only as she was being swallowed by a pack of bankers that I noticed she wore no coat.

2

When I was fifteen years old, Arthur Fields (né Feldstein), my father, went out for Newports wearing his captain's hat and bushy gray mustache and never came back.

About this, my mother liked to quote Leonard Cohen, the only man she said she ever truly loved: "I risked my life, but not to hear some country western song." She claimed to be more offended by being made the "butt of a cliché" than any dereliction or betrayal. As a result of my father's departure, my mother, a then-committed communist and ardent advocate of public education, was forced to abandon her post at Inglewood High School for a better-paying job at Intersections, an expensive and purportedly progressive private school in Santa Monica. About *this* she insisted that the shame and pain she felt serving the overserved was many times worse than that caused by her husband's disappearance.

My father, for all the time I knew him, was a salesman of a wide variety of items—siding, cars, meat, jewelry, loose diamonds—not all of which were his to sell. While he was around, at worst, my mother referred to him as a hustler and a dog. After he'd gone, she regularly referred to him as a "cowardly capitalist dirtbag." For my part, I remember him as warm and funny, a vague night ghost who smelled of cigarettes and beer, hiding squarely folded twenties under my pillow and between the pages of *Cuba for Beginners*. He was more ne'er-do-well uncle than father and, unlike my mother, I've never been able to muster much anger for the guy. I have always had a hard time hating the hapless.

"Your mother, kid," my father told me not long before leaving, "is no picnic." It was as close as he came to explaining his departure. He called her Char without any softness, hitting it hard like charcoal.

"Your grandfather called everyone 'kid,'" he told me looking wistful. "That's where I get it and maybe you'll keep the tradition going for us." Arthur's father, Benjamin Feldstein, a man long dead by the time I was born, once owned a flashy nightclub on Flatbush Avenue in Brooklyn. Frank Sinatra played there. Judy Garland. Johnny Mathis.

My father said Ben died under mysterious circumstances. My mother said there wasn't anything mysterious about the death of a man who doesn't pay his debts to the mob.

They had good banter, my mom and dad. Always chattering at each other. I liked to listen to them talk and when Arthur left, I missed them together more than I missed him alone.

"Good banter," my father told me, "is a Jewish thing."

For many years, I didn't understand what made us Jews. There was a mezuzah nailed outside our front door, but that was about it. There was no Shabbat, no Seder, no Hebrew school, no temple, no Bar Mitzvah. If there was another Jewish kid at Inglewood High, it was news to me. Not until my father left and my other shoved me into Intersections, that golden cauldron of Hollywood Jewry, did I know anything about "the Jewish community."

"We're secular Jews," my mother told me.

"Historical Jews," my father said.

"Atheist Jews," my mother said. "You know, Karl Marx was the descendant of rabbis, Soli. And he called religion the opiate of the masses."

For my eleventh birthday, she gave me that copy of *Cuba for Beginners.* Ché, Fidel and Karl in cartoons.

"How are we Jews if we don't believe in god?" I wanted to know.

"Soli, the Nazis didn't care what you believed," my father said.

"So that's why I'm a Jew? Because the Nazis would have killed me?"

"That's right, kid."

"Not so fucking simple, Arthur," my mother said. "There are other reasons."

"Like what, Char?"

"It's our heritage."

"Are we a race?" I wanted to know.

"No," my mother said. "Absolutely not."

"Of course we're a race," my father said.

"So, I'm not white?" This was a relief. I was one of about twelve white kids at school and I'd have given anything in those days to be black.

"You're definitely white," my mother told me.

"You're not white," my father said.

"Really? Can I say that at school?"

"If you want to get your jaw broken, sure," my mother told me and rolled her eyes at Arthur.

My father said, "You're Jewish because your parents are Jewish, and theirs before, theirs before that and so on all the way back, all right? And because of that you've got a certain disposition, a certain mind. You see?"

"What kind of disposition?"

"Scrappy, funny, depressed, anxious, worried, nervous, tough, nuts, smart. That you even want to know what makes you a Jew makes you a Jew."

"All Jews are like that?"

"No, Sol, don't listen to your father."

"All the Jews I ever met, yes," my father said. "It comes from our history. We are what we are because of the way we've had to live. If you spend thousands of years being murdered and mistrusted, well you're going to be different than people who spend thousands of years murdering and mistrusting. You see what I mean? Doesn't have anything to do with whether you believe in God or if you pray or where you pray. When they come knocking, you think they ask if you pray? Fuck no. They have a list, Soli, and if you're on it, you're dead. Ask Baba if you don't believe me. That's a woman who knows what it means to be a Jew."

"That's enough, Art." My mother couldn't stand her mother and she couldn't stand how much Arthur liked her.

"You ask why she calls herself a Jew, Soli. Next time Baba comes to visit, you ask her yourself. Your grandmother was raised to worship music and art and books. She never prayed in her life. What difference did that make?"

"Enough," my mother said.

The only thing they ever agreed upon was the importance of self-reliance. Any problem I had, I was to handle it myself. A bad teacher, a fight, algebra, a bully, whatever. Even permission slips bothered them. "You're twelve years old, make your own decisions," my mother said and taught me to forge her signature. "If you don't need anybody, kid, then you won't need anybody," my father told me.

On the other hand, after he disappeared, it turned out my mother *did* need somebody, and that was when Baba came to stay.

3

Baba was Karolina Klein, Charlotte's mother, my grandmother, Lina, who, maybe because she was scrappy, smart, and a little nuts, or maybe because she was lucky, managed, in the winter of 1940 to slip out of Berlin.

In October of that same year, her parents and two sisters were arrested and soon after, in Łódź, loaded into a highly efficient vehicle designed to use its own exhaust to annihilate its passengers. Lina, on the other hand, had gone to see a boy she loved, "a pretty goy painter with emerald eyes," when the Gestapo stopped by their apartment in Scheunenviertel. And because she was fortunate both in her timing and her beauty, her neighbor, Fritz Kurtz, hid her in his bedroom.

My grandmother used this word, hid, with a grin, raising those mean, black eyebrows, her only physical feature not soft, not light, not gentle, which made her startling, which offset what would otherwise have been an ordinary beauty. They served her as weapons of punctuation, accusation and comedy. When I was a child, I imagined all of her magic existed not in her bright eyes, which were the color of oiled pine, but there in her brows.

Fritz Kurtz hid her in his bed, until she escaped first his clutches and then the only city she'd ever known. From Germany she traveled to France, then to Spain, then to Portugal, eventually arriving alone on a crowded ship at New York harbor. It was the spring of 1941, a few days shy of her sixteenth birthday, and everyone she'd ever loved was dead or missing.

Fifty-eight years later, when I was myself nearly sixteen years old, she left New York for Los Angeles, where she did her best to take the place of my vanished father.

Thanks to Intersections, my mother had by then moved us from a grubby apartment in Playa del Rey, to a slightly bigger, slightly less grubby apartment in Santa Monica. Each of us had our own bedroom, but my grandmother and I shared a bathroom. She was restless, an insomniac, incapable of staying still, and in all hours of the night climbed into my bed, her voice still not yet entirely free of Berlin, offering aphorisms, advice and stories of her life.

When she'd first arrived in New York City, she bounced around the Lower East Side bereft, living with distant cousins, grandparents of old friends, people whose names had been written on scraps of cigarette packets and corners of ticket stubs. In the garment district she organized bins for a man she called "the king of fasteners, emperor of buttons, a dictatorial little fart."

I loved her for her irreverence, her refusal to modify language or subject for younger company. It was her wildness, her toughness, a perspective and humor that only suffering and abject terror can provide. She had an earned, inimitable quality, a stillness in the eyes. Unlike so many people I knew, who had suffered one terrible trauma or another, she had never gone dead blank, never lost her humor.

She was immune to my procrastinations, booby-traps, tricks and entreaties. She said, "Shut up, Solomon," and covered my mouth with her hand. "Against a survivor of the Holocaust, you cannot win. So, your father is gone. Poor you. The horrors of your homework? Your desire for ice cream? For sex? All meaningless. Now go to sleep." She pressed her lips to my forehead. "I love you, little rabbit."

I loved no one more. I have loved no one more.

After telling the emperor of buttons to go to hell, she took a job serving beer at Vasac Hall.

"Every Friday night after Shabbat services on Norfolk Street, I crossed Houston, walked up Avenue B to Tompkins Square Park, pushed my tits together and served beer and sausages to horny Poles ready for the weekend. You go out, Soli, into the night humming *The Song of Solomon*, what do you think is going to happen? Your mother won't ever forgive me for the way I lived. Never. But, I say, fuck her," she whispered, "I'd had enough of gloom and doom. I was after pleasure. I have always been. I will always be."

I heard some version of this last bit countless times. She was always for pleasure, for experience, for throwing everything she had in with the untamed and good-hearted. She loved artists and would eventually make her life with them. "I was a satellite, a groupie, a hanger-on, a model, a lover, a muse."

"Those are pretty words, Solomon," my mother said, "which all mean whore."

My grandmother laughed. "Charlotte confuses pleasure with sin."

I said, "Do you like art, Mom?"

She took a deep breath. I thought she might throw her glass at the wall, but instead, in her calmest, most terrifying voice she said, "If you don't work, if you have the time, it's nice to go to a museum, but don't ever believe, Sol, that your grandmother was *any* kind of artist."

"Tell that to the painters I fucked."

Lina Klein never lost those battles.

Later, after the yelling and the breaking of plates, my grandmother came to find me in my room.

"What artists do," she whispered, "I mean the real ones, is really the only thing that matters. Turning nothing at all into something beautiful. It is the essence of all wonder. If you grow up and find that you have no talent, Soli, get as close as you can to those who do. It's the next best thing. It might even be better."

From the minute she showed up, this is how she spoke to me. She said she loved *The Song of Solomon* because there was no mention of God. It's the most subversive text in the Torah, a little erotic poem some brilliant troublemaker slipped in among all the threats and fatherly disappointment. She went to Friday services because she loved that "dirty little song" and because she felt as if she were participating in a practical joke.

"Like a porno replacing a public safety film. The whole thing, Soli, is about sex, you know? The best kind of sex. Between unmarried people! Regular sex. Oral sex." And, she leaned in, raising those eyebrows of hers, and whispered, "one of them has dark skin, the other light. His thing is sweet as fruit, hers a garden of pomegranates. Pomegranates that need to be eaten! Their lips are honey and milk! Never shy away from sex, Sol. No matter what your mother says. Any chance you get, any variety you find, the stranger the better. There are two paths to joy—art and fucking."

And so, there we were in the summer of 1998, the three of us in a three-bedroom, two-bath apartment in Santa Monica, California. It was the summer of my father's disappearance and the beginning of my mother's slow, surprising transformation from Marxist-Leftist-Democrat to passionate Zionist and fervent supporter of the Israeli ultra-right.

"It's your mother's second adolescence," my grandmother whispered to me after a particularly nasty fight. "Don't worry. It's all to spite me, but you just can't out-Jew a Holocaust survivor."

"Oh, it's not like you survived the camps!" my mother said many times. But even this did not appear to disturb my unflappable grandmother.

Why did Charlotte hate her mother so much? Because Lina Klein knew my mother's father for about as long as it took to make my mother. Because she was beautiful, and my mother was not. Because she was unbearably lucky (aside, of course, from the small detail of her family being murdered, etc.). Because she was blithe and brave, bright and bawdy. Because she rejected a tedious moralism that my mother could not live without.

"And when a girl's mother is a bohemian free spirit, a hedonist, a little Lower East Side slut, King Solomon, well, then that girl grows up to have an asshole tight enough to crap diamonds. What can you do?" said Lina Klein to her sixteen-year-old grandson as they lay in bed together watching the dusty ceiling fan knock shadows around.

For three years, this was the woman with whom I shared a bathroom. The woman whose voice I heard both over the phone and in my mind as I lay awake those cold nights after my encounter with Plume, in the long, grim days leading up to the presidential inauguration, while Charity lay dead-still at my side dreaming of profits and purity.

In July of the first year of the new millennium the matriarchs Klein delivered me to LAX. My grandmother hugged me tight to her slight frame and said, "Solomon rabbit, you go enjoy yourself. Don't take any of it seriously. Pleasure above all. You'll never ever look back and wish you'd had *less* sex. More than anything, though, don't become a prick at that fancy school."

With this, she kissed me hard on the forehead, her favorite gesture of benediction, and climbed back into the passenger seat.

Only then did my mother get out to put her hands on my shoulders, look me straight in the eyes and say, "Sol, whatever you do, it's got to be for more than yourself. You have to do something for others, for the *world*. You have to. As you know, I'd prefer you act for Israel, but whatever you choose to do, it's got to be for more than money, for more than *comfort*, all right? That's all I ask. To hell with comfort, that queen bitch.

Change the world for the better a little bit, okay? And don't go joining a goddamned ashram."

They drove off then, my mother's eyes on the road, Baba's on me, both her arms extended out the window. "Pleasure, Solomon, pleasure!" she sang.

And with that, I flew east.

I expected my grandmother would soon leave Los Angeles to abandon my humorless mother and her awful new politics, to return to New York and her beloved apartment on the Lower East Side, which she'd purchased, pregnant, in 1951 with the "participation" of my grandfather, weeks before he faded into the crowd. Just another handsome hustler I'd never know.

If my grandmother is to be believed, regarding both the apartment and the man, she regretted nothing. "One of the best decisions I've ever made in my life, Soli. If a beautiful man wants to provide you both unspeakable pleasure and three bedrooms three floors up on Orchard Street, with so much sunlight streaming in, what kind of jerk wouldn't take it? What? I'd be better off *married*? Marriage is for deluded bores."

"You notice, Sol," my mother said, "she makes no mention of the *child* he gave her."

"Nothing's for free," my grandmother said and grinned at me.

"You're disgusting!" my mother screamed.

And so it went.

Each year I came home from college expecting peace, a slight thawing at least, but no. They were like an ill-paired couple who couldn't muster enough energy for divorce. My grandmother stayed. My mother let her.

Even after September 11, when my mother really lost her mind, they remained housemates.

By the time I graduated from college, tensions between

them were as high as they'd ever been. They flew back east to see me collect my diploma. All through those days, Charlotte made clear that it would no longer do for me to simply live a righteous, selfless life. Now I must devote it to the good of Israel. As the ancient "master plan" theories began to swirl and gather new force, joining together anti-Semites from all camps to make the same old simple argument (the Jews did it), my mother's attitude was just as simple: the world at large could get fucked.

Lina Klein on the other hand, was uncharacteristically quiet. I thought, at long last she'd lost the energy to fight. And who could blame her? There's nothing more boring than arguing with a zealot. Still, her silence worried me. I knew by then that the battles my grandmother waged against her daughter were only expressions of her war against orthodoxies of every stripe.

On the morning before they were to fly back, Baba took me to breakfast.

"Soon I'll be eighty years old, Solomon."

"So?"

"So that's a very long time to hang around."

"Do you feel okay?"

"Since when do you ask such questions?"

"I always ask you questions."

"Not like this."

"Like what?"

She pushed her plate away and drew my hand across the table so she could cover it with her fine, cool fingers.

"Soli, I have a little graduation present for you. I don't know what you want to do now or where you want to do it, but what I do know is your mother doesn't have any money and without your fancy scholarship *you* don't have any money, so unless you're going to go live on a kibbutz or join the IDF—are you going to join the IDF, Solomon?"

"No."

"Kibbutz?"

I shook my head.

"Okay," she said and slid two keys across the table. They were attached to a large opalescent button by a silver ring.

"What is this?"

"One makes you larger, the other makes you small."

"Funny."

"And the button is made of something fancy. I can't remember what. I stole it from the emperor himself. Pearl? Abalone? Goyim bone?"

"You're giving me your apartment?"

"What's wrong with you? No, I'm not *giving* you my apartment. I'm offering to let you live in my apartment. Assuming you'd like to move to the city to pursue your dreams, whatever they may be."

She knew exactly what they were. In many ways, she herself had formed those dreams with her heady stories of a lawless, bohemian New York City. For years, I had imagined a life like hers. Or, anyway, a life like that of her stories. By the time I came to be sitting across from Lina Klein holding those keys, my fantasy had been burnished by the work and lives of Joseph Mitchell, Frank O'Hara, James Baldwin, Alice Neel, and her various other heroes, many of whom she claimed to have known.

I was elated, but I also knew that the apartment was her single asset and for years she had used it to generate income to help pay the many debts my father had left us. Yet another compounded source of Charlotte's rage. God damn Arthur for leaving her his burdens. God damn Lina for coming out so well after an utterly selfish life. God damn her for abetting my meaningless existence, for tempting me away from the Levant.

"Can you really afford this?"

"Yes."

"You're certain?"

"When am I not certain, Soli?"

"Don't you need the money?"

"If I need the money, I'll put you on the street."

"Then thank you, I will move to New York."

All that missing light returned to her eyes. I slid around to her side of the booth. She put her arm around me so that her hand was on the side of my head and pulled me to her.

"I love you."

"And I you, Solomon rabbit."

I began to cry, but she couldn't see it.

"What will you do in that wonderful dream of a city?"

"I'd like to be a journalist."

She squeezed me tighter. "That's good," she said. "That's very good. What will you write?"

"Like Joseph Mitchell," I told her.

"You remember how you discovered him?"

"No."

She flicked my ear. "Little shit."

She had given me a copy of *Joe Gould's Secret* for my twentieth birthday.

"What a writer," I said, mimicking her.

"But such a disappointing lover."

I laughed and sat up to see her face.

"Did you really sleep with Joseph Mitchell?"

"Don't be insolent, young man."

4

Those early years in New York were the happiest of my life. Without having to pay rent, I needed very little. I was not Joseph Mitchell, but I managed to publish enough—about theater, about art, about books, about restaurants—to pay for food and drink and cigarettes and the thick surplus peacoat I believed was fundamental to a respectable life on the Lower East Side. At first, I published nothing more than five hundred words at a time. Then a longer profile of a young Senegalese artist known for using pollen in his paintings. This brought me some attention. Another piece on a socialist art collective squatting in Red Hook brought me a bit more. I came to know journalists and editors, artists and gallerists. I learned to write quickly and competently. I went to good parties. I was a regular at Judy's, a low-lit bolt-hole with no tables, a long lacquered-oak bar and comfortable stools. I did not want a new watch, or more friends, or true love. I wanted only to write something of consequence, something that might make Lina Klein proud, that might shut my mother up, that—I must admit this fantasy—might return my father to me.

Three years after I'd moved to New York, on a January Sunday evening at Judy's, a bull-like man sat down next to me and laid his thick hands on the bar. There were other stools available, but he chose the one to my right and so I glanced at him to get a sense of what might be coming—a rant, a come on, a plea for money, drinks, drugs, a meal—but what came instead was the outright shock of discovering that the man was Ernst Frankel.

My first instinct was to get up and call my grandmother, who worshipped him, who, before I went to college, often sat us in front of his famous marble sea, its waves so impossibly waterlike, on weekend afternoons at LACMA. She was still there, stuck in a city she didn't love, with her souring daughter, while I lived this life she'd handed me, a life in which a person can go out for a beer and find himself beside one of the world's greatest living artists.

I tried to be very still. I'd read recently in a novel that Americans in French cafés were easy to identify because they were always picking at themselves, while Europeans let their hands rest, doing only the work of raising a cigarette or a glass to their lips. I was a dead-skin-scraper, a nail-biter, a beard-scratcher and, at the time, I found this observation profound, as if I'd finally been slipped the secret to cool.

"Are you all right?" These were the first words Ernst Frankel spoke to me.

"Yes, why?"

"Well, you've stopped moving altogether. I was afraid you'd had some sort of event."

I hung my head and told him about the novel, which made him laugh, which made me very happy. It was a good laugh—thudding, full of bass and not too loud—and I was proud to have elicited it.

I was at the end of my beer and so he ordered Scotch for us both, without asking me if it was something I liked to drink. This would turn out always to be the way with him and I didn't mind at all. In those days, I often had no idea what I wanted until someone showed me.

"Are you alone?"

"That's a difficult question," I said, trying to be interesting.

"Is it? For my part, I find it quite simple. I am alone. I am not waiting on anyone, but yes, I suppose, since now we're here together, neither of us is alone. I apologize. Do you often drink alone?"

"I like to come here on Sunday nights and have a drink," I told him. "It's a ritual I've made for myself."

"Since when?"

"Since I moved here."

"And when was that?"

"Three years ago."

"You live in the neighborhood?"

"Around the corner."

"Alone?"

"Are you planning to murder me?"

He smiled. "I admire young people who are happy to be alone."

I nodded.

"But maybe I will murder you. Would you like me to murder you?"

"I don't think so, no. Though it might make me famous."

"Do you think?"

"Sure, for fifteen minutes or so."

"Wouldn't you like to be famous for longer than that?"

"You tell me," I said, turning my stool so that I could really face him.

"You want me to tell you what you want?"

"You've been famous for fifty years, Mr. Frankel. Is it something you think I'd like?"

He smiled at me then. Until that instant, he had been to me one of those people whose faces never quite settle in the mind. Each angle suggesting something new, each photograph presenting a slightly different person. But now, I thought, I knew what he looked like.

"What's your name?"

"Solomon. Sol Fields."

"Is it a burden?"

"I wasn't entirely named after the king, if that's what you mean."

"Who then?

"Also after Charlotte."

"The painter?"

"Yes."

"Different spelling, no?"

"Yes."

"So your father was for the king, your mother for the artist?"

"No."

"What then?"

"My mother was for the king, my grandmother for the artist."

"Your grandmother?"

"Maybe you know her."

"Why? You think all the old people know one another?"

"Because she lived around here for a long time and because she moved in your world."

"Which world is that?"

"Art."

"What's her name?"

"Lina Klein. She's a great fan of yours."

"No," he said. "I don't know her. At least, I don't know her name."

"You must know a lot of people."

"Tell me about yourself, Solomon. Where did you come from and why are you here?"

He asked me question after question. About my father, about where I'd grown up, about my mother, the schools I'd attended. My grandmother. It was the first time in my life I knew what it was to be interviewed and how disarming it could be. There are few rarer qualities than a true interest in the lives of others.

Only by the time we were halfway through our second Scotch, did he ask what I did for a living. "Now," he said, "I must ask the very most popular question in New York City."

"I'm ready."

"What do you do?"

"I'm a journalist," I said. "Trying to be."

"Are you writing about famine and war?"

"No."

"Poverty and oppression?"

"No."

"Corruption and deceit? The failure of the American experiment?"

"No."

"Don't tell me."

"All right, I won't."

"You're not writing about—" He leaned forward so that his spotty white beard was an inch from my mouth and then he whispered, "*Culture.*"

I laughed. "Alas."

"What a shame."

"Why?"

"This city is so full of sad, disappointed people. They come to write or paint or play guitar and, as you know, they mostly fail. And the ones who stay, they end up as critics and *journalists* and teachers. Often all three at once."

"You'd rather they leave town for good?"

"Oh yes. Or, even better, they become bankers and spend their money on art."

"But who would tell them what is good and what is not?"

"Is that what you want to do?"

"No."

"What do you want to do then?"

"I want to write about artists," I said, which wasn't entirely true, but it sounded good and certain.

"Write about me then."

I stared at my glass.

"Are you trying to be European again, Sol?"

"You want me to write about you."

"Yes."

"You haven't given an interview in ten years."

"Fourteen years."

"Fourteen years. You've never read a word I've written."

"So, I'll read a word you've written. There's a guy I know. An editor. I can't stand him, but I hate him the least. The magazine used to be good. I don't know anymore. The guy's relentless. He thinks I'm his ticket. He's terrified his whale will die of natural causes and he wants to be the one to do the killing. So, I'll bring you to him. I'll say only with Solomon Fields will I cooperate. Package deal. Take it or leave it."

"Why would you do that?"

"Because it'll drive the fucker crazy. Because it'll drive all those clubby little fuckers crazy. They'll say, who the fuck is Solomon Fields? And I'll say *this* is Solomon fucking Fields! I found him at Judy's. Behold! Isn't he magnificent?"

I tried to laugh, but I was having a hard time breathing.

He wrote his address on a Judy's matchbook, which I still have in a coconut shell bowl in my apartment. "Put something you've written in my mailbox. If I like it, I'll meet you back here next Sunday for our little ritual."

Then he stood up, pulled on his coat and ushanka and left the bar without offering to pay.

5

On the phone the next day, Lina Klein couldn't stop giggling.

"What were his forearms like?"

"It's January. He was wearing a sweater."

"His hands, then."

"Big. Strong."

She sighed. "Clean? Scarred?"

"We were at Judy's. It's dark in there."

"Jesus Christ. Was there paint on them? Plaster? Dust?"

"Not that I saw."

"Not that you saw. Are you a journalist or not?"

"It's a good question."

"What are you going to give him?"

"I don't know."

"Do I need to get on a plane and make sure you don't fuck this up?"

"He's not serious. You realize that, right? There are a thousand better writers."

"Solomon. You are in New York exactly for these moments. You are twenty-five years old. These are the days that matter. A door opened, now do whatever you must to get through it. Climb into his bed if you have to, but if you're going to live in my apartment, you're forbidden from being a coward."

It did indeed drive him crazy, but Frankel's relentless fucker relented and turned out not to be so bad. I worked harder on that piece than I'd ever worked on anything in my life and eight months after the great man took a stool next to mine, the magazine published my profile.

My grandmother came to New York and the two of us walked to a newsstand at Tompkins Square Park, so that she could see my name on the cover. "Look at this," she said, "I love you more than I have ever loved you, which is a lot of loving you." She bought every copy and took my arm and we began to walk west. "Now tell me, big shot, what was he like in bed?"

My mother over the phone: "I'm happy for you, Sol, okay, but you spend all this time and energy for what? Who does it help exactly? Writing about a multi-millionaire who turns pieces of rock into other pieces of rock while everywhere people are suffering. I'm sorry, but I don't see the use of it."

"Use!" Lina Klein said, disgusted. "Use! Listen to me. There are three true sins: utilitarianism, snobbery and orthodoxy. Right now, do yourself a favor. Ignore your mother. Pretend she doesn't exist. Say yes to everything, all right? Just say yes to every fucking thing."

I followed her advice. I went everywhere. The world appeared entirely apprehensible, containable, festive and open. I had a name, a career. Magazines were still flush then. I was paid well, and a great many people bought me meals and drinks. Editors and publicists, artists, agents and gallerists.

And then, six months after the publication of "Ernst Frankel: Shadows of Violence, Shadows of Stone" (title not mine) I won an award of some prestige. There were more parties, more dinners.

Frankel and I were photographed together in his studio, his heavy arm around my shoulder.

And then, a week after that image was published in our nation's paper of record, I received an invitation.

Josef Capo of Pale Advertising wore a black suit of obvious quality, and his hair snipped within an inch of his scalp. There was a military aspect about him, due in part to the haircut and the sharpness of his clothes, but also to his upright posture, his broad shoulders and rawboned face.

He told me that he was impressed by my writing, that he was looking for *creatives*, that Pale Advertising was the largest, most successful advertising agency in the world.

"Are you interested, Mr. Fields, in the world of advertising?"

Even before I'd reached puberty, my mother had been railing and raging against what she described as one of "capitalism's most despicable children." I was forbidden from watching television. Every billboard we passed was an opportunity for a lecture.

"No," I said. "I'm really not."

"Why is that?"

"I was raised by a Marxist."

He laughed. "Well, if ever you change your mind, the money is very good and you'd be welcome to give it all to the proletariat."

The obvious thing was to ask just how good the money was, but I didn't want to know. My mother never let me forget how hard she worked to support us, to pay off my father's debts, how close we were to being homeless, how corrupt the systems were, how imbalanced, how broken, how violent. As a result, I was always aware of how much money I did not have, how fleeting fortune could be, and exactly how precarious was my station in life.

So before he could write a number on a piece of paper and slide it across his lustrous desk, I thanked him and walked out of there with all the arrogance of someone who had yet to disappoint himself.

"Good for you, Soli, way to stick to your guns," Lina Klein said.

But then all of a sudden (or so it seemed to me then) we were in a recession. The money began to disappear, and my pursuers were less avid, less profligate. Except Josef Capo, who, with characteristically excellent timing, sent me a letter with an offer I could not refuse.

"*Would* not, Solomon," Lina Klein said, black ice in her voice. The number did not move her.

"What do you need money for? You pay no rent. Do you know how many artists would kill for what you have? So many have done with so much less."

"We're in a recession," I told her. "I have to think about the future. I have to make money."

"You sound like someone's grandfather and you're making a terrible mistake," she said and hung up the phone.

My mother was no more forgiving. "You could be a journalist and write about Israel at least. You could *go* to Israel and be a journalist. Or join the IDF. Or do anything other than sell toothpaste."

I don't know where she got it that I was going to be writing toothpaste campaigns, but for years it was the same refrain. To her mind, there was no better metaphor for the frivolity of our miserable nation than the oral care aisle at her local Safeway.

6

My first months at Pale Advertising were marked most notably by my having created the *Go Anywhere, Be Anything* campaign for an airline owned by a bald billionaire named Lucien Vega who claimed to have abandoned all material attachments. Aside from the rejection of desire, he was now convinced that the key to enlightenment was flight, which is to say, the key to selling tickets was the promise of enlightenment. It came to him in a dream.

Vega spent a week at Pale HQ interviewing the greatest minds the company had to offer, but no one, not even the celebrated car guy or the legendary orange juice woman could woo him. Then at the end of a long week of mind-murdering meetings, his famous blue eyes found me at the back of the great conference hall. I was the only one there who hadn't spoken. He rolled his chair down to my end of the table.

He said, "Nirvana by aircraft."

I nodded.

He said, "You understand."

I did not.

He peered into my eyes the way the soulless pretend to be soulful and said, "We will provide everything to our first-class passengers so that there will be nothing left to desire. For the duration of a flight, they should come to understand what I understand always. Wanting is foolish. Desire is deadly. I am happy because I no longer want."

It took some restraint not to slap him.

He said, "Give me your line."

All week long our very best had been lobbing slogans at him and he'd been batting them back with disgust. There was a palpable fear in the office that he would jump ship and take his billions as he went.

"Go anywhere, be anything," I said.

"Yes," he said. Then he was out the door and I never saw him again.

A few hours later the celebrated car guy found me at my desk.

"We're going with yours," he said, none too pleased.

The campaign was an enormous success. My star rose rapidly.

Those years at Pale changed me in many ways. First, they made me richer than anyone in my family had been since Hitler rose to power. Second, they changed my relationship to language. I was trained at the Pale black ops boot camp to write in alliterative sentences, ever seeking the clever and the wry. I learned to communicate in the flat language of conformity and commerce, of self-actualization and self-esteem. A language that descended precipitously from Esalen to advertising to journalism to politics, pooling and cooling in the common American lexicon, where it rests now, stagnant and stinking.

"Someday," Capo promised me, "the poets will speak like bankers and the bankers will speak like poets and we will all think like children."

The man was a visionary.

"I love you, Solomon rabbit, but you're being a jerk," my grandmother said. "You're squandering your gifts, to say nothing of *my* gifts, to say nothing of your life. Which, in a manner of speaking, is also my gift. The point is that these are years you will not have back. Do you understand me? Never. Have. Back."

"I'm happy."

"You are not happy."

"I am."

"What are you working on now?"

"Watches."

"What kind of watches?"

"Swiss."

"You're happy devoting your life to convincing rich people they'll be happier if they buy more jewelry?"

I laughed.

"And for the *Swiss*? They've not been much help to us, have they?"

"Baba—"

"You're wasting your life."

She hung up.

"You could do anything at all," my mother said. "And this is how you choose to help our people?"

If nothing else, the selling of my soul gave Charlotte and Lina Klein something to agree upon.

7

Twelve times a year, on the rooftop of The Pale Building, we reproduced one of our most successful campaigns. If it was thin people dancing to a dreadlocked DJ beneath strung bulbs made to look as if they'd been produced in the 40s, that's what we'd have. If it was an Italianate villa full of tall, unhappy-looking women drinking champagne, that's who we'd find solemnly pirouetting above the penthouse. Our actors and models were contractually obligated to participate, and each arrived in character wearing precisely what they had worn on set.

The evening I met Charity we were celebrating the sale of Nüdø Vodka (originally produced by Icelandic naturists) to an American beverage conglomerate. The Icelanders would become very rich, but to their shame, the spirit would now be gurgling to life in Tucson at the same beverage plant as Nasty Nancy's Naughty NaughTea and Captain Xtreme's Red Hot Spider Cider.

Charity was there, attractive in a black dress and luminous skin. Because she was standing by herself looking down on the city, I thought she might be interesting. I hoped she was contemplating suicide, or, at least, thinking about something other than hand-etched vodka bottles and bringing small-batch liquor to scale.

But she wasn't.

When I told her that I was employed by Pale, she pinkened, came closer and made risqué jokes about cobranding and synergy. She spoke feverishly of her branding work in the "beauty space" and the ways in which the sale of expensive alcohol was and was not similar to the sale of rounding-raising-tightening elixirs made from the semen of Angora goats.

We moved from the side of the building into The Ice Lodge and sank into a white couch of buttery leather. Inside we found faux fires crackling, rough-hewn wood, and trays of vodka carried by buxom women in bikinis apparently cut from pelts of polar bears.

For some reason, there were cigars available, a detail which struck me as incongruous, but Charity was unbothered. She took one and we walked back to the edge of the building where I'd found her. We passed it back and forth pretending to enjoy the stinking phallus while we looked out upon our city and its black river.

"There's no difference between this and art," she said. "None. Same thing. We are all *makers*. Art is art is art. There's as much beauty in this—" here she turned from the abyss and gestured at the lights, the fires, the actors reviving their roles "—as in any great play, any great film, or opera. It isn't just for the money. We are designing our very culture and the most talented among us will be more important than Andy."

Despite this argument, which I found abhorrent and idiotic, and despite what I saw and did not see in her eyes, I followed her home, where we had insipid sex. And I never really left. As simple as that. We were subsumed by our shared theater and together produced an extremely attractive life. From the sets to the acting, all of it was well-designed and expertly executed. She thought the trash I was writing for Pale was literature, an idea I allowed to please me for a while. She talked endlessly of "Andy," and took his work to be an unmitigated endorsement of our own. "Sol, you are as much an artist, as much a poet as anyone. Look around. The world has changed. All those old lines have been destroyed. We are *all* brands.

Everything is performance. Everything is advertising. We've been *liberated*. Now we can be everything at once."

"I'm moving out," I told my grandmother. "You'll have the rent money again."

"I don't need the rent money."

"Then Mom can use it."

"Your mother is sick of my benevolence."

"You could sell it."

"I don't want to sell it. Where are you moving, Sol?"

"I'm going to live with Charity."

"What are you doing with someone named Charity, Soli?"

"She has a nice apartment. I'm going to live with her."

"She's too skinny. She has no capacity for joy."

My grandmother met her the last time she'd visited me in New York. It was not a success.

"The personality of gelatin. Self-righteous. All that talk of diets. As much passion in that girl as a toenail clipping. What do I care what she eats?"

"She takes care of herself," I said.

"What are you doing, Solomon? I don't understand what changed so quickly. How is my only grandchild working for Pale and going to live with some half-empty bimbo?"

I laughed. "You spent an hour with her a year ago."

"More than enough. Much more than enough."

"Give her a chance."

"It is vulgar what you're doing," she said and hung up on me.

But against all advice, and instinct, I left that rent-free Orchard Street apartment and moved up and over to Chelsea where Charity and I would live together in her professionally decorated loft, where through her tall factory windows, I would look down upon Manhattan's most famous galleries of art.

There are various explanations for my cowardice: I'd grown up afraid of being poor. I was more or less friendless as a child and through college, so the lure of a slick life beside an organized woman with glowing skin and clear ideas in an austere apartment on the west side of Manhattan was a revenge too sweet to pass up. But there was, I suspected, something meaner and simpler than all that cheap psychologizing: I just didn't possess the kind of heart Lina Klein hoped I did. I was one of those people brave only in youth.

And while all across the greatest nation on earth people were losing their jobs and their money and their houses and their lives, Charity and I bought whatever we wanted to buy. We went to parties full of people who had done impressive things. Sometimes I would see an artist I recognized and feel such a shot of shame that I would have to turn away.

Once, Frankel entered the restaurant where we were eating dinner. I watched him cross to the other side of the room. It was a large, dark place, his eyes were bad, and I knew he couldn't see me. He was with two men. They all seemed very happy, laughing and gesturing and being very affectionate with one another.

While I was writing the profile, Frankel and I saw each other several times a week. I loved to be with him and even after it was published, after the award, we'd walk out to the East River and share a cigarette. Then he went to Paris for a show. He sent me three postcards and called when he'd returned, but by then I'd taken the job at Pale and I didn't have the courage to call him back.

"This is your mother in you, Solomon," my grandmother said. "I don't understand. Such a waste. Such a goddamned waste."

"It could be my father in me."

She hung up.

I stopped going to museums, or listening to music, or reading books. Each month we received stacks of glossy magazines. Charity encouraged me to read those made for men and soon, the only reading I did was of *GQ*, *Esquire*, *Maxim*, *Men's Fitness*, *Men's Health* and *Men's Journal*. I tore out exercise routines and diet plans. She suggested that I "set an intention," that if I did, I could "manifest" anything I wanted. She said I was getting soft, but that if I put my mind to it, I could get down to twelve percent body fat. It was a journey she thought I should take.

The magazines always used the language of destruction and I liked that. I liked that if I followed their commandments, I too might be shredded, ripped, and cut into a good new man. All that mortification of the flesh, the experts promised, would offer me a body for the beach, salvation by the sea.

"This is what happens when you fuck the Catholics," my grandmother told me.

For a while our mutual journey toward the heavens would draw us together and Charity and I would have sex more often than usual, but then one of us would fall off the wagon and the other would feel superior, disappointed and betrayed. We'd go back to avoiding each other by watching mediocre filmed entertainment while pretending it was important cultural commentary and therefore acceptable to spend so much time gaping at our titanic television, capable of the deepest, truest blacks.

In the end, what broke me, what slapped me out of my stupor, wasn't that I couldn't give up cheese, or sufficiently sculpt my ass, or achieve a celestial state of ketosis. It was just the same mundane things that eventually break everyone: the passage of time (in my case, beat out by the regular thud of *Maxim* magazine on our welcome mat), another party in another space, and the bewilderment of continuing to do for so many years what made me miserable.

And the election of our lunatic leader.

And that on the first day of February 2017 my mother called to tell me that my grandmother, at ninety-one years old, had opened her wrists with one half of a pair of serrated kitchen shears and bled to death in the chipped yellow tub of the bathroom we used to share.

8

I flew west and spent most of the flight watching myself appear and disappear in the cold plexiglass. Bedraggled. That's the word my grandmother would have used. I will add ugly. Lina Klein had killed herself only twenty-two hours before, and yet I looked as if I'd been mourning her death for months. I wondered if it was possible to mourn the death of someone who hadn't yet died. This seemed entirely reasonable, and I thought perhaps I looked so sickly because somehow I'd known her death was imminent. And then maybe it wasn't grief I'd felt, but guilt. I allowed myself the possibility that she hadn't killed herself, but instead it was me who killed her. This was an indulgence, I knew. A woman like Lina Klein doesn't bleed herself to death in a warm bath because her only grandson, the person she loves most of all on earth, is a disappointment.

I was embarrassed to have let the idea pass through my mind.

Somehow a very small fly had made its way between the two panes. Or maybe it had been born there, I thought, from an egg left by an adventurous mother who had decided to *Go Anywhere, Be Anything*. But then, I knew nothing of flies.

In the car from LAX, I was able to avoid my face by rolling down the window. The driver, a heavy, man in an orange watch cap, wasn't pleased to have all that air moving through the car, rustling his neatly folded newspapers. He sucked his teeth in disapproval, but I didn't care at all. The primary advantage of devastating grief is that one feels no compulsion to participate in the ridiculous traditions of human society.

There was a time when Charity and I would compare our IndentYaDrive ratings. In those days, which now held the vagueness of antiquity, I was very proud of my car service manner. I made a big show of being interested in our drivers' lives, whereas Charity said hello and fell straight into her phone. As a result, I had a rating of 4.9. Charity was a full point behind. Incredibly this disparity was the subject of several long arguments resolved only after an hour-long "Listening and Loving" session hosted by Mind GApp.

All that time lost, and now, as I felt the glare of the driver's eyes in the rearview mirror, I decided I would never see Charity or our impeccable apartment again. I held my phone out the window to feel the wind pulling at it, but I didn't have the courage.

As we came off the freeway and turned toward my second childhood home, I was sure that my mother would be in a fury, that she would believe the violence of Lina Klein's final act was pointed directly at her, as arrogant an idea as believing I'd killed her myself.

But I was wrong. It was unsettling to see her so empty of rage. Just as I touched the mezuzah, I heard my mother on the other side of the door, the chain rattling, the deadbolt sliding back. I had braced for war, but her face looked like mine in the window of the airplane at night. Pale, eyes hollowed out. I'd never seen her hands so still.

There were two mugs and a brown ceramic pot half-full of lukewarm black tea on the Formica table.

Once we were both sitting down, she said, "Here you are."

"Here I am."

I was having trouble focusing on her face. I kept trying to look her in the eye, but it was impossible, and I had to focus on the bits of metal or whatever they were glittering in the table she'd bought when I was seven at the Crenshaw swap meet because I loved how it looked in the sunlight. She did those things as well. Without warning, after long stretches of rejecting every request, she'd indulge me with something significant. Never a toy or an amusement park or a cake. It was always a little strange. Like a kitchen table. Or a milkshake maker, or a cuckoo clock.

I said, "Tell me what happened."

I didn't want to hear it, but I thought, if I don't ask her, who will? Everyone else was gone. She didn't have any friends. It was part of our family legacy, the foolish fantasy that joy was born from independence and isolation.

"I told you."

"You came home and found her?"

"Yes."

"What time was it?"

"Three. I came home early."

"Why?"

"There was an electrical fire at the school. They canceled classes after lunch."

"Strange."

"I came home. I was here making a sandwich. I kept talking to her."

"What did you say?"

"You sound like a cop."

"I'm not a cop."

"I told her about the fire. I'm sure I complained about something. Maybe you."

"Maybe," I said.

"I put the sandwich on a plate and sat down with it right here and then, suddenly, I got very irritated that she wasn't responding to me. I knew she was home. I could smell her perfume, the steam from the bath. I said something nasty. Are you not speaking to me now? Something like that."

"Had you been fighting?"

"Of course."

"What about?"

"I don't know. I really don't. I took one bite of my sandwich and then I pushed my chair back. Hard. To make a point. I was still chewing when I opened the bathroom door. She was there. The lights were off, so I didn't see right away. I mean the color of the water."

"You turned on the lights?"

"Yes. I was still annoyed. I said, 'Why are you such a child?' and then I turned them on."

The anger dissipated. I was able to focus on her face, but there was a thickness to the air. My heart seemed to beat only intermittently.

She shook her head as if I'd asked a question, but I didn't remember speaking.

"I'd rather you forgive me and we drink our tea."

I said, "You didn't kill her."

"That's not what I'm talking about."

"What are you talking about?"

"You do what you want to do, Sol. Just don't waste your time."

I thought, in my entire life my mother had never said anything like this to me. But then I thought well, this isn't my mother. This is some other woman and we're both falling through the floor and Lina Klein is still in the bath. She must be cold. One of us has to get her.

"Where is she?"

"In a box in the cupboard." She glanced at the cabinet above the refrigerator where the cereal was. Or where it used to be. It had been a long time since I'd been home.

I stared at her.

"It's what she wanted."

"To be cremated? Or to be kept next to the Shredded Wheat?"

My mother's face turned bright with laughter and the air lost its sludgy thickness. I was able then to see the two of us, mother and son, our kitschy kitchen table shimmering beneath our hands. I could not remember when I'd last seen her laugh like that.

In my memory, my mother had never helped me avoid pain or discomfort. In this respect, she was not of her generation. Never coddle, never protect, never inflate. There were few terms she hated more than *self-esteem*. "If you get punched, punch back. If you fail, work harder. If you're hungry, learn to cook or learn to steal. We live in the belly of capitalism and here, in the end, no one will protect, serve, save or defend you."

But when I stood up from the table that first day back and asked if I could use her bathroom instead of the crime scene, she said, "Of course, Soli. Use it whenever you like."

"Have you been in since?"

"Yes," she said. "I had to clean it."

"You could have paid someone."

"Why waste the money?"

I looked down at her hands.

"Anyway," she said, "it wasn't bad. A little bleach."

I slept in my old room, which was mostly the same—single bed, dresser, bookshelf, all in unfinished pine. I used my mother's bathroom and not once did she give me hell for it.

She was affectless and flat. She barely spoke but was affectionate in ways she'd never been before. She touched the back of my head, held my hand and sat close to me on the couch while we watched television.

She wanted Fox News, but I refused. I suggested we go out for dinner or talk about Lina Klein or have some kind of ceremony for her, but she refused.

Charity called a few times. She left messages full of healing lingo. I nearly replied when she sent a text message about my grandmother's suicide being an expression of the will of the universe.

Somehow, I maintained control and stuck to my promise: I will disappear.

And then one day over our Shredded Wheat, my mother said, "What are you doing here?"

"My grandmother died."

"Did she?"

"What do you mean what am I doing here?"

"I mean, what is the purpose of your visit? You've been here nearly two weeks."

If she'd had her old eyes, I would have thought she was being funny.

"The purpose of my visit is to be here for you."

"For me?"

"With you."

She shook her head. "I don't need you."

"I didn't say you needed me."

"You can't stay here."

"Why not?"

"You need to go back to New York."

"I'm not going back to New York."

"You don't have to go home, but you can't stay here."

In those weeks at home with her, she often seemed drugged. Sometimes she was abstracted and spoke in non sequiturs, other times the old withering acid returned.

"Why do you keep talking like this?"

"No Jew has the right to kill herself."

"Then who has the right, Mom?"

"The expendable majorities."

"What nonsense."

"Sol. Go live your life."

"Isn't that what I'm doing?"

"No," she said, getting up and putting her bowl in the sink. "You're living my life. Be gone by Monday."

I drove out to the beach and climbed onto our tower. Lina Klein had chosen number seventeen. I don't remember why, but it was ours, and she liked to come after the lifeguard shuttered it so that we could sit up there and watch the ocean. I tried to grieve, but I couldn't convince myself that she wasn't on her way to meet me and, aside from a sick, hollowed-out sensation in my chest, I felt nothing.

It was warmer than she would have liked for February. She always wanted it cold, the sky washed of the haze that made such dramatic sunsets, but those didn't interest her. It was the ocean she loved, and its winter waves thumping at low tide.

After about twenty minutes of watching the sky I thought, All right, you want me gone, I'll go.

I called Plume. I'd put her number in my phone the way I might have hidden away some money. Until that moment, I hadn't thought of her since she disappeared down Tenth Avenue.

She answered on the third ring.

"Plume," I said, "this is Sol Fields." There was a very long pause. "We met in New York."

Then she said, "I'm very happy to hear from you."

"If you'll still have me," I said, "I'd like to come."

"Yes. We'll still have you. When?"

"I can be there next week."

There was another long pause and then, "Yes, all right. Send me your flight information when you have it."

"I will. But Plume, I'm not promising anything. If I come, there's no guarantee. In fact, chances are, nothing will come of it."

"Nothing will be expected of you."
"As long as we're clear."
"See you soon then," she said and hung up.

That evening, I said to my mother, "Are you grieving?"
She looked up at me, a flash of the old blade in her eyes. "Don't start with that bullshit."
"What bullshit?"
"I'm sad, Sol. Are you surprised?"
"I've never seen you like this."
"Like what?"
"Bland."
She smiled at me then with an utterly foreign tenderness and touched my cheek.
"What do you want to see, Soli?"
"See? I don't want to see anything."
"What do you want to know then?" Now she took her hand away.
"What did you think when you found her?"
"You won't like it."
"Tell me."
"I thought, well, she always did love the water."
I laughed. "Really?"
Now a tired smile. "Yes."
"I like it," I said. "I don't know why it shouldn't be that, or why it should be anything else."
She nodded.
"Listen," I said. "I'm leaving tomorrow."
"Good. Where?"
"I'm not sure. I'll tell you once I'm there."
"It's not some fucking ashram is it?"
"It could be."
"You could do so much, you know."
"What if this is all I want to do?"

"What if it's all anyone wants to do? Then where would we be?"

I stared at the table. Then the fight went out of her again.

"You should do what you want," she said. "You're going to anyway."

"Is that really what you think?"

She looked out the window. She had an extraordinary profile. It was impossible to know my mother without seeing the side of her face. Straight on she was unremarkable, but from the side she was a woman from another time. I don't remember ever being unmoved by her long, straight nose, by the drama of her jaw, the bright hazel eyes, the lightness of which always struck me as spiteful of her constitution. Fierce rebels in a gloomy land.

She turned from the window to look at me.

I said, "Do you think you can stay here?"

"What do you mean?"

"Can you stay on. Can you live here after this?"

"Of course I can."

"Do you want to?"

"I don't want to move."

"You can now. You can go anywhere you want."

"Don't try to sell me like you sell everyone else. How could I do that?"

"Baba's apartment."

"What about it?"

"What do you mean what about it? It's worth a fortune."

"She left it to you."

"How do you know?"

"How do I know? Because it was never going to be mine."

"Is there a will?"

"Yes."

"You've read it?"

"Yes."

"And?"

"And she left it to you. And all its contents herewith or therein or whatever it says."

"Is there anything else?"

"Is that not enough? You don't look happy about it."

I had to count a full five seconds not to pick up my chair and throw it through the window.

"You think I should be happy about it?"

"It's a nice gift. You can add it to your portfolio."

I walked out of the house.

Part Two

I have always responded to art which jarred the senses and made one aware physically and emotionally of the shifting terrain on which we rest our beliefs.

—Kara Walker

10

On the screen in the seatback in front of me, I watched *Kung Fu Panda 3* and wept. I watched *Neighbors 2: Sorority Rising* and wept. By the time I looked out the window and saw the green island, my eyes were pink and swollen. I was dizzy and no matter how hard I tried I couldn't get a full breath.

They let me out just in time. It was better in the terminal, but the real magic came when I stepped into the velvet day. Even at the curb designated for passenger loading and unloading only, the silken air was honeyed with the fragrance of unfamiliar flowers.

I was so debilitated and disoriented by that perfume, by time, by sorrow and fatigue, that when I saw Plume leaning barefoot against her shining-white Land Cruiser, I couldn't speak. I let her kiss my cheek, let her toss my duffel bag into the back seat. There in the sunlight, so far from my freezing, furious city, she had become even more beautiful, her black hair full of light and more abundant than I'd remembered, her teeth whiter, eyes greener.

She piloted us from the airport, slaloming easily between vans and taxis, limousines and rental sedans, all the while smiling and talking and me not hearing a word, now glancing at the side of her face, now her brown feet working the pedals, and, as we gained speed, her hair, as if in celebration of my arrival, began to lift and dance about her bare shoulders.

Then the airport was gone, and we were carving through a

bright plain of sugarcane. To my right a massive mountain rose into bloodshot clouds, while to my left, yellow sand underlined seething white water which dissolved to milky blue and grew darker and darker as it extended to the black horizon line. I reached my arm through the window and dipped it into the sunlight.

For full seconds at a time I could not remember where I was. Beside Plume I felt barely human, a hideous creature made of heavy clay. There was no light running radiant beneath my skin; my hair was lusterless; my teeth did not gleam; my nails did not shine; the dough of my belly pressed tight against my belt; I was thick and slow; my clammy feet sweated in my shoes. I stank.

Plume took us off the highway onto a steep road shadowed on either side by tall eucalyptus trees. The lowland perfume blended now with this new air, rapidly cooling as we drove up and away from the ocean, and in it I was at last able to fill my lungs. Outside the trees raced past, straining for each other, forming a canopy high above us and then at last we came to a stop before an iron gate composed of two massive panels. Stamped through them in lean letters, was:

The Coded Garden

Bracketing the gate were two sturdy black lava rock pillars and from them tall walls in the same material unfurled in both directions.

There was a pause, a grumbling whir, then the sound of powerful gears coming to life, slack chains now stiff with tension and then in a soothing, ancient fashion, The Coded and Garden departed from one another.

After the iron panels came crashing to the end of their tracks, we drove between them, onto a concrete driveway and into a lush landscape seeming to spread infinitely before us.

There were other, smaller paths, pale veins twisting away from this one, which was bordered on either side by massive trees whose bark was streaked red and green, blue and orange in vertical slashes. Rainbow eucalyptus, their trunks nearly five feet wide, and a hundred feet high.

At the other end of the tunnel of trees the road pitchforked and Plume took the left tine.

She brought us around a sharp curve where a small wooden cottage sat surrounded by grass and tall bamboo. Here we stopped. She hopped out as graceful as ever, grabbed my duffel from the back and carried it up the sand path to the covered porch. By the time she returned to me, I was only just struggling out of the Land Cruiser, trying to fully extend my legs. She touched my shoulder and said, "You're home, Mr. Fields. Last order of business before I leave you to settle in; we require all our guests to turn in their electronic devices."

She produced a small black ceramic box and removed its cork top. I hesitated briefly but, really, I was thrilled to be rid of the thing. I turned it off and turned it over. She corked and wrote my name across it with a white paint pen.

"It's nice you're so quick to abandon yours. Not all our guests are so willing. No laptop?"

"No."

"Good, though I do hope you have a notebook."

Then she was gone, leaving me to stand in front of the house, waving like a fool, as if she were my lover gone off to war. Farewell my sweet, sweet Plume. Be brave. Be safe.

I was alone with singing birds, the breeze rustling palm fronds and clacking bamboo. From my porch, I looked over a gently sloping field scattered with flowering bushes. Here and there, lithe coconut palms bowed in the wind. And up to my right, at the top of a steep hill, stood a sugar-white house built in tropical plantation style.

On its covered veranda, far away through shivering green lines, stood the figure of a man in silhouette. He seemed to be extending his arms, outward or upward I couldn't tell, but then when I moved to separate the bamboo for a better view, he was gone.

11

Within the walls of my cottage was a wide platform bed well-dressed in white, draped in mosquito netting, pillows plumped, corners tight. There was a small kitchen in washed oak, on the countertop an automated silver espresso machine. A table and two chairs, a narrow desk set in the wide bay window, some built-in shelves and cabinetry all in the same austere wood. Everything spare and cool and generically chic, like an expensive desert hotel that liberally uses the words *Zen* and *wellness* in its marketing materials.

But there was no art. Neither painting, nor sculpture. The closest I could find, was a tasteful stem vase holding a red orchid beside the bed.

Outside through a sliding screen was a shower flanked by a stone wall ringed with purple hibiscus. I stripped down and stepped in. With that fragrant breeze turning those flowers, feeling it mingle with the warm water on my winter skin, pouring over my greasy face, taking the travel stench from me, I tried my best to free myself of the image of Lina Klein in the bath.

By the time I found the discipline to turn the knobs, pull myself away, throw on the fresh white waffle-woven robe (monogramed TCG in a satin dove grey), and return inside, there was a small envelope, the same color as the monogram, waiting for me on the table. It was propped against a white bowl inside of which lay a yellow passion fruit cut clean in half, its orange pulp and black seeds glistening obscenely. Crossing the fruit lay a small abalone spoon.

I dressed, sat at the desk and opened the envelope.

On thick cardstock: *Please come to the house once you've settled in. SL.*

Should it irritate me that Plume had entered my cottage without being asked? That the invitation made no mention of which house, or how I might arrive there, that no specific time was provided? But then, as I sat outside on the step, barefoot in winter, bowl in lap, spoon in hand, preparing to deliver passion fruit pulp into my mouth, I just didn't care. I was so tired, so sad, so disoriented by the shock of rapid upheavals, I'd have gone along with anything.

I dressed and set out in search of the house on the hill.

Down one path to join another around the bamboo where the property opened upward. More of those swaying skinny palms, long arrows sunk in the grass, trunks their shafts, fronds their fletching. Jasmine and frangipani, towering eucalyptus here and there, all variety of citrus trees.

The path steepened and swung around the white house where it met a stone courtyard trellised and covered in pink bougainvillea. Beneath it, a wide wooden door was open. There was no bell to ring, so I called out. But no answer came. I waited. Tried again. Nothing.

I stepped into a large entryway and then beyond it into a living room populated by deep white couches, all in the same muted style as my own cottage. Beyond them, at the far end of the room, a dining table long and wide enough to easily seat twenty. Teardrop ceiling fans turned slowly above. The walls were bare.

I called out another hello. From somewhere deep within the house there was, at last, a voice. I moved toward it.

"Come in," it called. "Farther along."

I followed a long light-filled corridor which cut between two rows of lemon trees flowering outside the glass. Toward the end of it, an enormous room, soaring ceiling, airy and empty save for a grand four-poster bed draped with fine muslin, roiling at the mattress edges. There was nothing else there in this inner sanctum: no art, no tables, no lamps, no books.

"Farther, a little farther."

I crossed through a blue tiled arch and there I found a long naked man reclining in a sunken, slate bathtub so deep that his shoulders were right on level with my bare feet. He wore a head of thick black hair blasted scattershot with grey. His face was tan, handsomely lined, crow-footed and sharply punctuated with common blue eyes, a straight, sharp nose, not quite Roman, and slim lips that gated a large mouth.

A wooden tray crossed the tub and on it lay a small tea service—iron pot, a delicate, yellow ceramic cup, a wooden whisk, some other sundry vessels, a plate of thick-cut mango, a bowl of almonds. His arms, long, brown, leathered and hairless, lay along the edge of the floor, inches from my toes. He made no gesture, no explanation or apology for his state of undress, only said, "Welcome. Mr. Fields, yes?"

I nodded.

"You're shorter than I imagined."

"Well, you're more naked than I'd imagined."

"A joke," he said gravely, as if I'd confirmed his worst suspicions. "Did you enjoy the passion fruit?"

"Very much," I said.

He shifted slightly and from beneath the bamboo tray, his penis emerged—a ruddy sea cucumber trying to escape the confines of its watery prison. I suppressed a laugh by looking through a window to the lawn where two shirtless young men dressed in loose white drawstrung pants carried shovels over their shoulders as if they were rifles.

"Did you know, Mr. Fields, that contrary to popular belief, the passion fruit has nothing to do with Eros?"

I shook my head. "You're welcome to call me Sol."

He smiled a toothless, self-consciously beatific smile common on the faces of those convinced of their own enlightenment, who believe they've renounced anger and jealousy, that their hearts are open, their souls pure. It is the condescending expression of the angry yogi, the wealthy unwashed, the newly spiritualized, the Lucien Vegas of the world who gaze down upon their former friends and workmates, mothers and fathers, brothers and sisters, with utterly unearned pity.

"What do I call you?"

"What would you like to call me? You decide and that will be my name but let us for now return to the subject of passion fruit. In Brazil once upon a time, Portuguese missionaries called it flower of the five wounds. Five stamens to represent each of Christ's injuries. The ring of purple and white above the petals, the crown of thorns. Anyway, the suffering of Christ, not the suffering of desire. Interesting, yes?"

"It is."

By now, the sea cucumber had returned to its lair beneath the tea service.

"What do *you* think of Christ?"

"What do I think of him?"

"Yes."

"I have to admit that I don't think of him very often."

"Would you hand me that robe please?"

It was identical to the one I'd found in my cottage. The same monogram. The same excellent cotton. I removed it from the hook and turned to find him rising from the water. He stepped up out of the tub and only then was I aware of how tall he was. Now he turned and I was confronted by his skinny, hairless buttocks, a bright white contrast to his tanned back and legs. He spread his arms as if preparing for crucifixion, and then inserted them into the sleeves.

"Come," he said, gathering the tie around his waist, never looking back, never thanking me. I followed him into the kitchen where he began filling an industrial blender with various fruits and vegetables, powders and potions.

"So, no thoughts on Jesus, Sol?"

"I like his wine trick."

"Another joke."

The blender leapt to life and, as it droned on, he gazed at me without blinking. Then he poured two tall glasses and carried them through the open living room, past the long dining table, and out onto the veranda.

I followed and we sat together, side by side on two chaises longues. Past his bare knees, his long bony shins, his pedicured toes absent all flaw and fungus, through the frame of rail and baluster, one could see all the way to the ocean. Far off to our left there were the high iron gates through which Plume had driven me. Down to our right, perched on a low ridge, was a weathered wooden structure resembling a barn. Farther away down that narrow spine, were smaller buildings, also in wood. There were gardens and chicken coops and grazing goats, greenhouses and orchards. Here and there, a pajama-panted, barebacked, barefooted man worked the land alongside long-haired women in similar pants, white bandeaux around their breasts. Together they bent in the sun, picking and hoeing, gathering and gleaning. Straight ahead, in the center of it all stood a tall tree blazing with purple flowers.

"This is it, Mr. Fields. Your home for as long as you want it to be."

"What kind of tree is that?"

"That's our jacaranda. You've come at a good time. It will soon be in full bloom. "

"It's beautiful."

"Beauty is what we do here. Above all else. Beauty is our

warrior cry. Beauty, our philosophy. Beauty, our act of rebellion against an increasingly hideous world."

"Beauty," I said, not knowing what else to say.

"It all may sound a bit abstract to you now. And given how tired you must be, how worn down from your travels, from your winter life, it'll take some time." He took a sip of his drink. "You are a great journalist, Mr. Fields."

"I'm not a journalist," I said.

"Once, always."

I said nothing.

"I know how disorienting it is to leave your little island and come all the way to ours, so I won't press you, but I've always believed that we can never un-be what we once were."

"What were you before you came here?"

"An artist. I have always been an artist, Sol. From the moment I was born."

"I look forward to seeing your work."

He bent his head. Then he said, "The problem with living here, with being so close to the ocean is that we are never far from disaster. We do not have the privilege of being insulated by hundreds of miles of land. One must keep somewhere in one's mind the knowledge that there is always danger brewing offshore. At any minute it might make landfall, might come pouring out of the jungle, come raging up the hill, might lay everything to waste. All of this destroyed. Always, there is the threat that outside our walls, beyond the gate, darkness is screaming to get in—beast, flood, or fire."

I glanced over at him wrapped in his robe, gazing into the blue sky. It was as though he was an actor who'd responded to the wrong cue.

"Right," I said. "Are there many storms?"

"Yes, Sol, there are many storms. In one way or another there are storms every day."

"I see."

"Perhaps you do. But my sense is not entirely. Not completely. Not really. But I also know that if you stay here long enough, you will."

Instead of replying, I stood and stepped to the railing. A group of young women crossed the lawn. They were laughing, two of them carrying wicker baskets piled with lemons.

"All these people live here?"

"They do. Though theirs is a slightly different arrangement than yours."

"How so?"

"They're all aspiring artists. They're here to learn. As such, in return for food, shelter and tutelage, space and time, they endeavor to look after our garden, which is, in and of itself, a kind of canvas. They paint. They pick tomatoes. They tend to the lawns, prune the trees. Food, of course, is only part of our harvest."

I laughed and looked over at him. He kept his eyes on his land, not a spark of mischief in his face.

"You'll soon understand. I have no doubt."

"I see."

"You will, Sol. But remember, beauty is brutal."

It was just slogan after slogan with this guy. I closed my eyes and tried to find a product for it. Maybe a diamond dog collar. Maybe an élite Las Vegas hotel, a slick nightclub, shimmering models slipping past the velvet rope while lesser creatures look on longingly. Black screen, dissolving white letters: *Beauty Is Brutal.*

"I guess it is," I said. Whatever I thought of this guy, his garden caused me a strange longing, the way perfectly ordered, polished places often did.

"I know your people have a taste for a certain style of humor. A tendency to irony. Here we're interested in sincerity, Mr. Fields, in purity of thought and speech and far above all, of art."

"My people?"

I turned and faced him.

"New Yorkers."

"You don't like New York?"

"It is a cruel and ugly place. Cigarettes and drugs and sarcasm and violence. You treat yourselves terribly and then call it art or fashion. No, I do not like New York. Why live that way? Eating badly, sleeping badly, reveling in ugliness and pretending the pig is a pony."

His lips were parted now, and he seemed to be slightly out of breath.

"When was the last time you were there?" I said.

"Why do you ask?"

"I think you might find that there's more juice and fewer cigarettes than you remember."

He made a doubtful grunt and stood up.

"I hope you're comfortable in your cottage."

"It's lovely."

"Here you will be left alone. You have access to the grounds, the library, the paths, the orchards. All of it. Whatever draws you in."

"Even the studios?"

"Not the studios, no. Those we must leave to our artists. But otherwise, you are free. You're welcome to our food. Come to The Barn for meals. Take what the trees offer. We'd like for you to be part of this community."

He stood then. I watched him interlace his fingers and stretch fluidly toward the sky.

"Do you know how old I am, Sol?"

"You look very healthy," I said.

"*Certitudo, sinceritas et sanitas*, Sol. Certainty, sincerity and health."

"Must be this," I said, raising my mostly full glass of muck. "Which, by the way, you'd find plenty of in New York."

His eyes darkened slightly, then his expression returned to one of reserve, to that wise, knowing disappointment. He filled his lungs with deliberate care. Perhaps he, too, was a loyal Mind GApp subscriber.

"There is no separating one from the other. You wish to uncouple art from the body, the body from the land, but you will see. I hope. I really do hope that you will see."

He tightened the knot of his robe and placed his warm hand on my shoulder. "I will leave you to your day. Please stay and enjoy the view. Rest. Sleep. Give yourself some time to acclimate."

He collected our glasses and left me alone. For a moment, I stood at the railing looking out over his garden, the jacaranda dazzling in the sunlight. Far beyond it and just to the west, at the base of a low hill, was what appeared to be a tight grove of trees greener than all the others. It was all lovely, but what was I doing? What had I done? Get out of here. Check into a hotel. Have a swim. Get some rest. Clear your head. Return home to your life of good fortune. But then I was struck by another wave of exhaustion and so I returned to my chair and closed my eyes. Only for a minute, I thought.

When I woke there was a cotton blanket covering my lap and the sun was casting long shadows across the grass. I dragged myself up and quietly passed through the darkening house in search of my bed.

12

There were still a few flares of pink hovering above the horizon line and all the limber palms were bending in silhouette against an abysmal blue sky. The neat paths had become lighted runways snaking this way and that, while Sebastian Light's understated buildings glowed like massive lanterns.

Now in the evening, the property appeared as a lighted map. It was astoundingly beautiful.

I wandered until I heard music, and then went in its direction. Soon, in the near distance, a large structure appeared, which I soon saw was the barn I'd seen from above.

It was not in my nature to arrive at a party to which I'd not been invited, but in the vaguest terms, I thought, I *had* been invited. Also, in the last twenty-four hours all I'd eaten was a single fruit of the five wounds and a mouthful of sludge. I was ravenous.

Outside, people sat together on the grass, others around the picnic tables arranged here and there beneath the trees. A man with long blond hair leaned against a palm tree, playing a guitar. He nodded and smiled at me as I passed. There were two young women sitting cross-legged on the lawn, plates of food resting on the canopies made by their skirts drawn tight between their knees.

I passed a discreet enamel sign screwed to the wall: *The Barn*, black on white, in the same script as the monogrammed robes. Inside beneath the heavy-beamed ceiling, a very long farm table was laid with food: cauliflower, purple potatoes, chopped purple cabbage, fresh lettuces, Japanese eggplants, a platter of sliced papaya and mango, wedges of limes and tangerines. A fat copper cistern full of water. Beside it, stacks of copper cups. There were cloth napkins and wooden plates and silverware. Young people serving themselves, settling down at tables inside and out on the lawn.

No one seemed in the least surprised to see me.

I filled a plate and turned to find Plume at my elbow, materialized from the ether. "We raise all of it here."

She took a smooth wooden paddle between her fingers, ran it across a plane of butter and slathered my potato. "You won't believe how good it is. Come with me."

I followed her toward the back of the barn to a small table where two others were sitting.

She introduced me with stilted formality, as if I had arrived in some nineteenth-century drawing room, but I barely registered their faces and didn't hear their names. I had to eat. The potatoes were sweet and dense, their skin crunchy, laced with garlic and salt. The greens were crisp and peppery. The water, cool and clear.

When I was finished, I found my two tablemates watching me.

"Sorry," I said. "I haven't eaten in days."

"Are you only a journalist or are you also an artist?"

In my hunger the two of them had barely been visible. Now I could see the one speaking. His small stature was only made more apparent in contrast to the woman sitting next to him. They might have been siblings. She had springy brown hair which she wore loose around her shoulders, while his was black and cut in a neat forehead sweep. They shared the same pale-pink skin tone, the same cool, black eyes. She wore a loose dress of cream-colored linen. His shirt was white, buttoned to the throat and cut tight in the style of so many compact urban men, as if by eliminating all pleats and billowing fabric, he might be mistaken for an NBA center.

"I'm neither," I said.

"What are you then?" the man asked.

"How to answer a question like that?"

"All right," he said, "what are you doing here?"

"My plan is to have dinner." The guy annoyed me immediately. Something so familiarly pathetic and petulant about him. "Sorry," I said, "would you remind me of your names?"

"Crystalline," the woman said.

"Theo," Theo mumbled.

"Right, yes. I'm sorry."

Plume returned to the table. I'd forgotten she'd been away.

"It's an unusual name," I said to Crystalline, who had a quality to her I liked immediately. Poise, a little ember of provocation in her eyes.

"We're encouraged," she said flatly, though perhaps with a whisper of sarcasm, "to rename ourselves while in residence."

"I see," I said. "How long have you two been here?"

"Six weeks," Theo said.

"Six months," Crystalline said.

"And you?" I asked him. "Did you choose Theo?"

"No. It was imposed upon me at birth. The name I'm making is not yet finished. I'm still building it."

I glanced at Crystalline, who may have begun a smile before she looked away and began fingering the black cowry shell that dangled from a silver chain between her breasts.

"It's probably the jet lag," I said, "but I'm not sure I understand."

Theo spoke up now, impatient, his voice loud and grating. "It means that to be an artist is to devote oneself to the work so entirely as to become it. As we make paintings, we make ourselves. As we make ourselves, we make our paintings. It is an eternal circle, an infinite loop. Only ego is the switch that breaks the circuit."

It was enough for one day. I stood up. "Well, I look forward to hearing your name when you finish it. Nice to meet you both. I'd better go get some sleep."

Crystalline smiled at me. Theo did not.

Plume who had been watching this as if she were our therapist, stood up as well.

"I'll make sure you find your way," she said.

We left the barn and walked out into the night air, which was somehow softer and sweeter than ever. As we turned up the path toward my cottage, she said in her feathery voice, "It might be best, Mr. Fields, to abandon all your entrenched ideas."

"Best for whom?"

"For your story."

"As I told you on the phone, I doubt there will be a story."

Now we were at the door.

"Of course. Are you okay? You don't look well."

"I just need some sleep. Just one good night's sleep."

"I suspect you'll need more than that. But we will see in the morning."

"How old are you, Plume?"

"Age is meaningless."

"Surely. But nonetheless how many years have you been alive? According to the Gregorian calendar."

"I gave it up."

"Age?"

"Yes."

"I see, and what about *your* name?"

"You know my name."

"I mean the one imposed upon you at birth."

"Plume is the only name I have," she said, leaning forward. For an instant I thought she would kiss me, but she only brought her lips to my ear and said, "Goodnight, Mr. Fields. Sweet dreams." Then she became a wraith in the dim light of my porch and disappeared.

That night I dreamed I was in a bed so wide I couldn't see its edges. Lina Klein said sweetly from the bath, "Solomon, don't you dare die, too. You haven't earned it you little *fuck*." She really bit down on the *fuck*, sounding like a movie gangster, which made us both laugh until we pissed ourselves and then all at once I was alone in our tub soaking in iridescent urine listening to her humming a tune I didn't recognize.

13

In the morning, I forced myself out of bed and into the shower. I drew three shots of espresso from the silver machine and drank them until I could see clearly. Only then did I discover on the table a basket full of croissants, a jar of passion fruit jam, half a papaya, a wedge of lime and another card: *Day one. SL.*

After I ate, it was all I could do not to get straight back into bed and give myself up to dreams of Lina Klein. But she wouldn't have allowed it. "Don't ever be a stupid tourist, Solomon," she said. "Not in a restaurant, not in a bar, not in another country. Go out, go everywhere, keep your eyes open, be smart and be curious." In this spirit, I went wandering, dizzy with jet lag and whatever other maladies afflicted me.

I took a path to the west, which brought me across the long base of the low hill I'd seen from the house. The stand of trees was in fact bamboo planted in spiral. There was a wooden sign on a post stuck in the earth which read, in trademark Garden font, The Spiral. There were two identical heads, which could have been male or female, waist high, sculpted from marble, resting askew on either side of the entrance, each with their eyes turned upwards in either pain or ecstasy. Curiously, there was no sign, no plaque indicating the artist or title of these sculptures. They reminded me immediately of Miller's *l'Écoute*, which I'd always liked, but Frankel thought was emotionless and generic. I suddenly wanted to walk that place with him. He'd have hated it but would have at least had something to say about my grandmother and, oddly, although it had been years since we spoke, I couldn't imagine talking about her to anyone else. And really, the only person I wanted to talk to about my grandmother's abrupt exit was my grandmother. Frankel was a second, but not all that close. A person's life begins to look a bit gloomy if he's approaching forty and one of the two people on the planet with whom he can conceive of conducting a substantive conversation is in a box above his mother's refrigerator.

A few hundred yards away from The Spiral, I came to a windowless building in the garden's weathered wood style, distinguished by a bright red door, above which was another of those enamel plaques: *The Library*. Creative naming, it seemed, was reserved for human beings.

The coffee was wearing off. My eyes felt too large for their sockets. Despite the constant breeze, the heat and light of the day was nauseating. That desolate hollowness I'd felt at the beach in Santa Monica was deepening. She would not leave me alone. Her eyes, her commentary. I was trying to walk away, but with the caffeine diluting and the loud sun, I couldn't shake her.

I was dragging now as I continued on, climbing toward a group of cottages straight ahead, each smaller and humbler than my own. I could see The Barn, a hundred yards away to my right. Somehow it was lunchtime already and the artists were congregating. I needed to eat, but I couldn't endure all that enthusiasm or another conversation with Plume or Saint Theo the Unnamed.

I cut off the path and found some shade beneath a tangerine tree. I leaned against its trunk, ate some fruit and gradually faded off to sleep like some fairy-tale princess. It was night in New York and I could see Charity arriving home, standing before the mirror, tying her hair back, beginning her pre-bed ablutions, the washing and wiping and brushing, the toner, the serum, the cream, the Mind GApp man whispering her to sleep.

When I woke it was dusk. A spider had bitten the back of my hand. Lina Klein would have made an obvious joke about new powers and the advantages of physical pain. If she were around, she'd have mocked me for grieving her suicide.

I stumbled home, intoxicated by time and grief, fell into bed and slept through until the next afternoon.

14

Lunchtime at the barn was a more casual affair than dinner. A platter of grilled fish garnished with lemons, lettuces, a bowl of millet. None of the artists were speaking—neither those sitting outside in the sun, nor at the shaded picnic benches. There was only the sound of the cardinals and the doves, the egrets and the plovers, wind in the trees and the quiet clatter of metal silverware against wooden plates.

I took my food outside, avoided Theo who sat alone staring into the middle distance, and found an empty table beneath the drooping branches of a pepper tree.

Soon a man appeared before me and nodded questioningly at the empty place across from my own.

"Sure," I said.

He sat and began to eat.

His black hair was pulled back in a loose ponytail. He had a narrow, dramatic, feline face featuring a full mouth underscored by a good chin and pale-hazel eyes.

"Are you an artist?"

He looked up from his food as if I'd just called his mother a whore.

"Wrong question?"

He pointed his fork at a plaque dangling from a hook: *To restore silence is the role of objects.*

"He's not big on attribution," he whispered, "but it's Beckett."

I smiled.

"We're supposed to shut up now, but maybe we can talk tonight at dinner?"

"Sure," I said. "I'll look forward to it," and ate my fish, trying not to let him see me watching his hands. He finished before I did, held my eyes a beat longer than he needed to, and left.

On the way back to my cottage, Plume came around the bend carrying a basket of flowers, her black hair rising on the offbeat, the fabric of her flowing sundress filtering the sunlight flashing between her legs.

"Mr. Fields," she said when she reached me, "you've had a nice day?"

"Yes."

"You managed to find your way to lunch?"

"I did."

"Good?"

"Very."

"Is everything okay?"

"Yes, why?"

"Well we didn't see you yesterday. I was concerned that perhaps you weren't feeling well."

"That's nice of you. I'm just a bit tired."

"Of course. And may I ask, have you enjoyed yourself so far? You're happy with your accommodation?"

"It's all very nice."

"And I understand you spent some time with Mr. Light."

I nodded.

"You should feel free to use everything."

"How do you mean?"

"If you choose to write about us. Our book is wide open."

"Ah. I see."

"Do you think you will?"

"It's early still, Plume. I can barely see straight. But as I've said, it isn't likely."

"Right. Well, I do hope you can be swayed. Mr. Light is a great fan of yours. And after all, here you are."

"Yes," I said. "Here I am."

"Why do you think that is?"

"It is an excellent question."

"Well, I hope you soon find an excellent answer. Mr. Fields, let me ask you something, if I may."

"All right."

"What is it that you love?"

"What do I love?"

"Yes. And I'm not speaking of the material."

"Oh I don't know. Passion," I said.

She smiled and this time it was of higher quality.

"Hard to come by."

"Yes," I said.

"And one must be careful with it, as well."

"Why is that?"

"Well," she said beginning to walk away, "every passion borders on the chaotic, Mr. Fields."

Because of the exhaustion, the image of Lina Klein's eyes, the disorientation, the strangeness of sudden change, I nearly stayed in bed instead of going to dinner. But there was also the man I'd seen at lunch and the thought of him and a plate of food got me to The Barn.

They were festive again. There were smiles and waves as I passed those outside on the lawn, as if I'd been there for years. I filled my plate and made my way out to the same picnic table.

And then, as he'd promised, there he was again, plate in one hand, copper cup in the other.

"Mind if I sit here?"

I wanted nothing more in the world.

"Please," I said.

He sat across from me. "Sol," I said.

"Siddhartha."

"Nice to meet you," I said. "Again. So, you're an apprentice here?"

"I am."

"Are there other ranks?"

"Well, there's Plume."

"And what is she?"

"Hard to say."

"I see. And Sebastian Light. What is he?"

Siddhartha looked up and met my eyes. "So this is what it's like?"

"What what's like?"

"Having dinner with a journalist."

"Who told you that?"

"It's general knowledge. It was announced."

"What was announced exactly?"

"You seem more like a cop to me."

I laughed. His tone changed constantly. Even mid-sentence. Now he was mischievous and ironic, now he was cool and wary.

"Should I stop asking questions?"

"Of course not. We're an open book."

"Yes, so I've been told. All right, how does a person become an apprentice?"

"He sends announcements to art departments, museums, that kind of thing. They're beautiful things. Black cards made of heavy stock. Gold painted edges. Gold letters pressed by hand. Each year he does a numbered limited edition. Each one is mailed off in a grey envelope along with a small hammered-brass tack. You have to understand the attention he pays to everything. Not a thing is left to chance. On one side the card reads or, at least, last year it read, 'Are you done with a living death?'"

"Come on."

"It's true." He leaned forward, "Then you turn it over, in the same gold letters, 'If so, write to us. In exchange for work, we'll provide room and board, wisdom and peace, light and revelation. All of these things will be woven in art.' Then a mailing address."

"Woven in art?"

"As blankets are woven in wool, my friend."

He was so charming. It was as if he could control the sparkle in his eyes, gleam his teeth on command.

"And that's it? You just wrote? There was no email address? No website? No name or number?"

"Nope. He's against technology. You had to turn over your phone, right? Even as a guest?"

"Yes."

"And you don't have some sort of tape recorder in your pocket?"

"Do you want to search me?"

He laughed.

"And so you wrote."

"I did, yes." He smiled, but this time with, I thought, some contrition.

"What? Do you regret it?"

"No," he said.

"What then?"

"Nothing. What's to regret? Look around. All this. And a studio and a bed and enough strangeness to feed an entire lifetime's worth of paintings."

I nodded. "All you have to do in return is work the fields?"

"More or less."

"What's the more?"

"I've never known a journalist before."

"Lucky you. I'm not really a journalist though."

"No?"

I shook my head.

"Well whatever you are, are you really going to write about us?"

"I doubt it."

He looked surprised and briefly thrown. He knocked his knuckles against the table as if he needed the gesture to recalibrate. Then he leaned forward and said, "It's not just working the fields."

"No? What else then?"

"Stay a while, Sol, and I'll try to show you."

He went back to eating. All at once I no longer had the heart for banter. I imagined showing my mother a card like that. My mother sighing, looking at me only when she was ready to begin her diatribe, one version or another of which I had been listening to since I took the job at Pale: *This* is what we dream of? *This* is what we have worked for? This pabulum? And what did I tell you about ashrams?

Ashrams, the word had become her metonym for any place that concentrated those with enough money to spend their days "improving themselves" at the feet of some quarter-baked maharishi. She hated all those people who'd gone off to Woodstock. She never felt she could afford to turn on and drop out.

"There was no one at home to catch me," she said, glaring at my grandmother. "So, I worked, Soli. While everyone else was getting high and fucking themselves stupid, I worked. So that we wouldn't be those people at the dying end of a fantasy, living in a van with an infant, pretending poverty was freedom. Only the rich insist the poor are pure. Our people didn't suffer through what they did so that we could bathe ourselves in a Chevron station bathroom. Solomon, all that nonsense your friend Charity babbles on about, self-*improvement*, self-*esteem*, self-*care*, it's a setup, a long con. The same old cruel and poisonous crap hucksters and grifters and corporations have been slinging for centuries and it's going to destroy a once-great nation. Good luck to you."

If she'd been a mob boss, *good luck to you* is what she would have said before putting a bullet in your brain. And if she ever decided to kill herself, that's exactly how she'd do it.

Sid was looking at me.

I didn't want to, but I spoke anyway. I was afraid that if I didn't, I might dissolve right there in the sweet evening air. I said, revving myself up for conversation, "Do you still have the card?"

"In my studio." He looked relieved. "Come by and I'll show you."

"Sure," I said. "Why not?"

In those last years at Pale, I came to detest the people I was being paid to fool. How else to survive a job whose mission was cruelty? Those people desperate for access to some imaginary stratosphere of gratification, those simpletons masquerading as sophisticates who so easily fell prey to a letter printed on creamy stationery, a bottle of fifty-year-old Armagnac, compliments of the management, an exclusive invitation to our private viewing fête, an opportunity to *experience* an apartment in some monstrous building. The world-famous architect will speak. There will be canapés made by the executive chef of BoboCouCou. Studios start at three million dollars.

"What did you write in your application? If you don't mind my asking."

"Oh, I wasn't clever. I told him what I did. The work I wanted to do."

"And then?"

"And then I received a letter in return. All the specifics. Or most of them. How to get here, what to bring."

"And you were a student?"

"No. I'm older than everyone here. Except for you, maybe." He grinned.

"Maybe. So, if you weren't a student—"

"Chance. Divine intervention. Who knows? I was teaching a class. I saw the card in the art department, and I stole it. The thing was beautiful. And by that point in my life, I guess I was ready to stop living a living death."

We both laughed.

By now the sun was near setting and most of the others had gone off to whatever went on after dinners.

"What do you do all day?"

"There are hours for the fields and hours for painting, though he would say there's no difference. The work we do in our studios and the work we do in The Garden are both in service of art. Is what he says."

"You don't buy it?"

He began to nod, though not in affirmation. It seemed a tic, a nod of consideration. He was weighing possible responses. Then he stood up.

"You want to walk a bit?"

He took me along a path that swung around the back of The Barn and down a hill toward a vast pasture which, at its end, maybe half a mile away, abutted a darkening forest. The sun was gone now, the sky turning pink and then, as if they'd come to life just for us, little flickering lights appeared to form an illuminated runway weaving in easy arcs toward the trees.

"Is that the property line?"

"It's on the other side of the forest. There's a wall there along the edge of a ravine."

"The same wall that starts at the entrance?"

"Yes. It runs the entire perimeter. Can you imagine how much time that took? I think it's the most incredible part of this whole place. A masterpiece, really. It was made by people whose ancestors have been building these walls for six, seven hundred years. Some of this one is maybe four hundred years old. Those sections are through the forest there."

We broke from the path, crossed the dark pasture and entered the trees. For nearly five minutes neither of us spoke. When we came to the wall, he laid his hand against the stone.

"There's no mortar. It's all dry-stack masonry, all gravity and artistry."

Standing there with him, our hands on the cold lava, something shifted, and he said, "I should get to my studio," and quickly as we'd come, we were making our way out of the trees.

As we began walking back up the hill, I couldn't bear the idea of going back to my cottage.

"Should I come now?"

"Come where?"

"To your studio. To see the card."

I was immediately ashamed.

"Not tonight," he said, though not unkindly. "Maybe tomorrow? Get some rest. You must be exhausted."

At The Barn he turned down the ridge toward his studio and I walked on home, where I lay in bed staring up at the fan and, in half-sleep, felt as if the room were turning on an axis. I thought of Siddhartha and those pretty rock walls. I dreamed of Plume leaning over my table, her fingers wrapped around the handle of a long chef's knife, its blade glistening as she sliced a fruit of the five wounds into perfect halves. They fell upturned from that fire-forged steel, rocking at the bottom of a sparkling white bowl where drops of water fell from her heavy hair while Lina Klein sang to me in German.

15

For two days, or maybe three, I did nothing but sleep and eat the breakfast that was there when I woke. I went to lunch once, but when faced with that sad old school cafeteria problem, I carried the plate back to my cottage. I'm nearly certain that for a full day I ate nothing at all. My appetite came in waves. Or perhaps it was grief that came that way. My dreams were stranger than time. I didn't see Siddhartha. Plume left me in peace, but Lina Klein, alone in the bath, would not.

On the fourth morning, as I sat outside on my porch, there was Sebastian Light coming in fast, sweeping toward me, arms outstretched like a preflight egret.

"Good morning, Sol. We've not seen you around much. Everything okay?"

He took the chair next to mine.

"Yes," I said, "thank you."

"Excellent. Good. Listen, I know you've done some exploring on your own, but, if you'll allow me, I'd like to give you a tour. The grand tour. Are you willing?"

"All right," I said.

We walked down my path and around the screen of bamboo so that we could look up at his house on the hill. "The first structure," he said. "Goes all the way back to the beginning."

"You built it yourself?"

"More or less. On January first of each year we repaint it white. A ritual of renewal."

"What was here before you came?"

"Nothing," he said. "Jungle. Brush. Just savage land. We had machetes. For months we hacked away. All that was so long ago."

"How long ago?"

He ignored my question and gestured for me to follow him, clasping his hands behind his back as we walked. When we came to the top of the hill just below his veranda, we stopped.

"This view," he said, "was almost entirely obscured."

Where we stood, the grass was shorn short and neat and fell away. The symmetry of it all, the green of his garden, the ordered buildings and pathways, all those clean lines made it seem impossible that it had ever been anything else.

"What I hope, Mr. Fields, is that you will produce something true."

Then I was irritated. "Listen, I know you want me to write about you. You brought me here for exactly that reason. Why be so coy?"

I could not crack that serene face. He only shook his head and looked out over his world. "I want you to write, not about me, but about this, about us. I want it to come organically. The way that a painter wants to paint because he has no *choice*. He has an inexplicable need to express what *is*. I'm not being *coy*, Mr. Fields. The transactional pains me. It always has."

He turned and looked at me directly, holding my eyes, expectant, waiting.

When I was very young, maybe eleven years old, I followed some boys to a park where there was a half-built building made of cinder block. They were older and I wanted to be something to them. The one I really admired, a boy who was even then muscular in a way I could never imagine being, who I can still see shining in that edge of light that cut through an unfinished window, turned and slapped me across the face. I was so surprised. I'd suspected nothing. One minute I was going off with my new friends. The next they were all standing there looking at me to see what I'd do. I couldn't understand it. They wanted a fight, so I fought. It was the only way out of that place. I walked home ashamed and furious that no father waited for me at home.

Lina Klein was there, though, and she cleaned the blood off my face and held some ice to my eye and said, "Even assholes like that, Soli, you've got to look at them and see their bones, their stupid eyes and weak little brains bouncing around in their ugly skulls and know that's all they are. Nothing more. Just like you. Just like me. It's the only way to get through a life."

I understood, even then in my shame, what she meant for me to know about the world. "You must never fall for the myth of the absolute villain. No matter what happens, no matter how ugly it gets, always close your eyes and see their bones."

I looked at Light and tried to decide what he was, whether he was himself some kind of a villain, or rather, a bombastic artist in the throes of performance. And how did he see me? As journalist or audience or both?

I said, "As I told Plume, I can promise you nothing."

He said, "Look, Sol, look at this place, so clean, so soothing to the eye. It was not always so. This is, we believe, what beauty *is*. We must take madness, chaos, wildness and turn it to art. At its very core. That is why we're here. The pride I feel is immense. I'll never tire of it. And why? Why all the work? Why all the suffering? We do it all for beauty."

"For beauty," I said, as if hypnotized into repeating the Garden mantra.

"Yes. We built this place for beauty, to make a center for our philosophies *of* beauty which is to say for our philosophies of art." He was really starting to preach now. "To stand up and raise our fists and say *this* not *that*. To say *here* is beauty and *there* is ugliness, and we will not, will *never* cower beneath the safe tarp of ambiguity. I know it's not fashionable, but we believe in absolutes here, in *taste*, in *standards*. No, we will not be swayed by some vagary, received wisdom, that says *anything* can be beautiful. No."

He was panting a little bit now, a brilliant bauble of saliva balanced on his lower lip.

To defend against such a tide of bullshit was beyond me, so I said, "It's strange, but for all this talk of art, I've seen so little."

"Look around you. What is this then?"

"Well, it's very pretty. But I wonder if I might see some of the paintings."

"Of course." He smiled. "You will. Of course. And I'm pleased to know you're interested. That is a very good sign. A very good sign. But remember, Sol, to look for beauty everywhere. Beauty, Sol—" he was repeating himself now—"is why we're here in this garden and why, if you'll allow me, we're here on earth."

At that moment a figure appeared on the path, rounding a gentle curve. The timing was so perfect that for a second, I imagined Plume backstage, black turtleneck, headset, cued by his terrible line, whispering *go, go, go*.

"Ah," he said, as the figure became clear. "My dear Crystalline."

She was far less neatly arranged than the last time I'd seen her. She wore loose jeans stained with paint and a tattered black tank top. She was barefoot. Her corkscrew hair was piled, twisted and bound atop her head.

There was an aloofness to her still, an assurance. She moved, as Lina Klein would have said, like she'd never been hit.

"Crystalline, this is Solomon Fields. He is—"

"Right. We've met."

"Ah yes," Light said, smiling benevolently. "At dinner, wasn't it?"

"I think so," I said. "The days are a bit of a blur."

"You know, my grandfather was named Sol," she said, smiling at me.

I laughed. "It's not a common name these days."

"You mean with people under eighty."

Her eyes ironic, crackling, never once shifted to look at him. "Well, I'm going to finish my walk, Sol. My regards to all your grandchildren. Nice to see you Mr. Light." And then she was off.

"She doesn't mean it," Light said, as we watched her exit.

"I don't mind at all."

"In general, we prefer to avoid that kind of thing."

"What kind of thing?"

"The New York languages, cruelty in the guise of humor, violence in the form of sarcasm."

I laughed. "I like it."

"Cruelty and violence?"

"Humor and sarcasm."

I was slightly bored with him, his tour and tired platitudes. I wanted to be walking in the other direction. I wanted the darkest wit. The cruelest humor. I was so sick of perky optimism and cloying hope. Joy lies in its many opposites, I thought, parroting my grandmother. If New York was what Sebastian Light seemed to imagine, I would never have left. But the city had begun to seem to me like nothing but performative sobbing and self-righteous droning, as if everyone we knew believed all had been rosy until that asshole came lurching into the White House.

We passed The Barn on our right and came up onto a ridge along which lay thirty wooden studios. "The Ridge. I think of it as a necklace, a long, beautiful strand and in each gem, an artist lives and works. I'll do them the courtesy of not invading their space, but you can get a sense as we pass."

"Beautiful," I told him and meant it. In that moment, the

elegance of the place was enough to make me ignore his metaphors. "Which one is Siddhartha's?"

He looked pleased. "I'm glad you met Siddhartha. One of our most promising."

"And Crystalline? Is she any good?"

"With some discipline, she can be excellent."

The next stop on the tour was The Library, which Sebastian Light invited me to use anytime ("You may find it a sanctuary in which to write") and finally he brought us to The Spiral and its twin-headed entrance. He slowed down, and I got the sense that this would be his dénouement.

I followed him between the marble heads into the circling track. Bamboo stalks knocked against each other, making the sound of water drawing rocks along a riverbed. In the center was a low marble bench and before it a six-fingered hand covered with verdigris resting on a pedestal apparently cut from a single tree, the diameter of which perfectly matched the beginning of the wrist.

"This is very pretty."

"I find it's a good place to sit, to think. To just breathe."

"I meant this sculpture."

"Ah," he said.

Again, I tried to get a bead on him, but I was met with that same odd smile, which might have been ironic or might have been sincere. Then he started talking again.

"It was your focus on the sculptures that I loved about your profile of Mr. Frankel. There was none of that, his childhood was like this, his father like that. You wrote about the work. Your words brought the work into song. Those extraordinary sculptures took over, and the man, he fell back into darkness."

He looked down at me, those grey-green spearhead leaves stabbing in the wind behind him and the sun full on his face. I thought, This is what he wanted to say all along. Perhaps he is being sincere. Or maybe I was ripe for flattery, and he had realized that the only way through was via my fickle little ego.

"As I recall, I wrote about Frankel's childhood," I said.

Though it was true that I had tried not to use that same moldering formula, wherein the great man arrives late to a fashionable restaurant, says something enigmatic, then a rote description of his profound charisma. A cigarette is lit, the brand essential. There is small talk. The man must treat the waiter with warmth and humility, and this should be a humanizing surprise. Then back to the tortured childhood, the overbearing mother, the absent father, signs of precocity and genius, a wild misspent youth, minor success, moderate fame, a turning point, some visionary curator or gallerist, and then international reverence. The cigarette has become three, crumbs on the table, sediment in the wine glasses. Now he is gathering his coat, now we are outside on a Manhattan corner. Another cigarette, something enigmatic is spoken, he bows his head and down 10th Avenue he vanishes.

I tried to do a little more than that, tried to say something about the sculptures that hadn't already been said. I'd come to love Ernst Frankel and I didn't want to embarrass myself. I had the sense that Light knew he'd thrown me off-balance and was delighted by it.

"Very little, Mr. Fields," Light said. "Very little. What I would like, my great hope as I come to the end of a long life, is that you will do for me, for this, for us, what you did for him, which is to reveal not us, but our work."

"And nothing about you? Where you came from? Your history?"

He pushed the hair back from his eyes and said, "I am nothing, Mr. Fields, but what is here."

And then he was gone, our tour concluded in a cloud of cliché.

16

After he'd gone, I sat for a while in The Spiral before I went up to The Barn looking for the woman who called herself Crystalline, who I sensed was something other than the rest, but no luck. Instead, I found Siddhartha sitting at our table drinking the familiar green goo from a slim glass.

"Cleanse day," he whispered. "Last meal you'll get until tomorrow."

I sat down. "Think I'll give it a pass."

"Listen, let me finish this thing and we'll talk after."

"Right. Sorry. Silent lunch. Must obey the rules."

Fifteen minutes later we were walking toward the studios where all the front walls were retractable and as we passed, one of them was open wide enough for me to catch a glimpse of Theo né Theo standing before a blank canvas. He held the top of his head with his right hand, apparently deep in thought, or seeking inspiration, or trying to find the right pose.

He was wearing white overalls splattered with paint. Difficult to tell whether the stains were the result of frantic painting, or if they'd been designed by the latest prodigy of bohemian chic.

When he turned, I waved. In return, he rolled his door closed.

"You've met Theo?" Sid asked.

"And Crystalline."

"Right. The celebrated Crystalline."

"You're not a fan?"

"She's very talented."

"Diplomatic of you."

He smiled and changed the subject. "Unless you're invited, it's better not to engage with the artists while they're in their studios."

In this gentle reprimand, he sounded very much like Plume.

He took me to a studio a few down from Theo's and rolled back the door. His canvases all faced the wall. There was a wide table in the middle of the room where he'd arranged cans of brushes, and pencils and all other paraphernalia of the painter. A little fridge in one corner. A deep chair in the other. Two red Jielde floor lamps. Through the glass wall was a tricolor flag of sky, forest, and grass. It was the same pasture we'd walked, but in the daylight, from this angle, it was easier to measure its massive scale.

"You'd be amazed how different it looks in the morning, in the evening. I'd put up with about anything for this place. It's incredibly rare."

"I can imagine."

I hoped he would turn one of his paintings around.

"It's very tidy."

Frankel's studio was the most chaotic place I'd ever seen, which was the opposite of what I'd anticipated. People came and went constantly. Phones rang. There was always music playing. Live and recorded. Often simultaneously. Everything seemed expendable. Nothing felt fragile, but before I saw it, I had the idea that it would be austere, that to make what he did, he would toil in monastic calm. His work, everything from the notebooks to the major installations, no matter the period, no matter the subject, possessed an uncanny amalgamation of stillness, violence and softness. Underlying all of it was something solid and eternal, as if whatever he produced immediately carried the weight of the ancient. That was the great mystery, I thought, the magical, ineffable thing that allows a piece of art to seem both contemporary and infinite.

The first time I went to see him on Hester Street, a band was set up in the vast front room where the almond-colored leather couches and aquamarine rugs were spread over the worn plank floors. The East Eggs: two studiously scruffy young men—one on bass, the other on drums—and a striking woman with a shaved head, a bit older, strapped to a red Rickenbacker 360. She called herself Malice. When I walked in that late afternoon, she was snarling her way through The Jam's greatest hits and whenever I hear "In the City," I think of those kids, their eyes closed in that wide-open atrium, the pink winter afternoon sky pouring down on them through the skylights, playing for an audience of artists and stragglers, everyone dressed and posed to make a point.

I was very happy there, even if I was aware that it was all a bit too cozy for an untrained, undisciplined journalist. Painters or sculptors or musicians or actors or models or poets, they all knew who I was and no one who hung around Hester Street in those days was there just for the pleasure and family of it. Everyone was striving, and they all believed having their names in print would carry them closer to empires of their own, but, for the most part, I only wanted them as color. I was always there for Frankel, and I was jealous of the hours I spent with him alone.

Now Sid looked around his own studio and shrugged. "Mr. Light doesn't approve of disorder."

"He doesn't approve of disorder?"

"He prefers us to keep our studios clean."

"Right," I said. "And you?"

He gave me that slightly embarrassed smile. "I wouldn't mind a bit of a mess."

"But?"

"These are small prices to pay. You want tea?"

I did. He flipped on a kettle and when he was finished—Earl Grey, milk and sugar without asking me—we sat at the table before his lovely view, looking through the glass. There was a tin next to a pencil can and from it he produced a roll of gingersnaps. "Contraband," he said.

"What about the cleanse?"

"You look hungry."

"Nice of you. Where'd you get them?"

"There's a little town not so far. Nothing much."

"Is it worth the walk?"

"There's a bar. Good burgers. I like the guy who owns it. Sunny."

Now he looked away from me, as if he'd made a mistake, stepped out of line.

"Why do you hesitate, Sid?"

He picked up a thin brush from the table and took a deep breath. Then he said, "You might like to talk to him. That's all."

"Why would I want to talk to him?"

"It was his family who sold the land to Light."

"How would Light feel about me going down there? About you telling me this?"

He looked at his tea. "That's not really the story you came to write, is it?"

"Why not?"

"It's the same one we've heard a thousand times."

"Which is?

"Where are you from, Sol?"

"Los Angeles."

"And before that?"

"New York. Russians. Germans. Jews. And you?"

"I was born in Chicago. First generation."

"And your parents?"

"Bangalore."

"I see you've managed to change the subject."

"Not at all. My grandparents were loyal subjects of the Crown. How many times have we heard the same old story? Pink men with money get sick of the cold, head out into the world and take what they want."

"That's an awfully concise history of the world."

"The difference between your people and my people is that we never managed to do our own colonizing."

"What's Kashmir then?"

He smiled. "Fair point. Though our history isn't quite so simple."

"Neither is ours."

He laughed.

"Have you ever asked Light about Sunny?"

"No."

"Why not?"

"In my experience, he doesn't like to be questioned."

"And you want to please your master."

"I want to stay and paint, yes."

"Well, it's nice that Queen Victoria allows you to leave from time to time."

"We're not prisoners here."

"But leaving is not encouraged."

"It is not."

"Strange, this garden of his."

"He says, 'To leave The Garden is to leave the muse.'"

"Come on."

"Art is all. He's an absolutist. You are either devoted to the work, or you are a fraud. No middle ground. I know he may seem ridiculous—all the koans, rules and rituals—but I really do believe the same thing. The work must become an obsession. As the man says, 'It requires the passion of the pilgrim.' And I understand, too. I'm not fucking around with this. You know, a lot of people here take it for granted. As if this isn't rare. As if being given a studio, food, a place to sleep is part of life. And it is for a lot of them. They have parents who will give them whatever they ask for. But I've got nothing to fall back on. I haven't spoken to my parents for fifteen years. I have four thousand dollars in a checking account. That's it."

"Does Light know?"

"Know what?"

"How little you have."

"I'm not looking for sympathy. What I'm saying is that while all this might seem a sort of silly lark, a kind of brief adventure with an eccentric, it's a lot more than that to me. Painting is all I have. I'm sorry to sound a cliché, but it's true. Too late to turn around. So, when it comes to the lectures, the evals, the rituals, I'll swallow it. And I'll do it happily. It doesn't make any real difference. My war is elsewhere."

"What's an eval?"

"Each week he drops by a studio and looks at the work. Gives his impressions."

"And what do you think of his taste?"

"I've never seen a prettier place."

I narrowed my eyes at him, but he looked away and when he did, I was struck both by his beauty and an abrupt flatness in expression.

"Have you ever seen his work?"

"I don't know."

"You don't know?"

"Some say the sculptures at the entrance to The Spiral are his."

"But he doesn't claim them?"

"I've never heard him claim them. But I've never asked."

"Why not?"

"It's difficult to explain. He doesn't spend much time with us except for in—"

"Official capacities?"

"I guess so, yes. He doesn't eat dinner with us. He generally keeps to himself."

"Do you believe he's an artist?"

"In one way or another. And if it's true that the sculptures are his, then all the more so."

"You're a cagey fucker."

He looked up and smiled. "Would you like to see the card?"

"Why are you so evasive?"

"Why are you so suspicious?"

"I don't know. A mysterious man sends a beautiful woman to deliver a personal invitation to his garden paradise. Why would I be suspicious?"

"I meant why are you so suspicious of me?"

"I don't know. Maybe you're a honeytrap."

I didn't know where that line had come from, and I certainly hadn't meant for it to sound so absurdly sultry, but it brought his eyes to mine.

"A honeytrap? Are you afraid I'll seduce you, Sol?"

"A joke," I said, but there was a spinning in my chest and this time it was me who looked away, pretending to study a can of turpentine.

"HinJew," he said. "You know the expression?"

I laughed. "No."

"My sister married a Jew. It's a thing, you know. The HinJews. They say we share many similarities, our cultures. Whatever that means. We've established that both peoples use a history of oppression and the threat of terrorism as an excuse to oppress, but do *your* people ride elephants and work in call centers? Are *you* born with magical insight and a direct connection to medical schools and spirit worlds?"

I liked him so much. I missed sarcasm and sharp irony. Even in New York, it was falling fast out of fashion. Caution and fear of offense had replaced rough irreverence. Charity never said a cruel word against anyone. No one did, no one dared. Except for the obvious and group-sanctioned villains, everything and everyone was *amazing*. Nothing destroys humor like fear, and God were we terrified by the time I flew.

Charity did not respond well when I fell into my boring funks, when I grumbled about the vacuity, the stupidity of all that hope and cultivated enthusiasm, its languages and those of craven capitalism shamelessly Vitamixed into a bland slurry. I hated the wholesale rejection of rancor, hated more our terror of uttering the forbidden word. "What the world needs now is rage and revolt, not another credit card, Charity, not another pair of pants, day rave, *small batch* bourbon or chakra workshop," I said, while she yawned and rolled her eyes. "I am so sick of those people," I told her after another soul-flattening dinner, frantic for even the slightest sympathetic smile. But she only sighed and told me to practice loving kindness. Sipping from her steaming cup of fair-trade Night Coma, she said, "What's wrong with being cautious, Sol? Why do you have to offend people?" I stormed around the bathroom shaking my fist, trying to talk over her yowling supersonic platinum-edition toothbrush. She just spat and rinsed and yanked a long line of CBD-infused floss from its silver dispenser. "Go to bed, Soli," she said, tightening the two ends around her fingers until they turned purple. "Get some rest."

And while she slept so easily beside me, I lay awake and remembered Lina Klein raising her eyes from a cup of tomato soup, saying, "It's all a little much, Solomon. Enough with the doom and the gloom and the self-righteous blathering. It's tedious. I warned you about her. I warned you about the job. I told you what happens when a Jew shares a bed with a Charity."

So thank God for Siddhartha, peppercorn in the Splenda bowl.

"Let's see the beautiful business card that launched your ship," I said.

Siddhartha stood up and moved across the room while outside, the pasture grass convulsed in the lashing wind.

That night I sat outside in my robe watching the sky, remembering my grandmother telling me, for the first time, the story of my half-namesake, her great artist hero, Charlotte Salomon. She was visiting from New York and had taken me to The Getty, a place she found ridiculous.

"Another ruthless bastard trying to pretty his soul with art. Look at this place. What is it with the rich and their need to reproduce what already exists?"

We were sitting on a bench in the sculpture garden sharing a Snickers bar.

"After Kristallnacht she went to live with her grandparents in the south of France. They hid for a while in a villa there owned by yet another American millionaire. It must have looked something like this, with columns and statues and pretty views over the water. Then they moved to Nice, where her grandmother tried to hang herself. And you know what her grandfather told her after they got her down? That her aunt, *her* namesake, had committed suicide at eighteen. Charlotte's own mother, too, who until that moment she'd believed had died of the flu, jumped out a window. A year later her grandmother did the same thing while Charlotte looked on. And then? Her grandfather insists they share a bed together. Just like my charming savior in Berlin, Soli. She despised him. More than Hitler. He taunted her. Said she'd be the next to kill herself. Encouraged her to do it. And after all this, you know what Charlotte does? Despite the French sending her and her pathetic grandfather to a camp and then surviving it? Despite her grandfather's hands? She paints. And you know the question she said she was trying to answer?"

I shook my head.

"'Whether to take her own life or embark on something quite insanely extraordinary.' That's what she said. It was suicide or do something 'quite insanely extraordinary.'"

"And what happened to her?"

"Well, after a while she can't take her grandfather, so she gets a room in a little hotel and while the Vichy cowards are coming, and the Gestapo and the Italians and her neighbors and all the rest of the awful world, she sings to herself and she paints and paints and paints. She takes it all, Sol, and she makes something beautiful."

It wasn't the first time she'd rhapsodized about an artist, but there was something in her face this time that was different.

"So she moves back to the villa and marries a man she doesn't love, who was once the American millionaire's lover. The Nazis found them, of course. They're sent to Auschwitz. She's five months pregnant. They gas her the day she arrives. And then that's it. As if she's just nothing."

Lina Klein handed me the rest of the Snickers bar.

I could feel the chocolate beginning to melt between my fingers.

"I like to imagine you're named after her."

"Am I?"

"No. Different spelling. Your parents were thinking of the king if they were thinking at all. But when I look at you, I often imagine her."

"Is that good?"

"Of course, it's good. She was something outstanding."

"What happened to the paintings?"

"They survived. And they weren't just paintings. It was a novel. An opera. A memoir. It was everything at once made of everything she had seen and read and heard and loved and despised. Painters, musicians, poets, filmmakers, fascists, murderers, sadists, lovers, geniuses, fools. She painted it to music she heard only in her mind. *Leben? oder Theater?, Life? or Theater?* That's what she called it."

Before that moment, I don't think I'd ever heard my grandmother speak a word of German.

"But what happened to it?"

"Before she was taken, she'd wrapped it up and gave it to a friend. A doctor. '*C'est toute ma vie*,'" she told him. "It's my whole life."

17

That evening I dressed for dinner, but found The Barn shuttered. I'd forgotten it was the day of the intestinal pogrom, when all toxins were to be eliminated by the furious green stormtroopers of Sebastian Light's concoctions.

I did not want fruit. I did not want my food woven with philosophy or morality. I did not want to think at all. I wanted to fill my body and no number of passion fruit would do it.

Siddhartha had planted the seed. Whether he'd done it on orders or in an act of treason, I couldn't tell but I would find that bar.

The night was darker, the lights dimmer and there was a strangeness to the world. No one was out. No music played. Wherever they'd all gone, I had not been invited.

I arrived at the closed iron gate. It appeared there was no exit. Short of scaling the stone or vaulting the rusted metal, I could see no way out. But then I found a small, hammered-silver knob. I turned it and a narrow door swung open toward the outside world.

I hesitated as if leaving were some major transgression.

Absurd. I stepped into the dark night and its eucalyptus air. The road was unlit and beneath the dense canopy filtering the moonlight, I could just barely make out the shoulder. It felt good to be free of the Kingdom of Light, moving forward through darkness.

I looked up from time to time to navigate by the silhouette

of branches against the sky. Ten, fifteen, twenty minutes and nothing but VapoRub wind and the sound of my sandals slapping on asphalt. The journey began to feel more like falling than walking. I wondered if Siddhartha had been kidding about a town. Maybe it was a setup, a test.

I was so weak and dizzy with hunger now that the prospect of trudging back up the hill without having eaten was inconceivable.

Eventually I stepped out from beneath the canopy into a landscape tinseled with moonlight and at last the world was delineated. There was the highway. I gambled and turned right.

Now and then a car would race past, but otherwise it was eerily still. After about ten minutes I was sure I'd been fooled. Had it been some challenge set by Sebastian Light? Had Sid been sent to dangle false promises of fast food to test my purity and resolve? But as I was descending into increasingly complex fantasies of betrayal, I saw yellow light glowing behind a rise.

Soon a narrow road breaking from the highway came into view and not far along it, lights. In a few minutes I was standing on a wooden walkway, which ran maybe fifty yards on either side of the street. All the buildings shared the same style, the same wooden façade.

Martin Brockett's Tack and General was closed. Mercifully, Sunny's Bar was open.

I walked through that door as if I'd spent all day on a horse, a foreign man from a foreign land. I was prepared for leathery cowboys, red-faced ranchers, Johnny Cash on the jukebox. It seemed that kind of a place, but the music was slack key guitar and not a single person, not the big guy behind the bar, the few in front of it, or the others shooting pool, was white. They all turned when I came in, but not as if I were wearing a black hat and a silver six on my hip. It was just a quick sizing up, and then back to their game and their drinks.

I took a stool, said hello, asked the bartender if they were serving any food. He nodded to a chalkboard above him, which featured burgers and fries and nothing else.

The place and the menu so perfectly corresponded with my waking dream; it was as if I had willed it into existence. The absence of cultivated style, mystery and millet provoked in me a powerful wave of pleasure. What discovery, what sanctuary.

The burger and fries came hot and fresh. The bartender dried glasses while I ate, and when I'd finished, he smiled.

"Good?"

"Fuck," I said and ordered another one.

After he came back from the kitchen with the next round he leaned against the register. Tall, broad-shouldered, strong, but not particularly muscular. He had a bit of a belly swelling his clean white apron. But despite the neck-down fleshiness his face was drawn sharp and lean, his remarkably round head shaved close to the bone.

"Where you visiting from?"

"L.A."

"You staying up the hill?"

"At Sebastian Light's place."

He grunted.

"I understand that it was yours once."

"My mother's. You an artist?"

"No."

"You're friends with him then?

"Definitely not."

"Uh huh. You want another beer?"

"Sure."

He poured me one.

"Sol," I said.

He took his time drying his hands before we shook.

"Sol like sun?"

"Like Solomon."

"You a wise king?"

"Neither sunny nor a king."

"As it happens, I'm Sunny."

"Good to meet you," I said.

"What do you do, King Solomon?"

"Now, I'm unemployed. I just quit my job."

"What was that?"

"Advertising."

"Got to make a living."

"Right."

"No shame in that."

"Plenty of shame."

"I guess you're right," he said and then after a long pause, "Sebastian *Light*."

"Not his real name, I take it."

"That sound like anyone's real name to you?"

"You know the real one?"

"Nah," he said.

"When he bought the land from you, he used that name?"

"As far as I know. He bought it from my mom. I was a kid."

"Why don't you like him?"

"Why don't you tell me what you're doing there if you're not an artist and you're not his friend?"

"I used to be a kind of journalist."

"All right."

"He wants me to write about him."

"And say what?"

"I'm still working that out. Either he's a generous man and a great artist who has made a sanctuary for promising young painters, or he's a sly, brilliant performance artist who has orchestrated an incredible living installation for my benefit."

Sunny nodded but he was clearly unconvinced of either.

"But there's a third option," I said.

"What's that?"

“That he’s an empty, talentless narcissist who lives in a closed loop dependent on the constant adulation of a bunch of desperate sycophants.”

He laughed at this. “Not likely he’d choose the third option.”

“No, not likely. Anyway, I don’t know if I’m going to write anything at all.”

“Well, if you do it, do it right.”

“How would you do it?”

“I wouldn’t forget that people lived there long before he showed up.”

“Tell me about them.”

With his thumb, he rubbed away a smear of grease from the bar.

“I’ll tell you what, if you decide you’re going to do this, and you don’t turn out to be one of those desperate sycophants, you come back here.”

Then he walked into the kitchen. I waited, hoping he would return. All the others were gone now, pool cues crossed atop the table. The jukebox was playing Willie Nelson.

I could see him back there, scrubbing the grill, his broad back to me.

“What do I owe for the food?”

“Forty,” he said without turning around.

I put a fifty on the bar and walked into the night.

When at last I came half-drunk, sweating and panting to the gate, I found that I was locked out. There was no knob on the outside. In the dark, I couldn’t even find the outline of his trick door, or even the words cut through his gate. For a moment, I tried to read them by hand, but no luck.

I didn’t like the prospect of scaling the wall. It frightened me, though I wasn’t sure what exactly I feared. Hidden razor wire? Some apprentice on night watch armed with an Uzi and a klieg light? So, I pressed the button Plume had pressed all those days ago. Eventually a green light flicked on and a camera began to murmur and hum. No one spoke and if there were an audio system, it was only being used to listen. Then, after too long, the great grinding gears moaned, the iron panels split in two revealing a perfectly illuminated Plume in a nightgown of green, graceful dignitary awaiting the arrival of her bumbling foreign guest. I stepped through, the gears kicked in, and I was returned to the muted, underwater quiet of The Coded Garden at night.

"Thanks for the welcome party," I said.

She smiled her bloodless smile and the two of us walked together toward my cottage.

"You had a nice evening?"

"I did. Is there a way for me to return here without disturbing you?"

"Leave, yes. Return, no."

"So, each time I leave we'll have to go through this?"

"It's really the only way."

"I'm a prisoner?"

"If I'm not mistaken, you left rather easily. It's getting in that's slightly more difficult."

"One might argue," I said, doing my best to match her irritating register, "that being constantly monitored is a kind of imprisonment."

"Oh, now I wouldn't say you're being constantly monitored, Mr. Fields. And after all, there's not a good hotel in the world that doesn't note their guests' comings and goings."

"And yet this is not a hotel."

"No, but we like to look after our guests as if it were."

"You are saying there's no key available? No code, no clicker?"

"There is not."

"I suppose I'll have to speak with your supervisor."

"As you like."

"Do you ever break character, Plume?"

"I hope you'll come to understand there is nothing to break."

By then we'd come to my cottage. She turned to me. I was immediately weakened. Her very form was a blow. She wrinkled her nose.

"Mr. Fields, you smell of hamburgers."

What a sentence. I laughed as naturally as I had with Siddhartha that afternoon. No mockery, no dismissal, and she seemed for a second to come to life. Was there not a new brightness in her face, some twinkling joy in her eyes? Would this be the moment that she'd speak with a semblance of sincerity? Could we now have a human conversation?

No.

She clenched her jaw then said, "Mr. Fields, I wonder if you'll write about us."

I sighed. She was as unswerving as every fanatical publicist I'd ever known.

"What would I write? It's nice, but nobody needs another fawning piece about another nice place. I've seen nearly no art. Your man won't answer my questions. On the other hand, you know where I might find a good story?"

"Where?"

"Down at the bar. Unsurprisingly, it turns out there's more than one version of your origin story."

She said, "I appreciate your candor, Mr. Fields."

But my response seemed to have shaken her. Her eyes darted about in her skull, as if rebooting, then she raised her chin and walked away, green gown fluttering as she blew off into the night.

"Go back to the artists," Lina Klein told me a year before she closed her life. She'd come to New York to see me and was staying in a fashionable hotel around the corner from the apartment, which she'd been renting for a fortune since I'd abandoned it for a life of Pale and Charity.

At the hotel bar she said again, "This life you're living up there, what's it for? You're miserable. And that woman, Solomon." She shook her head and watched a floss-thin waitress drift past.

"What should I do instead?"

"I've told you. Come back here with the artists. Please don't live without them."

"You think these people are *artists*? Paying twenty-six dollars for a scotch? And you *rented* the apartment. To a guy who works at a fucking hedge fund. Which is the only kind of guy who can afford to pay the indecent amount of money you're asking."

She laughed.

"The artists are gone," I said. "They can barely afford to live in Brooklyn."

"So, go somewhere else then. I want you to be happy, Soli. Move to Guam. I don't care. But you will not be happy like this. You will die vacant and alone."

"We all die vacant and alone," I said, regretting it as soon as I saw her expression.

She rolled her eyes. "Why'd the chicken cross the road, Solomon?"

"Why?"

"To die alone in the rain."

I laughed.

"Supposedly it's Hemingway's joke, but you are not Hemingway. You are my grandson and I love you and I want you to be happy and this is no way to be happy."

"Have you thought that maybe I am happy?"

"I'm an old woman now."

"You're the youngest person I know."

"As an old woman, I am entitled to certain demands."

"And you're demanding that I leave the love of my life and a lucrative job in the middle of a recession and go back to a dying industry?"

"Writing is not an *industry.* You sound like *them*. And the love of your life? Please. I'm telling you not to waste a life that a great many people would kill for. If it's all over here, then go somewhere else. You know damn well the place is not the point. I fear for your heart."

"Sounds dire."

She pushed her scotch out of the way, leaned toward me and took my hands the way she always did when she needed to make herself understood. "This is not a joke. I am telling you the truth. Despite what you imagine, there is really no more time left. If you keep on like this, you will never come back. You'll never get out from under it. You'll be too comfortable. Your brain will rot. Your heart will harden and freeze. *This* is that moment you have heard about all your life. Now. *Now*. You have to decide. Do you understand me?"

"Baba—"

"Do you understand me?"

"Yes," I said.

"Solomon, do you fucking understand me?"

"I understand you."

"Okay then. I won't tell you again. Now let's go. I want a sandwich."

18

The next day, or maybe the day after that—time was rapidly losing its meaning and I could not perfectly keep track of its passing—I went for a long walk around the grounds. Coming up the wide sloping pasture, the blond guitarist was parading a small herd of goats in my direction. It was a lovely image: the lithe, shirtless, blue-eyed shepherd smiling as he came, golden hair lifting in the breeze, teeth as white as the animals' coats, both shining bright in the afternoon sun. It was often difficult to believe that these living tableaux which so frequently materialized before me were spontaneous.

As I parted his sea of goats, he said, "Greetings. Are you enjoying?"

I waited for him to finish, but that was it. Everything was shorthand here, everything was hashtag, which only intensified the sensation of living within a highly controlled and virtual world.

"I am. Are you?"

"I am so blessed," he said, beaming. "Look around us. Look at these animals."

He laid his hand on the head of the tallest goat and blinked at me.

"How long have you been here?"

"Long enough to see myself. Long enough to be renewed."

"And you like it here? A lot of time to paint?"

"Oh, brother, you can't imagine. It's as if this garden is communicating with my brush. It's a very special place."

I nodded.

"Listen, I've got to get these little ladies milked, but if you need anything, you just ask me, okay? I'm here. I'm right here." Then he quarter-bowed, said, "Blessings," and continued on down the pasture and I watched him go wondering why I was so shaken by such a barren exchange. Was it because there was something else at play beneath the deathly language? Or because I had abandoned everything for a place utterly devoid of meaning?

At The Library, where I was hoping to be alone, I found Theo and Crystalline reading in the warm glow of the green-shaded lamps. I'd taken too many steps inside to politely turn around, so I slumped into a chair and, hoping to avoid conversation, reached for the first book I could find, a five-pound tome of Helmut Newton photographs resting at my elbow. I regretted it immediately. What kind of person charges into a library and immediately drags a pile of nudes onto his lap? I could feel Theo's eyes fix on me.

"Good evening, Sol," Crystalline said, glancing up from her book.

"Hi," Theo said, returning to his as soon as I looked at him.

"You like Newton?" she asked, smiling.

"Not especially," I said. "What are you reading?"

She raised the book so that I could see the cover. "*The Renaissance Portrait.*"

"You're far more serious than I am."

"Probably. Though some might argue that photography is more serious, that it has made the painted portrait obsolete."

"Do you believe that?"

"No, but I've never been interested in those questions. Someone is always saying something is dead."

I laughed. "Yes. And you, Theo?"

"What am I reading?"

"Yes." He raised a slim paperback, "*Out of Shade into Light: Painting Through Trauma.*"

"Interesting?"

"I'm sorry," he said, "but I'd like to focus."

Crystalline said, "Don't be sour, Theodore."

He didn't answer. She grinned at me and said, "I hate Helmut Newton."

"Why?"

"It's as if he sets out to murder his subjects. All those beautiful women. When he's done with them, they may as well be desks or teacups. There's nothing human left."

Theo said, still without looking up, "I've always liked him."

She turned to him. "Is that right? Tell us why, Theodore."

"I think he can do both. Give and take life."

"Fascinating," she said.

He flushed. "Can I see the book?"

I handed it to him.

"They're beautiful photographs," Theo said, turning the pages. "They're frightening. Powerful. They clearly deal with death."

Crystalline rolled her eyes. "It's all too polished, too organized, too aspirational. Too easy. Did he ever photograph an ugly woman? An ugly anything?"

"So, you condemn him for his subjects?" I said.

"I condemn him for a lack of imagination," she said. "He was a technician, not an artist."

Theo shook his head. "Newton himself said that in photography there are two dirty words: art and taste."

"Convenient for him, isn't it?" Crystalline said. "Funny how art and taste are dirty words, but he clearly had no trouble with money."

Theo nodded at her book. "You think those Renaissance painters you love so much weren't doing it all for the money?"

He took a Kleenex from his breast pocket and wiped his nose.

"Theo has a cold," Crystalline said. Never had such a simple statement of fact sounded so cruel.

"And Crystalline dreams of her integrity, while she goes on taking everything she can from our patron."

She closed the book hard, as if killing a mosquito between its pages. She seemed amused. "And what exactly is the conflict there?"

"You don't agree with anything he says. You think he's a fraud. And yet you keep your mouth shut. Every single eval you listen, and you smile, and you say nothing. You play the game. You even changed your name."

"But I paint. I paint, don't I? Which is more than I can say for you, who claims to adore the man."

This last blow seemed unnecessarily mean. He was odious and pathetic, but clearly, he was in love with her, weaker, and, I was certain, less talented. My commitment to conventional morality was weak, but I despised bullies and I was afraid she'd go further. I didn't want to see it.

So I said, "I was once at a party with Ernst Frankel."

This stopped their bickering.

"Come on," Crystalline said.

"Why?" Theo did not seem grateful for my intervention.

"I wrote about him. It was a long time ago."

"For a magazine?" Crystalline leaned toward me.

I nodded.

"Which magazine?" Each time Theo spoke, it was with more disdain.

"Let him talk, Theo," Crystalline said, but it was clear she, too, wanted the answer. The quality of her attention had changed.

"It was very crowded. We were in SoHo. In a big loft. Of course. Every art party cliché in the world. He introduced me to a Greek woman. Very beautiful. Strange, unforgettable face. She was probably ten years older than I was. Big black eyes, spring-loaded hair. I liked her immediately. Enough not to notice right away that Frankel had abandoned us on a couch by one of those big windows. It was very cold out and I remember her tracing waves through the condensation on the glass. At the time, I was still impressed by New York and totally unsure of myself, so I was happy to be sitting there with this woman who was one of those people who seems to know more than anyone else does. We talked for a long time, but really all I remember of our conversation, aside from the thrill of it, the scene, the wonderful sense that I was in exactly the right place doing exactly what I should be, was that she took my hands in hers as if she were going to impart some profound knowledge. She really took her time and I thought, maybe because I was drunk, or because I was vulnerable to wise, beautiful women, I thought, my God, she's about to change my life. But you know what she said?"

Crystalline and Theo—because no one, not even Theo, could resist the mystery of an ending—were rapt.

"She said, 'The whole world is burning and you're trimming your pussy'."

Crystalline began to laugh. Theo slunk down in his chair.

"It's always calmed me down," I said.

It was true that Frankel had introduced me to a pretty woman at a party in SoHo, and that we had sat together on a couch and talked and smoked a joint and had walked back in the cold to her apartment and that she was ten years older and that for a while she had made me feel very calm and very happy, but she wasn't Greek, she was married and she hadn't said anything about the world burning.

That bit was Lina Klein's story, which she'd told me when I was fifteen or sixteen and my mother wasn't home. She came into the living room from the kitchen, a can of beer in each hand. As was often the case when she told stories, she'd forgotten what else she was doing, so instead of handing me mine, she was talking a thousand miles an hour, moving like a sugared-up hummingbird, the hem of her red robe twisting this way and that, always a little slower than her body.

"We were at a party together at the apartment of a writer who had just published a novel everyone was talking about but of course he's dead and dust and now no one including me can remember his name."

I believed she withheld nothing from me. There was such fluency between us—a deep sense of mutual comprehension, which felt musical.

"I can't even remember the girl's name. Doesn't matter. I was sad and scared and sick of nearly everyone I knew, and this gorgeous girl takes me into a corner and holds my hands and I'm sure she said a great many things, but what I remember, what I've always remembered is the Greek expression. Well, no, I have no memory of the Greek, but in English—" and then my grandmother grinned the way she always did when she was about to say something she knew would embarrass me. "Soli, I thought it was the funniest thing in the world and it always calmed me down. Oh, I really loved that girl. So much time lost. Anyway, remember it whenever you're trimming your pussy," Lina Klein said, giggling, coming at last to land beside me with two sweating cans in her hands while I hid my head in my arms.

Now as I watched Crystalline laughing, and Theo simmering, I tried to see my grandmother at their age, tough and lonely in New York City sitting with the beautiful Greek woman, hearing the expression, which, for all I knew, wasn't a Greek expression, or an expression at all. It, along with the girl herself, may have been partly, or entirely, invented by my grandmother for the purpose of making me happier than I was.

And now I felt sorry for poor Theo. I was sure he'd been following the same pattern since he was a teenager. The same sad fate of so many small, lonely neurotic boys. "Always the friend, never the fucker," as Lina Klein would have it. The same old story, time after time. The inevitable drunken confession. The girl, always so much taller, always searching for someone self-assured, experienced, saying, *I'm sorry, but*, and then Theodore the Furious, enraged by sexual frustration and universal unfairness, would howl at the stars, storming off to sulk before threatening suicide. Over and over and over he would enact these dramas and now, so poisoned by rejection, he had found himself in The Garden, determined, as were we all, to begin again.

He would be patient and kind. He would never blame a woman for her indifference, for her preferences, for her failure to love him. And yet, here he was repeating the same mistake, unable to paint or, even, build his new name, knowing full well that he didn't stand a chance with towering Crystalline no matter how many hours a day he spent before his easel or working through the tongue exercises he memorized from Maxim.

"I think I'll leave you two to your reading," I said and stood up.

Crystalline looked at me with something more focused than friendliness and said, "I hope you'll come and see my work soon, Sol."

"I'd like that very much. And yours, too, Theo," I said, but he only grunted, as I headed for the door.

In the balmy night, out of the cold library air I felt energized and fully awake for the first time since I'd left Los Angeles. Perhaps it was Crystalline's attention, or believing I'd defended Theo, or because I'd adapted and performed Lina Klein's story, or because the jet lag was fading at last.

Whatever it was, instead of walking home, I entered The

Spiral and wound around in the dark until I came to the six-fingered hand, lit from below, its shadow fracturing in the shifting bamboo. And then Siddhartha stepped out of the dark-green night.

"I'm sorry," he said, when I jumped. "I wasn't trying to scare you."

He sat next to me on the bench.

"Come here often?"

"Cute," he said.

"Are you following me?"

"Just passing by."

"This is good, I think," I said nodding at the hand.

"I like it, too."

"Is it his?"

"Depends on who you ask."

"And the heads outside?"

"As I told you, some people say they're his. Some say Henry Moore."

"I doubt that."

"He's got the money."

"But does he have the taste?"

"See for yourself. There's an eval tomorrow," he said and then, after a long moment, "Are you happy here, Sol?"

"I'm glad I came, if that's what you're asking."

"People have been good to you?"

"Yes," I said. "Though I don't think Theo is all that happy I'm here."

Sid leaned forward, all at once alert and focused.

"No? Why do you say that? Did he insult you?"

"No, no. Of course not. Forget it. It really makes no difference at all."

"All right. Do you think you'll write about us?"

"Us?"

"This place. Him. Whatever."

"I don't know. I'm not sure what there is to say, really. As I've told the Director of Communications."

Again, he didn't take the bait.

"You're loyal to him," I said.

"How can I not be?"

I was tempted to answer his question, but I didn't have the energy for it, or for a conversation at all. I'd have been happy to sit with him there without speaking, watching the greening hand and its ever-changing background. I wished then that he'd put his arm around my shoulders, which surprised me. The desire and its intensity.

"Well," he said, standing up, "I'm sorry to have bothered you."

I shook my head as if to say, don't worry, but I don't know how he translated it. Then he was gone and I stayed on and thought of Lina Klein drifting into one of her darker moods at the end of her SoHo story, "All those people gone, Soli, disappeared from my life, most of them dead. And after all their chatter, their philosophies and opinions, I can't remember a single one of their names. Sometimes, what I'd really like is to just stop talking altogether."

"You mean forever?"

She shook her head as if to say, forget it.

And now I thought, More than anything else, maybe that was her reason. Just for the silence.

19

It was a dark and stormy night and all along the ridge, The Garden's artists stood before their studios. They wore summer scarves and buttoned shirts, cotton dresses and black denim, Birkenstocks instead of bare feet. Crystalline sat outside her studio on a tall yellow stool all dressed in bluish grey, one leg thrown over another. It seemed impossible that she didn't have a cigarette slotted between two fingers, or, at least, a phone in her hand. It was striking how different the world was without those contemporary props of diversion, how their absence altered the states of both solitude and assembly. It forced our chins up. It kept us still. Or most of us. Pacing in front of his studio was put-upon Theo, who appeared to be on the verge of combustion. He moved like a man one avoids on the subway.

As for my own phone, from the instant I was sealed into that airplane at LAX I'd stopped paying attention, but it wasn't as if in New York I was deeply invested in worlds outside my own. I let the news go the way of books. I gave up watching those synthetic-skinned sermonizers diving after our nation's own supreme leader deeper and deeper into the oily catacombs, prattling on and on, more and more befuddled between the incessant ads for pharmaceuticals.

Do not take Abilify if you're allergic to Abilify.

One day after the next, our surrealist tragicomedy strained the bounds of credulity and after a while I changed the channel and moved to the insane nation of Bravo, where at commercial breaks, I was more likely to be confronted by my own handiwork.

I wish I could say that I stopped paying attention because the horrors of our time, the sociopaths we deserved, and all those cabinets of cowards caused me too much despair and pain.

Really though, as Charlotte Klein loved to point out, the problem was my *own* cowardice, my utter failure to do a single thing about any of it.

After I'd moved in with Charity and stopped responding to my mother's constant barrage of increasingly conservative op-eds, I told her that I'd given up.

"I liked you more when you were self-righteous," she said.

"But have you ever watched *Revenge Body*?"

She was not amused. "How long have I been telling you how little your *feelings* matter? Other people's suffering depresses *you*. You're *tired* of it. You don't like the way you *feel*. You're bored and your *feelings* are hurt because some cop beats a man to death? And then you come home parroting your goy girlfriend and lecture me about what I can and can't say? And now you quit altogether?"

I'd heard these lectures so many times before. They always ended with the same rousing conclusion: do something for someone else. First the someone should have been anyone who had less than I did. But later, she modified her directive to, "Above all, a Jew. A Jew would be a start. All the Jews would be better. Israel would be ideal. But at this point I'll take anyone. Anyone other than your precious little self."

The three of us at the beach together. A rare outing. Cloudless winter day, too cold to swim, but warm enough for mother and daughter to sit on the sand and yell at each other. I was maybe eleven years old, before my father went out for cigarettes. I had, as I always did when they fought, a stomachache and complained. She burst into a rage. "I don't give a fuck how you *feel*," she said. "I'm so tired of hearing about your feelings. Go puke in the bushes if you need to, but you're not the only one here."

Lina Klein looked at me and shrugged, which always meant, you see what she's like? As if I didn't already know. Nearby there was a scrubbed family sitting on a big Navajo blanket having a picnic. The parents gaped at my mother while their kids stared at me.

"Go fuck yourselves," my mother said.

They swept up their blanket and scurried away. And after they'd gone, Charlotte Klein said to me, "I don't give a fuck about *you*. It isn't *you* we're concerned with. The individual will be the end of us all." A little Marxist parenting at the seaside.

My grandmother kept her eyes on mine, perhaps trying to mitigate whatever damage was being done to my spongy mind. Always that slight smile on her face, which for so long I took to mean wisdom and kindness but would only later come to understand as something else.

Other times, my mother was gentler. Though she would never explicitly apologize, later she'd come into my room and rub my back as I pretended to sleep. "Sweetest of dreams," she'd say sounding just like her mother, something I don't think she ever understood.

Now she was vivid in my mind while lightning veined the horizon and I waited with those pretty painters for her least favorite kind of man. I missed my mother and felt an abrupt and awful sense of guilt for having abandoned her alone in that apartment where she had knelt to scrub pink tint from the yellowing porcelain. I should have never come here. Not after, for the first time in my life, she told me to do as I pleased.

But then there he was, sweeping down the hill, chin high, dressed all in white, arms spread as if for flight, and as he slowed to a stop, I felt moved in a minor way. Here he stood before us in the flesh, the guru, the master himself. And what was that feeling if not, when all was said and done, hope? Didn't he carry with him the possibility of better lives, better selves? Answers to impossible questions? Antidotes to sadness and suffering?

"Come, come, my friends. Gather around, please," and all the artists made a crowd in the light of The Barn. Once they had settled, he took a breath and began to speak. The man, it seemed, could do nothing without first giving a speech.

"We are all cowards, my friends. Even I, after all these years of life, am a coward. We, all of us, must understand the direct, indisputable correlation between cowardice and failure. This is crucial. It is not just that you are afraid. Understand: cowardice is not fear, cowardice is failure to act in the *face* of fear. In all the ways we are cowards, that is, in all the ways we fail to act, each instance of paralysis constitutes a sharp point of loss. You must understand this. It is essential. Let us consider commitment, let us consider devotion and engagement. When we fail to commit—whether to art or to love—we shall be punished for that failure. Fail to risk heartbreak and you will be punished with solitude. Fail to devote yourself to beauty and you will be punished with hollow work. Devotion is total. Risk is total. There must be no equivocation. Too many of these failures and you will be left angry, regretful, vacant and in the end, at the very best, if you're very lucky, you'll be left warning others not to make the same mistakes you did. Of course, if your failures of courage are few, if your accomplishments are many, then you may have the luxury of both, you may stand before an audience of young artists offering well-earned advice and wisdom gained from years of devotion and risk."

Here he bestowed upon us, a bright, knowing smile. I could just see the top of Crystalline's head. There was no sign of Plume. Siddhartha was standing toward the front looking particularly striking, the soft orange light enhancing the line of his jaw.

I tried to decode Crystalline's face.

Plume appeared then at her master's side looking alert and professional, hair drawn back in a tight ponytail, revealing the full proportions of her elegant neck. I saw not a flicker of humor in her eyes.

"Come," Sebastian Light said, "let's begin." He floated through the crowd and his flock followed. He passed the first studio and raised his hands at the second. We all stopped and then from the crowd stepped the slender man I'd seen playing guitar in front of The Barn, the man whose very fingertips were connected to The Garden.

He entered the studio and in the bright light looked out at us with his snow-blue eyes.

"Saber, are you ready?"

"Flow, flow," Saber said with that familiar California-rich-boy-burnout-twang that says I'm so relaxed even the full expression of complete words is taxing. And so, *flow flow* was pronounced *flah flah*. He bowed and swept his arm in welcome. Light entered, and we all pushed forward behind him.

I stood behind Siddhartha, close enough to smell him. Over his shoulder, I could see Crystalline in profile, her jaw set. Toward the back was an easel draped with a white sheet and just to the side a metal folding chair.

Light raised his chin and began again. "I will approach this painting as I would a painting in any gallery. I will not consider my personal relationship with Saber, such that it is. Perhaps as patron, I will be harsher than the average critic, for his success will also be mine. I will look, I will absorb, and I will respond. I hope that it will not only be Saber who learns from this experience, but all of you. I hope that you will see through my tired eyes, which have seen terrible things and wonderful art, terrible art and wonderful things. So much of both. Have faith that my intentions are pure. My aim is to educate and elucidate, to use my experience, my knowledge, my love of beauty, of you and all your potential, to inspire. I do not wish to cause pain, but when I *do* cause pain, and pain is often caused, I do so with tremendous regret. Please know that. Please know that I understand the terror, the hope, the desire, the dream. In the end, what I want is what you want. Beauty, my friends, beauty."

Somehow the crowd was transfixed, not, incredibly, because its members were witnessing an astonishing outpouring of dreck, but because they were moved. It seemed impossible that the man was serious, that any of them were, yet no one broke character, no one laughed.

I looked over at Crystalline, who looked back. She grinned just barely, but it wasn't clear if it was flirtation, or some acknowledgement, some agreement that the whole thing was, yes, absurd. Then Light was speaking again.

"Come," said our Susan Sontag of the palms, and Saber stepped forward to present his smooth, shadowless Germanic face, upon which everything was revealed—no darkness beneath the eyes, no furrows, no hollows in which to hide secrets or perversions. He was the Light ideal—skin taut, heart red. No, there was no chance Saber went home to torture his Chihuahua or masturbate in a moose suit.

"I am undefended. I am free."

Sebastian Light turned and drew the sheet away with a little flash of flair. Then there it was, a single painting exposed to the air, to the eyes of us all, to the expert gaze of our supreme critic. A silence fell. We waited for the answers: good or bad? art or not? beautiful or hideous?

There were our swaying palms rendered with slight impressionistic style set against skies of sunset colors, planted in seas of fire, in which floated various words dashed out in a loose cursive: *soul*, *live*, *dance*, *forever*, *truth*, *believe*, *gratitude*, *sing*. Saber had slashed his name in the blue sands beneath the flames.

I looked at Crystalline. She'd sunk her shining front teeth into her bottom lip. There was loathing in her eyes. I leaned to my left in hopes of seeing Siddhartha's face, but no joy.

"Well," Light said, as he began to move around the painting, "this is something extraordinary. A gorgeous balance between the glory of the physical world, *our* physical world, and an attitude, a philosophy of openness and hope, optimism and light. You see, here in the flames, we find danger at our feet, always lapping at our knees, but above us there is freedom, there is life. Even in the terrible fire below, we may find our souls, our faith, the will to live, to dance, to believe. Not only have you revealed *yourself*, but in so doing you have revealed a love for the natural world. This painting incorporates passion and fear, scale and scope. And it is true. What you have achieved is *beauty*. I'm proud of you, and so should we all be."

By the time he'd finished, Saber was sobbing. This was the only sound. Were the others impressed? Did they share our critic's opinion? Did anyone, too, believe that this shit in any way resembled what Light had described?

"Anyone?"

"I like it," said a muscular blond woman with magnificent teeth.

"Yes," whispered a wiry, wire-haired woman, her stern mouth in argument with her lively eyes. "It moves me in ways I can't explain."

"Mmmm," agreed her neighbor.

"I love the words. The words draw the piece together."

On they went, the soft oohs and gentle ahs of inoffensive concurrence.

And then Crystalline spoke. "Come on."

Light turned on her. "Yes, Crystalline, an opinion?"

"It's always the same thing, isn't it? More kitschy trash."

Light stepped before the painting as if protecting a weaker

man from violence, leveled his eyes at her, but said nothing. She held his gaze.

Was he displeased? Was it part of the show? Was her little rebellion staged for my benefit? It was impossible to know.

"Saber," Light said at last.

Saber stood up from his chair and joined his hands. "I have no room in my heart for hatred," he said. "I am here on this earth for beauty, for love, not for anger. If you have something better to show, Crystalline, then bring it with you to the Biennale." This last he did his best to pronounce with real Italian gusto, really hammering on that last syllable.

Crystalline squinted at the painting as if it were a plate of rancid offal.

I glanced at Sid, who was watching her with an unsettling coldness.

Light said, "This is a lesson to be learned here. Not everyone will like your work. Some will despise it. Out of jealousy or true differences of aesthetic tastes. Perhaps Crystalline spoke out of turn, but another artist's sharp tongue is something to get used to, for the art world is as cruel as any other. We must survive it or die. As I said from the outset, as I've said before every evaluation, there will be pain. And here, I can only imagine, that Saber is in pain. The question now is whether he will be defeated by the brutality of his compatriot. Or will he use suffering as fuel?" He laid his hand on Saber's shoulder. "I maintain that what you have created is a superb work and I hope that's worth something to your heart. Before we finish, I want to say something about cruelty. We are not compelled to like what we see, but here at least, we do have the responsibility to be kind in the transmission of our opinions. I will *urge* you, Crystalline, to calibrate, to consider the way you communicate, to think about what is necessary and what is not. Now, does anyone have anything to contribute before we move on?"

Silence.

"Good," he said and began to move through the crowd, which drifted after him. When Sid passed me, he smiled but said nothing and we continued into the night.

We followed down the ridge and then Light stopped before Theo's studio. This was, apparently, unexpected. There was some murmuring, some worried glances. After a moment, Theo extricated himself from the crowd and said, "It's not my turn."

Light said, "Now's the time, my friend, now is the time."

"Could I have another week? Just one more week. I'm not ready."

"Open the door and submit."

And then we all waited like a mob out for justice while the artist, head down, rolled his door open. We crowded in after him, but there was no covered easel. There was only a high-backed wooden chair. Theo sat in it, and I found a place next to Crystalline.

Light said, "Do you have anything to show us?"

Theo was pleading now. "I'm not ready. You didn't tell me."

"Enough." Light turned and faced the crowd. I watched Theo close his eyes as our critic-in-chief began yet another sermon.

"Art, my friends, is made by the committed. And it is those of you here who have sacrificed everything, those of you who give your souls, your blood, yourselves, you who will be artists. Is it enough? No, it is not. It is the minimum. Talent and imagination and an ability to truly see, these are all required. Passion is not enough, love is not enough, no more than loving another person is enough for that love to be reciprocated, but it is essential and those of you who do not have it, those of you who live in fear, those of you consumed and blocked by your own egos, you should go home, for you have no chance."

Then he turned and stepped to the side so that we could all see him turn his eyes on Theo.

"Those of you," he said, quieting his voice, "who've not managed even to choose a name, to make a single painting, who complain, who are *inhospitable*, who are jealous and spiteful, who cannot harness your anger, your pain and translate it into art, but instead turn it to more anger, more hatred, more jealousy, more *ugliness*, it is time now for you to become something else, something safer, something that requires less spleen and more mind."

Theo remained motionless, eyes shut tight.

I thought, What does he mean, inhospitable?

"Go, Theo, go back to New York, where cowards are celebrated, where meanness is mistaken for intelligence. You're not fooling anyone here. Enough. This is not your home."

It was the first time I'd heard him speak the poor kid's name.

Silence.

And then, Theo, without raising his voice, said, "Fuck you." Only now did he open his eyes. "Fuck you all."

He looked around the room as if searching for someone to join him, to come to his defense. But, of course, no one did. I said nothing. Crystalline, her shoulder touching mine, said nothing. Sebastian Light said nothing. Theo took a deep breath, paused and then screamed in our faces, as we all stood still watching this single sad person alone in his chair.

When he ran out of air, his fists fell open and his shoulders sagged. Then he stood up, pushed forward through the crowd which followed him outside to watch his slight silhouette growing smaller, moving in the direction of the studios.

Light turned to us. "Well, my friends, on that unhappy note, let us bring this evening to a close. Even in The Garden, life is always life."

And with that bit of scintillating wisdom, he strolled off in the opposite direction, Plume following a few feet behind.

As I began to extricate myself from the gossiping scrum, Siddhartha appeared at my side and nudged me in the ribs.

"There's something to write about," he said, smiling as if he'd done me a favor.

"What happens to Theo now?"

"Who knows? You didn't like him anyway."

He said this a bit too casually, as if Theo's trial had meant nothing at all and for the first time, I didn't entirely like Sid.

"I only said he didn't like me."

"It doesn't matter. I'm sure he has a trust fund. He'll be fine."

"So bitter."

"You met him. You want me to feel *sorry* for him now?"

"You know, it occurs to me that you haven't changed *your* name. Doesn't Light give you shit about it?"

Sid leaned forward and whispered in my ear, "He thinks my name *is* made up."

I laughed. Siddhartha of the wit and charm. "I'll see you tomorrow," I said. "I'm exhausted," which wasn't true. I was just tired of talking and of Sebastian Light's silly show.

As I walked away, I thought, I should leave here. It's enough already. Beneath the shell, there is nothing alive. Nothing I didn't already have in New York. It was all banal. Go home. Go see your mother. I thought of the desperation and fury of Theo's scream. I wondered how long he'd been calling himself an artist. Maybe he really had the talent and the will and the patience and the ego for it, but I didn't think so. On this, my instincts aligned with the head gardener: this night was the end. And now he'd have to find something else, something new to call himself at parties, and whatever that was would never be quite so beautiful.

Still the image of him being driven away, being abandoned at the airport like a failed contestant on some shitty television show bothered me and I wished Lina Klein were there to walk me home, to talk about it. I wanted her eye, her assessment. I wanted her to sit with me there on the porch before bed and tell me where to go, what to be.

"Be a proxy. When I can no longer be there, be there," she said, and I swore I would try. During her life, I believed those entreaties were born only of the regret of an old person with a young heart. But she must have meant, *when I end my life in your mother's bathtub*.

"Frankel," I so assuredly wrote (and she so proudly quoted to anyone who would listen), "as do all great artists, always maintains an area within himself of pure wildness, a place wholly free of control, of moral logic, of any logic, any law at all."

Was there some pure wildness, some real art, in her final moment? The planning required no courage, no originality of spirit, concept, or character, but the *doing* was something else entirely. To choose to draw a blade with enough pressure along her wrists, to make such an unrelenting, unequivocal decision, yes, I thought, there must be some art in that. Even some beauty.

"Proximity to beauty, Soli," she told me, "to talent, even if you don't have it yourself, is what's necessary for any kind of a good life. Get yourself as close to passion and genius as you can. Conform to nothing. Move back downtown." *Downtown*, Lina Klein loved to say. Even if that mythical place barely existed, even if, as my mother gleefully reminded us, it had long ago been decimated by the *capitalist machine*.

I wanted to ask her if this, Sebastian Light's bizarre little wonderland, counted as downtown, if she'd approve, or how she'd read the place and she was so present in my mind that it wasn't until I was a few steps from my porch that I saw Plume waiting for me on the top step.

I recoiled. I wanted the other side, the unfastened, the irrational, the unrestrained. No more marketing, no more publicists.

"I was passing by," she said.

"Just in the neighborhood?"

"Would you sit with me, Mr. Fields?"

I sat.

"I'm wondering whether you've considered writing about us."

"Jesus, why does it matter so much to you? Won't he pay you otherwise?"

"He's a man approaching the end of a great life. I want him to have what he wants."

"And he wants a profile?"

"Yes." Now she reached down and ran the nail of her right middle finger across the top of her left foot. "Though," she said, sitting upright again and dropping into a confessional register, "between us, I think it's a mistake."

"Why a mistake?

"It will only disappoint him. Even if you were generous, you'd never quite get him right, or this place, or us. And then until he dies, he will feel—"

"What?"

She shook her head. "Sullied. This is a man who notices every dead flower, every pebble out of place. So, we go through with it. The profile is published and then he will read what you've written and will be forced to see his life's work in some other way."

"Which is something you don't think he should have to do?"

"He's an old man. What good is it? He made this extraordinary thing, changed the lives of so many artists. He used his money in such benevolent ways. Why cause him pain?"

"Where did that money come from?"

"You're always asking the wrong questions."

"Have you considered a life in politics? You'd make a superb press secretary."

She shook her head. "I've never understood your humor. People like you. I try. I have tried. But I just don't understand why you'd want to move through the world like this. Why must everything be mean and cold?"

I glanced at her. She seemed genuinely frustrated. I was trying to find some indication of performance, some tell, but I only saw an unhappy woman shaking her head and looking at the sky.

"You want me to write about this man—"

"I don't want you to do anything."

"Okay, okay. He wants the profile, but without me having any of the information I'd need to do it."

"Why are you so seduced by that idea?"

"Which idea?"

"That you must know everything. That you have some obligation to show us our flaws, our failures. You want to break them across our heads. You take such pleasure in ugliness."

"You're not interested in those things?"

"I don't think there's any reason to show them to an old man. What good will that do him? You want to bring him pain in the name of what, *truth*?"

"I have no interest in causing anyone pain," I said, and wondered if that was true.

"Well," she said and looked down at her golden feet, "I don't know what you're interested in, but I don't imagine you're likely to write something purely kind."

"If I were to write about him, about this place, no, I wouldn't write some letter of adulation."

"But why not? Why not return his hospitality with kindness?"

I laughed. "Let's remember that you brought me here. You came to me. Not out of kindness, but because you *wanted* something. It's not as if I was some hungry traveler whose car broke down and you took me in."

"Isn't that exactly what happened?"

"Oh, for fuck's sake," I said. "I like you so much more when you're not reciting from your sacred book of saccharine."

I liked that line, but she didn't even smile.

"It's not up to me," she said after a long pause and with a new sadness in her voice. "This is what he wants."

"And you don't want to see him wounded."

She raised her head now and looked at me with the softest expression I'd ever seen on her face. "Yes. That's right. I don't want to see him harmed at all."

"Why do you think this profile is so important to him?"

"Because as is true of so many old men, he's concerned with his legacy." Then again, her voice fell into that confessional whisper, its sincerity impossible for me to determine. "And with revenge."

"Revenge?"

She looked away. "This is off the record."

"All right."

"He tried you know. This was years ago. He went to New York, had a studio, a gallery for a while."

"He was a painter?"

"Yes. He spent close to ten years there. They nearly destroyed him. They were all so cruel and smug and mean. So certain of their own perfect taste."

I nodded.

"They gave him a show in a fancy gallery. They built him up and convinced him he was something different from the others. Then they attacked him."

"When was this?"

"A long time ago."

"When?"

"Not so long that he's forgotten. Still, he was a different man then. Different name."

"What name?"

"It doesn't matter."

"It does if you want a profile."

"He'll tell you what he wants to tell you."

"And this profile would be his revenge?"

"That's the way I believe he sees it, yes. He'd never say so. But yes, it's what happens when a wound doesn't heal right. You make terrible decisions for reasons that are beneath you."

"Why me, Plume? He could have chosen anyone. I can think of any number of journalists who would come here and happily produce precisely what you want."

"Well, as I've told you several times, he admired the way you wrote about Ernst Frankel. He's really never forgotten it and—" Here she hesitated for a moment. "And they knew each other."

"No."

"Yes. In New York. Early on."

"And?"

She sighed. "Frankel was ruthlessly ambitious, cruel. He betrayed him."

"How?"

She shook her head. "I don't know."

"Come on."

"That's all he'll tell me."

"And so the idea is what? That I write a glowing testament to Light's brilliance and Frankel will remember what terrible sins he committed thirty, forty years ago?"

She shrugged. "He has the idea that it has to be you. That somehow it'll be more potent."

"A little thin, don't you think? And awfully petty for the priest of prettiness and love."

She looked as if she might agree with me for a moment, but then she closed her mouth.

"Why are you telling me all of this, Plume? Why be so suddenly forthright?"

"Because I think, in the end, you'll write about him. Whatever his motivations, whatever yours, and even if you don't know it yet. Also, I believe that writing about him will save your life. Which is to say, he will save you as he's saved so many. I'm telling you these things because when you do begin to write, I hope you will do so with tenderness. I hope that you won't make a human being who has been alive for many years, who has suffered, who is imperfect, who once had a father and a mother, who was once a child, who is as complex and strange and beautiful as anyone, into something flat and simple to be destroyed."

"I have no interest in destroying anyone."

"Perhaps not, but you seem as interested in ugliness as you are in beauty."

I nodded.

She shook her head. "You adults who claim to be drawn to chaos, to violence. To what you call the *real*. It's very childish."

"Like most of the art I've seen around here."

"Mr. Fields, I'm not here to argue aesthetics. To be honest, I don't care what you think of the work you've seen here. Technique, originality, *talent*, it's just not the point anymore. What matters now is service, is *utility*."

"I thought what mattered was beauty."

"That is what beauty is *for*. Nothing for the sake of itself, Sol. Those days are done. Art without aim, without argument? All that is nothing more than decadence."

I imagined Lina Klein listening to Plume incanting the Garden lines. How gleefully she would have filleted her. But because of the lovely lime blossom air, or for some other reason, I couldn't muster the appropriate indignation. And who was I to argue? Perhaps there *was* nothing more beautiful than service. In a manner of speaking, was this not what my mother had been arguing all my life? That my very existence was tantamount to decadent performance art, that real meaning, real beauty was achieved through devotion to others?

But was my silence an affront to my fiery grandmother? A woman who, for as long as I knew her, cultivated an incandescent hatred of "mealy, lovey-dovey, gutless bodhi tree bullshit made by pathetic painters obsessed by their precious little traumas?"

Lina Klein loved to make pronouncements about art. As do so many who fail to produce it themselves. In these pronouncements and, more generally, in her increasing demands that I should live in a way she found admirable, in the last years of her life, I'd begun to see something in her I didn't always like—a desperation, a fragility, an intellectual thinness. Worse, and much harder to confront, a pure black loneliness.

"So," I said to Plume, "art is like the electric company or the sanitation department?"

"Of course. Do you not see that there's beauty in the electric company? In the processes, the systems, in the machines and the people who, while you sleep, silently take your trash away."

"You obviously have never lived in New York."

Not even a smirk.

"You're trapped," she said. "You've tied yourself to those awful old ideas and they will drown you."

"And you believe Sebastian Light's ideas are better, faster, newer?"

"I think a wiser man might grant him the possibility."

"I'm surprised to find a woman like you so devoted to an old billionaire living in a gated community."

She sighed. "And what am I like, Mr. Fields?"

"I have no idea, really. You're clearly intelligent."

"Is that all I'm like?"

"Aside from being strange and withholding and obviously playing a role?"

"Sure. Aside from all that."

"Well, you're staggeringly beautiful."

She turned to me. "That's a very nice thing to say."

"It's pure truth."

"I'm sure neither of us believes in such a thing."

"Certain truths are very pure," I said.

"All of us live our *own* truths, Mr. Fields."

"Doesn't it make you feel dirty to repeat that shit?"

For the first time, she seemed genuinely angry.

"Are you bothered that I don't have more interesting things to say? Do you believe that cynicism and anger and skepticism and pessimism and fury and disenchantment and mistrust are any better? Are you under some illusion that you're *not* a breathing cliché? Aren't you your own little refrigerator magnet?"

"You're right," I said, now turning, smiling, meeting her eyes. "You're right. I am a cliché. I confess and it breaks my heart."

"But why is it so important to be original? You must know that we were born far too late for all that."

"Because of my former life. Because I hate jargon, cant, sloganeering. Lifeless language. I want surprise. I want shock. I don't want to give in to the kinds of people I used to work for. Or lived with."

"First of all, there is no *former* life. There is only the one, Sol. But tell me, what would surprise you here?"

"Something out of place. Screaming and yelling and broken glass would surprise me. Jesus, a single misspoken phrase."

She nodded. "Is that why you're looking for trouble?"

"Trouble?"

"Is that why you're running off at night?"

"You talk as if I'm your teenage son."

She laughed at this.

"Maybe we think of you that way."

"There's that *we* again. I wonder who you mean exactly. The fatherland? Our glorious leader? Whatever, I'll be very disappointed to learn you think of me as your son, teenage or otherwise."

"My advice," she said, "is to stop looking for trouble."

"That's terrible advice," I said. "Are you really going to get rid of Theo?"

"His time here has ended."

"Just like that? You'll what? Send him to the airport tomorrow?"

"He's already at the airport."

"Incredible. Punishment is swift on fantasy island."

She stood up. "It's not a fantasy, Mr. Fields."

"Who drove him?"

She ignored my question.

"Sleep well. Or as well as you do."

"As well as I do?"

"We learn a great deal from the way a man sleeps, Mr. Fields. Someone who kicks and moans and calls out, who gnashes his teeth, is not a happy man, does not have peace in his heart."

I was left sitting on the porch trying to work out just how frightening, how dangerous they were, his army of acolytes who followed me, who watched me sleep, who cast out dissenters. But it was all too campy, too silly. I tried to imagine Sebastian Light as David Koresh, the apprentice hordes as Moonies, Branch Davidians, Heaven's Gaters. Were they planning to commit group suicide? A subway sarin attack? A virgin sacrifice? No. At best, it was an elaborate piece of performance art, all a riff on the violence of unrelenting hope, on the corruption of language, on the deadening effect of caution, of groupthink, cults of uplift, empowerment and peppy art-world citizenship, on the sanitizing of culture, the sterilizing of art. Wouldn't that be wonderful? To find that soon, one way or another, they would line up and take a bow, tear off their smooth masks, their colored contact lenses, their dental veneers, to reveal wrinkled skin, brilliant bloodshot eyes, cracked yellow teeth.

How much sadder it would be to find all The Coded Gardeners sincere.

As I lay naked in my bed, I imagined Plume watching over me while I kicked and moaned and clicked my worn teeth.

A storm woke me in the morning and for hours I lay listening to rain thrashing the tin roof.

My breakfast was there as ever and, ignoring today's card, I took it back to bed and ate it for lunch and drowsed beneath the white muslin like some grieving viceroy.

When I woke again there were three papaya seeds stuck to my cheek and it was late afternoon.

20

At some point in the night, I woke to the hope that when the sun rose Theo would be at his easel trying to paint, counting his slights, searching for a name. But later, I went up to his studio and found no sign of him. All the brushes, the cups, the bottles, the cans, all gone. His chair was pushed square to the table. I don't know how they could have done it so quickly, but the boy had been erased. In his place was an empty canvas propped on a clean easel, like some interior designer's idea of a room where art is made.

I sat on the floor looking out the glass for a while. I liked being there in the quiet, with the door closed. Even the simulacrum of art held the power to move me.

Frankel said that when he first began working, everything he did was a response to death. Every idea, every sketch, every sculpture was, in some way or another, a form of memorial, which was to say that everything he did was a reference to what no longer existed.

"In those days, I demanded a silent, isolated studio. I was obsessive about it. Unless I was working alone behind a locked door, I was paralyzed."

"What changed?"

"I became a revolutionary," he said, patting my knee.

We were on a bench in Washington Square Park drinking coffee from paper cups.

"What were you revolting against?"

"Death," he said, in a quiet voice, as if revealing a secret. "It had never occurred to me before. But then, all at once, I saw that I had more interest in the living, that as long as I always knew I could die, *would* die, the new sculptures could never be empty of death, but they could become driven by, and evidence of, my futile, joyful war against it."

While I was working on the profile, Frankel gave me free access to the studio. I could come and go as I pleased. Speak with whomever I liked. I drank with them. I got high with them. I tried to separate the artists from the stragglers. I stayed into the early morning and sometimes slept on a couch. I was happy either way. I loved waking to see the nests they'd made and I loved walking home with a cup of coffee just before dawn, still a little drunk, always writing. There was less litter in the space between my mind and my work then, the lines more direct. Really, I couldn't make it stop. I'd unlock the door and go straight to work for hours at the table by the window without even taking my coat off and in my last years at Pale, I came to see that it was the absence of those moments of singular focus, of possession, of gleeful obsession, that made my life unbearable. Every day they seemed to drift further and further from me and at the end I knew that if I didn't jump, I'd never have them back again.

That evening Plume arrived toward the end of dinner to announce, in uncharacteristically casual style, "Mr. Light would love to have everyone to The Library for a brief celebration."

I followed them down and halfway there, Crystalline, who hadn't been at dinner, was suddenly at my side.

"Hello, Solomon," she said, bumping my hip with hers. "Going to do some reporting?"

"You're awfully cheerful."

"Why shouldn't I be?"

"Your sidekick was exiled."

"Yes, well," she said, without any indication of regret.

"That's it?"

"He was an angry, stunted little man who had no sense of himself."

"May I quote you?"

"So, you are going to write about this place?"

"What do you care?"

We were nearly to The Library now.

"Why don't you come and see my work?"

I laughed. "Everyone thinks I'm going to make them famous."

"See you later," she said, and walked through the door before me.

All the light was dimmed except, conspicuously, Sebastian, who stood before a bookshelf, his teeth bright in a single spot cranked to ten. Next to him stood an easel. A white cloth covered what one could only assume was another masterwork. But whose? Would Maestro Light reveal, at long last, his own creation? This seemed unlikely, for if the man knew anything at all, it was that the seat of power is made of shadows.

He began to speak, and I braced myself for another onslaught.

"All of you here have proven yourselves to be serious and determined. Not only do you have talent but you're willing to fight, to take off your shirts, pull out your shovels and *dig*. Just as important, you have an appreciation, a passion, for this *land*, for its beauty, for the effort that has gone into nurturing it. Those of us here tonight love this soil and the blood and the tears that have fertilized it. You love the buildings and walls, its gardens and orchards. It is you who make this place what it is, who believe in its greatness, you who reject defeat and cynicism, who respect our origins, our culture, our shared values, who understand what it means to take an empty, godforsaken chunk of dirt and turn it to sanctuary, an Eden. You who fervently believe in this experiment, our Garden, our homeland, our haven. You and those who came before, who are willing to defend it at all costs. Thank you."

The guests stirred. Even Crystalline appeared rapt. Her coconut flesh glowed. With a childlike smile, Saber cracked his tragic artist mask. The powerful blond woman with the teeth whose name was either Citrus or Duckling pressed a rosy hand to her breast and looked upon our leader with desirous devotion. They all appeared roused by this spirited call for unity, by an idea of identity that did not begin with their arrival in The Garden and surely would not end there. Now they were trading in the eternal. They had toiled to build and plant and paint their way toward this utopic present and right on through in the direction of a celestial future.

I studied him and it was difficult not to believe that he was sincere, that his heart swelled when he spoke, his chest full of pride. And yet it had to be theater. It had to be art. It must be. Because if not, what then? The alternative was too sad to contemplate.

He turned to Plume, Sebastian Light's own Vanna White, who pulled the sheet away.

It was an intricate map of The Coded Garden as if drawn by Long John Silver, the lettering twisted and curled, the paper dipped in black tea. *Antiqued*, in the patois of New York City's gentleman farmers, the edges uneven and carefully charred. There was the whole of the property detailed down to each sculpture and palm. Beyond those walls the whimsy began. Here was the ocean, a snarling sea creature rising from its depths, tail lashing at the waves just beneath an old-timey compass. There were green mountains, sharp as shark teeth, rising into the golden sky. Our narrow road descended to the coast and there in each direction, a highway dissolved into nothingness. There were no other signs of a history predating our own, no towns, no buildings, no Sunny's Bar, nothing but mythical beasts and threatening terrain.

"My friends, here is your world, your sanctuary, your home. It is where you live, where your names, and hearts, belong and begin. Gem?"

The wiry-haired woman stepped forward, arranging her dour mouth into an unpersuasive smile.

"I made this map," she said before she faltered and looked down at the floor. "It was, it *is* important for me, to do honor. It is. I wanted to celebrate this land, this whole universe that I've been, that we've been handed. Given. Gifted. I owe so much for it and I will, I want to repay that debt. Happily, I mean."

The audience waited for more, but the sour expression returned, and it was evident that there would be nothing else. It was excruciating to watch her bumbling through that speech not because it was a failure, but because she was so nakedly desperate for Light's love.

"Thank you, Gem," Light said. "I had thought to begin our Biennale this way, but in light of last night's sad events, I thought it best to give you this gift now. As you leave, Plume will offer you a small reproduction of the map."

Reverently they stood in line, each passing before the map, touching, smelling, feeling, communing. I stayed where I was, watching him provide abbreviated bows to the artists as they left The Library, rolled scrolls like batons in their fists. Life or theater, I saw in him a new fatigue, a rounding of the shoulders as he gazed upon his subjects, a slackening of his chin, a papery quality to his skin. He is weakening, I thought. He might be unwell. Had he been granted only a month left to live? Was this the story? After all, performance is grueling. Beauty is brutal.

I waited until the last player had left the stage and when Sebastian Light turned from the open door to look at me, I was sure he saw the change in my eyes. But did he see pity or possibility? He gave me an odd look, which I couldn't quite parse—pleading, sad, defiant—but whatever it was, in that instant I found him touching.

He raised his hand so that I could see his wide palm as if he were saying farewell from across a great train station. Then he turned and left.

I stood before his collection, reading the spines—*Drawing in the Kingdom of God*, *Painting in Paradise*, etc.—trying to figure out what he did and did not mean. Soon, I took my map and went out into the night where I found Siddhartha waiting for me, looking handsome and crisp in a white t-shirt and jeans.

"Go for a walk?"

"You people are always showing up, pretending not to want anything."

"You people?"

"Denizens of this insane place."

"You meant Indians, didn't you?"

"Yes," I said. "You're all the same."

He smiled. "What do you think I want?"

"Who knows."

"Who else shows up?"

"Crystalline most recently."

"Crystalline," he said, and I noted the same disdain as before. "Did you like her little performance last night? You looked impressed."

"You don't like her."

"She's a good painter, but she's ambitious."

"Are you not both of those things?"

"Not like her."

"You're not as good or not as ambitious?"

"Both. Neither."

"Really?"

"I don't want anything from you."

"No?"

"No."

"Tell me something." I nodded at the scroll in his fist. "What am I supposed to make of that map? Are we calling it art?"

Up until then, we had been standing in the soft light above The Library door. Now he started walking and I went along.

"No comment?" I said.

"Would you like to go for a walk?"

"Are we not walking now?"

"Well, yes, we're walking, but we're not *on* a walk."

"You fucking people," I said, shaking my head.

"Pedants, all of us. Tomorrow after dinner, if you like, we could go for a walk."

"A formal date?"

"A formal walk. There's a place I'd like to show you."

"No end to the mysteries."

"No," he said, "none. That's what art is for."

Then he kissed me on the cheek and strode off.

They were always appearing and disappearing. Always punctuating their arrivals and departures with dramatic gestures, poignant moments, final words of wisdom. Excellent exits at The Coded Garden.

21

The following evening, I waited on my porch. I found that I was nervous and a little nauseated by the same anxiety I'd always felt in all the schools I'd ever attended—the anticipatory dread of rejection, of violence, deception, humiliation. I worried Sid was very wealthy. Despite his claims of having nowhere else to go, no one to catch him, he had a certain unhurried aspect which recalled so many wealthy people I had known. An inbred confidence, a nonchalance. Factory set. Whether they were those who pretended to be poor, or those who flaunted their wealth, the aspect was always the same, the calm could never be broken, and I could never quite grant them the benefits of doubt. I'd been suckled on suspicion—of money, of state, of men—wary since the first memory of memory.

When I came home from college repeating the lines I'd learned there, my mother clicked her tongue and said what she always did, "Evil comes from money. The issue is class. Hatred is born of imbalance. It is never more complicated. It will never be more complicated."

"Are you denying racism exists? Sexism? Homophobia? *Antisemitism?*" I screamed, doing a little late-adolescent pearl-clutch jig.

"Symptoms," my mother said, unimpressed. "Too much in the hands of too few."

This was, of course, in her days of *Das Kapital.* Days before she replaced Marx with Israel, when workers became Jews, before the sweet comforts of an even more rigid politics, but by then I had already been formed by her early lectures, my vanished father's legacy of debt, and constant questions of whether and how we might pay our rent. Days before Lina Klein's California arrival, before she became a landlord (much to her daughter's white-hot ire), before the barbarians invaded my grandmother's beloved Lower East Side allowing the three of us a theretofore unknown security.

I have begun to see a line between my mother's conversion from one orthodoxy to another and my own transfiguration from downtown chronicler of bohemia to whatever ugly thing I became at Pale. Both were driven by fear. But also, some pathetic, latent instinct to rebellion. These theories are incomplete and underexamined, and I can't say precisely what it was that so frightened Charlotte Klein. She despised disorder, that's certain. Do not arrive at noon when you promised 11:45. Do not put the milk where the orange juice belongs. Unless she was in command of it, even music unsettled her. A car racing past, its stereo blaring, would practically debilitate her with rage. I know she loved how deep under the skin her rightward drift burrowed into her mother's flesh. Finally, though, I think she found real comfort there in the simple fictions and furies of Tucker Carlson and the Likud. And maybe I wasn't so different when I went to Pale. I couldn't shake the fear I'd absorbed from my mother—of instability, of poverty, of eviction. My degree, the apartment, even Lina Klein did little to obliterate my early education. And there was my father, that charming deadbeat. He, too, left his marks. And loath as I am to admit it maybe I wanted to throw a few jabs at my grandmother, as well. So certain of herself, so easy in her philosophies, so appalled by "dead lives," maybe I wanted to show her I wasn't hers.

We were all such fools.

And now in the dusk of my thirties, I was still incapable of shaking my mistrust of those who never once wondered if the money would come. Yet if there was anyone to change my mind, it was Siddhartha the Handsome, striding now up my path. I didn't then entirely understand my response to him, but it was the kind of deep-seated need that has long made me do foolish things in its service. Was I not *still* there in The Garden because all these blithe and pretty people were clamoring for my attention? Wasn't it why, in part, I succumbed to Robert Capo and Pale? Ernst Frankel? My grandmother?

Lina Klein: "So easily seduced by the flattery of an invitation, Solomon. Because someone says come, isn't reason to go. You're not a Labrador."

Which was a total contradiction to her always-say-yes advice, but, of course, she never imagined her grandson would sell his soul in such spectacular fashion.

Whatever, I always went. Just as I did with Sid that balmy evening through Sebastian Light's secret door onto the black road where the day's damp heat rose from the asphalt to meet the cool air descending through the rainbow eucalyptus.

We walked side by side down the hill. Through the canopy the sky looked lacerated, as if it might at any moment begin to drip between the branches. I closed my eyes and tried to move blind for a while. This only exaggerated the strangeness I felt being with him alone beyond the kingdom. I opened my eyes and said nothing. I did not ask where we were going or why. The nausea passed. The sky dissolved to violet.

It must have been ten minutes before he spoke and when he asked why I was really here, his voice startled me.

"My grandmother died," I told him without hesitating. I was surprised by my straight answer.

"I'm sorry. Had she been sick?"

"No," I said.

"An accident?"

"No."

I had no great desire to tell him my tragic tale, but I also did not feel entirely in control of myself. I thought of Plume. Perhaps she was right. Perhaps they all were. I will abandon irony and cheap sarcasm. Now, I'll just go along, try not to be cruel, try not to lie.

"How did she die?"

"She killed herself."

"Your grandmother?"

I laughed.

"Why do you laugh?"

"Because you seem so incredulous."

"I'm sorry."

"Stop apologizing."

"Okay. You found her?"

"No, my mom."

"How?"

"How did she do it?"

"Yes."

"In the bath. She cut her wrists."

He turned and looked at me now, but I kept my eyes on the road as if I were driving, not walking.

"I'm sorry. Do you really mind my saying that I'm sorry?"

"It doesn't mean anything, but I don't really mind."

"You don't think I mean it?"

"I don't know what any of you mean."

He made a sound as if to begin a sentence and then stopped himself. A few seconds later he began again. "You two were close?"

"Very."

"I *am* sorry."

"Thank you."

"Do you mind talking about it?"

"No."

"Really?"

"I don't know," I said.

If ever I had been, or might one day be, a journalist of any quality, it was because I derived no pleasure from talking about myself. Not because I was generous of spirit or large of heart, but because I had long found myself utterly tiresome. Charity, who found herself utterly captivating, could not understand this. She saw it as a tremendous deficiency, for which I should be treated.

Sid asked, "Have you talked about it much?"

"No."

"Where was this?"

"California."

"At home?"

"My mom's apartment."

"Are you close with your mom?"

"In certain ways."

"But you were closer with your grandmother?"

"Yes."

"Do you always talk like this, Sol?"

"Like what?"

"So matter of fact. So directly."

"For most of my life I've done the opposite."

"And now?"

"You must change your life."

He laughed.

"Do you know the poem?"

"Yes," he said.

"Really?"

"You think I'm as stupid as the rest of them?"

"I don't think you're stupid," I said, this time glancing at the side of his face.

"Then?"

"Then nothing. I'm glad you know the poem."

"For here there is no place/that does not see you. You must change your life."

Siddhartha was very beautiful in the near dark.

"It was her favorite."

"Your grandmother?"

"Yes. She loved the idea of it."

"What?"

"Confronting great art and having no choice, but to dramatically alter her life."

"Was she an artist?"

"I guess that depends on what you mean by the word. She wanted to be. More than anything else, she wanted to be."

"She tried?"

"For a while."

Sid made a sigh of sympathy. Several times, I'd wondered whether Sid had meant what he'd told me about his devotion to art, or if he, too, was playing a role. But now I thought, There's no way he's not a real painter.

"She was never angry though," I said. "Never bitter."

"Never?"

"Not as long as I knew her. Not as long as I can remember anyway. She was always sanguine, always honest about her lack of talent."

He waited for me to go on.

"I've known a lot of people in that world," I said. "Rarely have I met anyone—artist, critic, gallery owner, straggler, groupie—who wasn't seething with envy, hatred, frustration. She loved art too much to hate anyone who made it well. And she satisfied that love by proximity. She believed that the only life of any value was lived as close to art as possible."

"Lately I've been thinking that the only life of any value is lived as *far* from art as possible."

I laughed. "Well, that's the advantage of abandoning one's dreams. She was able to become an admirer, a true fan. It granted her a generosity that ambition would never have allowed. She believed the world is always being destroyed by striving, passionless men."

"It is. She sounds wonderful."

"She was."

"So, what did she do finally?"

"For a living?"

"Yes."

"Her daughter would say she was a whore."

"Jesus."

I smiled.

"But—"

"But you want to know if she was a whore?"

"Yes."

I waited. It was too dark to see his face, but I relished the idea of throwing Sid off-kilter with stories of suicide and a promiscuous grandmother. It was a relief to talk about her, but I wondered if it was a mistake. Would he take it all to Sebastian Light? Would they in turn edit the script? If Sid were one of them, could I survive the humiliation of my confession? What difference did it make? None.

"No, she wasn't a whore. She was poor for a long time. She was alone in the city. She was beautiful. She made her way how she could. She had a tremendous capacity for joy, for pleasure."

"I'm sorry she's gone," he said, and I believed him.

We came now to the silent highway, crossed and then instead of continuing toward Sunny's we entered a keyhole in the jungle.

Quickly the sky disappeared, and we were traveling through a tunnel of vines. I wondered if he might be leading me to slaughter: a meadow, all the Coded denizens hooded and gathered around a great fire, Lord Light wielding a glinting poleaxe. Immortalize me within your glossy pages, Solomon Fields, or lose your head.

But no meadow appeared. Instead, the path delivered us to

the edge of a bluff above a wineglass bay where far below waves collapsed against a beach I could not see.

There was a log split lengthwise and propped on two boulders to make a bench. We sat on it together.

Sid said, "I wanted you to see this."

"You know all the magical places."

"You don't really think I'm like the rest of them, do you, Sol?"

"I don't really know what the rest of them are like."

"You don't make this easy."

"What is this?"

"I'd like to talk to you," he said.

"Talk then," I said, pretending to be tougher than I was. The stillness and sharp clarity of the stars stamped into the blackness was nearly unbearable. It was as if the physical world were knocking me into submission. But to whom?

"But you don't trust me."

"No."

"That's strange."

"You think it's strange that I don't trust you?

"Yes. What reason have I given you not to trust me?"

"Listen, Sid, if you didn't ask such stupid questions, I'd be more inclined to trust you. But it really doesn't matter. Whatever your motivations, I'm happy to play along."

He sighed and seemed relieved. Another man might have insisted on his purity, would have beaten the subject into the ground, refused to continue until we'd agreed upon some lie of perfect innocence and understanding. I would not begrudge him his motives, his obligations, his contracts. There before that boundless black sky, whatever lies he told, whatever roles he wanted to play, whatever his divided allegiances, made no difference to me at all.

"Are you surprised?" His voice startled me. It seemed a long time had passed since he'd last spoken.

"Surprised by what?"

"Your grandmother. Her passing."

"No. But if you want to talk, then please don't talk around it. No euphemisms. No fucking jargon."

"All right. Why do you think she killed herself?"

"Because there was nothing else she wanted to do here. The same reason you might leave a job, or a city or a party. You're bored to tears. It's time to go. Greener pastures."

"Simple as that?"

"Of course not."

"What else then?"

"The same reason you've wanted to kill yourself."

"I've never wanted to kill myself." He said this immediately, as if it were the truth.

"Strange," I said.

"You think it's strange that I've never wanted to kill myself?"

"Very."

He took a long breath and then said, "Doesn't it bother you that she left you behind?"

"Bother me? I'm not sure that *bother* is the right word. But I'm not angry at her for it. I've never liked that response to suicide."

"Which response?"

"Anger."

"You're not angry at all?"

"Not at all. I'm sad. I'm very, very sad. I miss her. But I'm not angry." I wondered if this were true.

"Why do you think she did it the way she did?"

"As opposed to what?"

"Something, I don't know, more discreet. Less dramatic. Why do it at home?"

"She was angry."

"At you?"

"At her daughter."

"You don't think it's selfish?"

"Of course it's selfish. But it's also very painful. In fact, it's one of the most painful methods of suicide. And the least likely to succeed."

"And so?"

"So she was willing to suffer for that image."

"Which?"

"The one she left her daughter."

"And you, too, no?"

"I never saw it."

"You hardly needed to see it to see it."

"You sound like your master."

He laughed. "He's not my master."

"Employer?"

"No."

"If you say so."

"You really don't feel betrayed?"

"No," I said. "She died just the way she wanted to. Just the way she did most things. With conviction, with courage."

"You think it was brave?"

"Of course it was brave. I certainly don't have the courage for it."

"If you did, would you kill yourself?"

"I might, sure. I like to keep the possibility as a viable option. That's the way I've come to think about it. Like moving to Nicaragua or becoming a doula."

Sid laughed and the sound vanished so fast over the cliff it made me shiver.

"Are those the three options?"

"Yes," I said. "Suicide, Nicaragua, doula."

"I like you, Sol," he said. "You're tough."

"I don't know how tough I am. I'm just not easily outraged."

"I like that."

"My grandmother hated outrage. 'To be outraged,' she said, 'is to be shocked and to be shocked is to be naïve' and she despised naïveté in anyone older than thirteen."

"Do you agree?"

"Yes. Outrage in adults is theater."

"Nothing outrages you?"

"I feel anger, rage. Disgust. Disdain. Revulsion. All of that. But no, not outrage. As she would say, There's nothing shocking left."

"Nothing?"

"Nothing. I know that's hard for you artists to hear."

"It is," he said, "it is. What else about her?"

"You could see it in her eyes. A coolness."

"I can imagine her."

"Are you a good artist, Sid?"

"I don't know. I want to be."

There was an innocence to his response, which touched me.

"But you're an artist, right? You're not some kind of—"

"Fraud?"

"I was going to say actor."

"You mean, am I a poseur? You'll come see my work and decide for yourself."

"I'd like that."

"Do you really like art, Sol?"

"Very much."

"And your grandmother, she was really no good?"

"I've only ever seen two of her paintings."

"Where?"

"In her apartment in New York."

"And?"

"They were unremarkable. Portraits of men. Lovers."

"And that's the end of it? Judgement cast?"

I liked that he was coming to her defense. One painter fighting for another.

"I would love to discover her a genius. But those are the two I've seen. And I don't think she would have lied to me. She was not one for false humility. She knew she was beautiful. She knew she was smart. She saw herself more clearly than anyone I've ever known. There is another painting, one she sold in a show when she still believed she might have talent. That one I've never seen. Someday I'd like to track it down. Still, she harbored no fantasies about herself. She was never one of those ugly little people so critical of the work of others, while producing nothing of their own, pretending one day their true virtuosity will be revealed when they finally settle down to bang out their masterworks."

"You've spent too much time in New York"

"That's true," I said. "But they're everywhere."

"I know, I know."

Then there was a burst of high-pitched barks which warped on the wind. I jumped.

"Deer," Sid said.

"I've never heard that sound."

"Doesn't seem quite right for such beautiful animals," he said. "They sound more like something from the sea. Dolphins or seals."

We listened to them getting fainter and fainter.

I took a breath and said, "It's strange, but lately I've begun to think of her as the thing she made."

"What do you mean?"

"She chiseled away and chiseled away and chiseled away until the woman she ultimately destroyed was as exquisite a human being as I had ever known. As if all her life she'd been crafting this person she came to be. Her character, the way she moved, the way she responded to the world, what she was to me, the way she carried herself, the way she dressed, all of it down to the way she held a cup of coffee or moved a saltshaker across a table. She was so controlled. She was so composed. I mean that she composed herself in the sense that she ordered and arranged her entire person to be a thing she believed was beautiful. Or, more, something finished. I know that partly it was all a way to survive, something she learned to do when she was very young and alone in New York. She told me as much. 'Do not accept chaos,' she said. But what I mean is that in all of that was a kind of art. And that by destroying what she had worked so hard and sacrificed so much to make—this self of hers—she controlled it to the very end, told the story precisely as she wanted it told. She had finished it. Edited it. Given no quarter. No false gods for her. No sentimental romance. She would be victim to no whim. In the end, there would be nothing but what she had been, what she had made. No humiliating decline. No abandonment of taste, of style, of elegance. No weakening of the mind. No, she spent a life making something she believed to be beautiful and then she destroyed it."

Sid didn't speak, which was a relief, and for a while we sat watching the sky, listening to the ocean.

Then I said, "The last thing Houdini said before he died was 'I'm tired of fighting.' I've always liked that, but I believe my grandmother meant the opposite. It was not a giving up on a life, but the completion of one. But who knows? Maybe it's the same thing."

"I'm glad you came here, Sol," Sid said. Then he put his arm around my shoulder and kissed the side of my head.

I didn't know if he did this because he knew that I was crying in the blue dark or because he felt some true tenderness for me or because he was fulfilling some obligation to Central Command.

I didn't know why he'd brought me there to sit above that beautiful bay.

It didn't matter at all. I liked to feel him against me, and I was glad to be there, to have said what I did. It was enough that he'd heard it, enough that I had said it and that afterwards, listening to those words, I still believed them.

We walked home together through the tunnel, along the highway, up the road and all the while I thought not of Lina Klein, but of Ernst Frankel and his studio and all those people coming and going, and how I might one day open his door and sit in one of those ravaged club chairs and wait for him to see me.

Sid rang the bell and soon enough, there was our lady of The Garden letting us in with a smile, offering no wisdom, not even lingering to sniff around. Tonight, she was more bellboy than general manager, though I was nearly certain she exchanged a meaningful glance with Siddhartha.

Once she'd glided off, Sid said, "I'll see you, Sol," and hugged me like he meant something by it.

I watched him vanish in the direction of the studios and then just as I was about to turn away, there was a quick change of light beneath the jacaranda, which was just coming on bright in the rising moon.

I went toward it, and as I came closer found Saber staring into the branches. I thought maybe he'd taken a handful of mushrooms and whatever he saw in the tree would be invisible to me, but then something flashed amongst the flowers.

At first, I thought they must be small fluttering birds, but as I approached, I saw they were figures made of cardboard, identical cutouts, maybe fifty of them, like patterns for gingerbread men, each hanged by a raw rope noose.

"What is this?"

Saber looked at me, his eyes wide and frightened. "I don't know, man."

"You don't know? This isn't one of his—"

"I'm going to find Plume," he said and then he, too, ran off into the night.

I bent a branch and drew a figure down. It was imperfect—cardboard cut quickly with a pair of scissors, or even a jack-knife—but the noose was impeccable, as if taken from a fine dollhouse gallows. There were two red Xs for eyes, but otherwise the face was featureless.

As the wind came up and whipped those strangulating dolls into a frenzy, I let it go. They were quite beautiful, I thought. Or the installation as a whole was. But it was incongruous, not at all in keeping with the Garden aesthetic. Could it have come from outside? Who would bother to slip into the walled city under the cover of darkness to do something so fanciful? Was it an act of sedition? A gesture of rebellion? A way to get my attention? Was it Theo back from the dead? Was it Crystalline? Sid? A twist of the plot?

I watched them dance in the moonlight until Plume arrived in a long, loose dress made of some weightless red fabric printed with large black chrysanthemums.

She stood at my side, her lips parted. Then slowly, as if afraid of being electrocuted, she reached for a noose. Once she had its little head in her fingers, she snapped it from the tree.

"Not a very nice way to treat a piece of art, Plume."

"I don't know what this is."

"It's the most interesting thing I've seen since I arrived."

She wound the loose end of the rope around her finger and looked at me.

"You're telling me," I said, "that you have nothing to do with it?"

"You think this is interesting?" Was that a spark of something good in her eyes?

"Yes," I said. "By comparison."

The spark died. "Always the caveat."

"I wouldn't think the Supreme Leader would sanction so many lynchings."

"This wasn't made by any of our artists. They know better."

"Then who did it?"

"I don't know."

"You expect me to believe that?"

"You'd should go to bed, Mr. Fields. You look tired."

She pocketed the cardboard. And then, yes, another exit.

I walked home shivering from something I didn't recognize, something which seemed to have been provoked by the jacaranda gallows, by the moonlight, by my conversation with Sid, by the growing distance between a former life and the one toward which I was traveling, and still there was something more, a thing which was not sadness exactly, nor was it joy, but an expansiveness, a filling in, an amplifying of the senses. Something, anyway, that wasn't blankness.

All at once, The Coded Garden no longer felt so absurd, so anodyne. I found now as I climbed into bed that I was rooting for Sebastian Light. May all this be designed. Let it all be directed. May it be his swan song, a final installation. It's what Lina Klein would have wanted, so it was what I wanted, too. From the lectures to the rock walls to the hanging to my very presence there, may it all be orchestrated, may it all be art.

22

The next night, The Barn was abuzz. There were lanterns on the grass, candles on every table. An enormous, blurry ballerina moved in slow motion across the broad outside wall, a projector buried in a hibiscus bush beaming its light through the air. Other than her slippers and a black tutu, she was naked, hair tied in a high knot.

Saber leaned against the doorway, his guitar gently weeping.

The first thing I'd done that morning was check the jacaranda, but it had already been cleared of its figures. No sign to be found of those heretical gingerbread men.

Inside, Siddhartha sat alone in a chair against the wall looking glum. I waved, but he made no sign he saw me, so I walked through the milling apprentices to Crystalline, who stood alone by the cistern of magnesium water.

"No dinner this evening?"

"Apparently not."

"Did you see the tree last night?"

"No. I heard about it though."

"Too bad," I said, watching her carefully, "it was good."

"You saw it?"

"Yes. A little evening art."

"You think that's art? Dangling cardboard from a tree?"

"Depends on the cardboard. And the tree."

"I hope you're not a sucker for stunts," she said, looking across the room at Siddhartha, who was staring at the floor.

"Does it bother you?"

"I don't confuse kitsch with art," she said.

"It was something to see. My grandmother liked to say that experience is all."

"Nice slogan."

"She had many."

"Speaking of experience, despite my invitations, you never come to see my work."

"You want me to just show up?"

"You don't need an appointment."

"All right," I said. "I'll come tomorrow."

"Promise?"

"I solemnly swear."

"Good."

"The figures in the tree," I said. "Plume claims none of the artists were responsible. According to her, Lord Light knows nothing about it."

"Oh?"

"Do you really think that's possible?"

"Honestly, I have no idea."

"What do you think he'll make of them?"

"I think you're about to have your answer." She raised her chin at Sebastian Light, who was just then arriving, dressed all in white linen.

And then the lights dimmed and the room fell to a hush. He stepped onto the platform and looked upon us. The collar tonight was Nehru, the pants draped easy on his long legs, the miraculous black hair framing his face.

Man, he was a handsome man, a ready-made guru, and the minute he laid his foot on the boards, he transformed that humble stage into something grand. For a long moment, he didn't say a word, just stood, patriarch preacher before his progeny. But when he spoke, there was anger in his voice, and it seemed to me that it was real.

"My dear friends, last night our beloved jacaranda was

vandalized, desecrated. How many of you were exposed to this ugliness, I do not know. I do not know how many of you, without warning, came upon that exquisite flowering tree, expecting its calming beauty, and were confronted with a such disgusting shock." He took a breath, apparently calming himself. "I cannot pretend to know what that experience did to your psyches, to your hearts, but one thing is for certain, we are all of us, even the perpetrator, in need of purification, of cleansing. And so: let us forget what we saw last night. Stand up. Come. Let us walk together now."

Then there was The Garden's great beauty wearing a tranquil smile and a loose white dress, hair braided and bound, at the door raising her hands above her head. The mob began to churn and drain from The Barn into the night air behind her.

"What's going on?" I asked Crystalline.

Crystalline was grinning, an expression of good-natured sadism.

"You'll see. Coming?"

"I wouldn't miss it," I said and soon we were out of The Barn and into the black.

The hushed column moved across the lawn following our general to the pasture where we zigged and zagged down to an edge of forest, further than I'd ever been. Here we entered a leaf-strewn path and were soon consumed by the trees.

Two rows of glass lanterns lit our way in amber light to a tight clearing which contained a hut swathed in cream-colored canvas. The air smelled of cedar smoke.

Light passed us all and stood at the entrance next to Plume.

"My friends, it is time now to begin again, to cleanse ourselves."

At which point, our gracious host dropped both trou and drawers, allowing the privileged among us to take in the sight of his ageless body, his low-dangling nuts, before he disappeared through the flaps.

"Last chance," Crystalline whispered. She was pulling off her dress. "Run for the hills or strip down."

"Is this a joke?"

"Define your terms, Solomon."

One by one the naked disappeared.

"Does he mean it?"

"You'll need to be more specific."

I did not want to take my clothes off. I was preparing my excuses.

"Maybe you should ignore your grandmother's advice and go back to your room," Crystalline said, and there was a note of pity in her voice. "Whatever he means, the things we do in there shall still be done."

"Profound," I said.

She had her hands on my back, driving me toward the dark chamber, her mouth at my ear.

"Into the oven you go, Solomon."

She ducked her head, gave me a white-ass wink and dove forward into the dark hole.

Gem undressed and entered.

The line was dwindling now. All around the entrance were knolls of organic cotton still warm from the auras of their owners.

I continued to waver until Sid, without looking at me, passed on the left—bronze and smooth as a porpoise. And because of that snub, or the beauty of his body, or simply the dread of being left behind, I stripped off fast and plunged on.

Inside, I felt soft blankets underfoot. The smoke stung my eyes. I groped for an empty spot and sat. Quickly I was sopping with sweat. The panic of claustrophobia was coming. I pressed my back against the canvas. I felt flesh against my knee, my shoulder, my elbow.

I kept thinking. Stand up, walk away, enough is enough.

The dim light coming from the door was stolen away by a loyal minion who must have been given the job of holy hut-closer.

All the rustling stopped. There was a settling.

All I could hear was my pounding, poisoned heart desperately trying to cool its polluted body, the crackling of burning cedar and the sibilant sighs of all the pretty perspirers.

"Once upon a time," came Light's voice from the darkness. "Human beings had fire. The coyote had no fire. The coyote said to the wolf, 'Go, steal a flame from the humans.' So the wolf went to the village. The humans gave the wolf a bowl of sugar. He forgot to steal the fire. And that is everything."

More shadows, more breathing, some panting.

"My friends, never, never forget to steal the fire."

Impossible that this is real, I thought. Impossible.

This was apparently the final lesson, for he stopped talking and the crowd fell silent.

Sebastian Light dipped a rag-wrapped baton into the smoke and from the coals was born a flame. All the wet-faced acolytes appeared in the carroty firelight. It took me a moment to recover from the jolt of finding myself roasting in a tandoor packed with hemp-hearted, magnesium-watered, free-range bodies, sparkling eyes, crisscrossed legs framing thick-thatched triangles, long, well-postured backs, flowing brooks of glistening hair.

Here was Crystalline, eyes closed, torso long as a dragon's neck, nipples skyward, hair damp and matted to her pale forehead. There was Saber, hands gripping his knees as if evaluating grapefruits.

"Who would like to begin?" Sebastian Light again.

He swiveled his great stallion head until those unsettling beacons of his lit upon a quiet kid who looked back with frightened crocodile eyes. Now in the firelight all his dramatic features seemed tripled in power. He was one of those who might have been hideously ugly, but thanks to the miracle of millimeters, managed to be strikingly handsome.

"Ridge," Sebastian Light said.

Ridge shook his head.

"Please," Light said without any note of pleading.

Ridge closed his eyes and took a long time emptying his lungs. Then he said, "Heaven."

There was a murmur to my right, and everyone fixed their eyes on its source—a thin woman I was nearly certain I'd never seen before, who opened her mouth but made no noise. Maybe she was new.

I looked at Crystalline across the fire. She smiled, but it wasn't her usual. It seemed to me a look of apology.

"Good," Sebastian Light said. "Go, Ridge. Empty her."

"But I didn't see it," Heaven said, lowering her chin, her voice quavering. "The tree. I didn't even see it."

"We are a single body," Sebastian Light said. "Go."

Ridge began to crab his way around the coals and soon he was fitting himself behind Heaven.

Light pointed his burning baton at her. "You are free, Heaven. You may leave. No one will stop you. But if you stay, you must mean it. It must be true."

The flame drew closer to her face. She might have been sweating or crying.

"Grab hold, Ridge," he said.

Ridge brought his hands between Heaven's thighs.

"Grab hold," Light said again. "Grab hold."

Ridge drew his left hand higher, while the other lifted away to cup her breast in his hand. She shut her eyes again and let her head fall back against his chest.

Ridge's left hand began to move in time to a quiet, guttural, rhythmic groan, which emanated from somewhere between Light's chest and throat. Soon nearly everyone was following along as he increased the pace. It was all so absurd, and yet in its absurdity, its utter lack of originality, there was also something ugly, polished and pitiless. The whole thing like a sinister, dizzying ballet.

Heaven began to sigh.

"Let go, let go," Light said.

Ridge worked harder, she sighed louder.

"Yes," Light said, "yes, let it be true, let it be free."

And true or not, Heaven cried out and convulsed, shook and moaned until she was quietly sobbing while Ridge whispered into her ear. The humming stopped. They both looked so unprotected, so ashamed. I was sorry for Heaven. I was sorry for Ridge, whose whispering, though I couldn't make out a word, struck me as sincere and kind.

"Exquisite," Light said. "Exquisite. Heaven, you are brave, and you are selfless, and you are beautiful." She had been coerced into a public orgasm and for her troubles, another slogan. "But the images of desecration will not be wiped away so easily. There is work to do yet."

There was a long period of silence then. Crystalline kept her eyes closed. Siddhartha wouldn't look at me. No one seemed to be very happy to be there. For the first time since arriving at The Coded Garden, I had the distinct impression that Sebastian Light was behaving in ways that surprised even his most loyal soldiers.

"Crystalline," Light said.

"Yes?"

"Who?"

She tightened her lips and rose up. Any second, I thought, she would tell him to go fuck himself, but instead a look of real trouble and mischief appeared on her face, and she said, "Him."

Then there she was looking directly at me.

"As you like," he said, and I could not tell whether he was pleased.

She shifted her weight, tilted her torso forward over her

crossed legs and tipped onto hands and knees, her face close to the coals. Around the embers she came with challenge in her eyes.

"Accept from this woman whatever she will offer you, Solomon."

I could have left, but I didn't.

When she arrived at the banks of my lotus-legged self, she took my knees in her hands and pulled herself up. For a moment she towered above me, her face vanished into shadow and then she returned to earth, whispering loudly, theatrically, "Will you accept what I offer?"

I couldn't read her expression. I couldn't tell if all of it had been programmed, if she were doing it for her ambitions or his or simply because she wanted to fuck me.

And what choice did I have? What does a broken man in a lunatic's sweat lodge do when a pale dragon asks him whether he will accept her offering? What he does is try to breathe, is try to bury the modesty his mother wove into him to spite her own mother's shameful, saucy self, is try to disconnect himself from himself, is try to convince that self it is as free and as liberated and as open to carnal pleasures as Lina Klein. What he does is force a sound of consent from his dehydrating body, through his arid throat, across the desert of his tongue.

A sound which provoked in Crystalline a gentle growl, and then with the quickness of an Olympic wrestler she was behind me, my legs locked down by hers, those wily orangutan arms moving beneath mine, her nipples teasing my shoulder blades, cool hands flat on my chest, and down my belly until one of them, or both, what did I know by then, wrapped around my cock. And now before an undressed audience, its members slick with sweat, watching, smiling, began to hum their locomotive beat.

I closed my eyes. Not in ecstasy, but in an effort to disappear from Crystalline and Siddhartha, from Plume and Saber and Gem, from Ridge and Heaven and Citrus/Duckling, from, above all, Sebastian Light. I was naked, captive, sweating, tumescent, submissive to the power of his most brazen octopus. I closed my eyes and listened to them sing, "What she offers, what she offers, what she offers." Faster they chanted while Crystalline grazed my left ear with her lips whispering to me, only to me, her filthy encouragement.

"Come for me, come for me. Give me what I want," she hissed, her slippery thighs vising my hips, her hand closing tighter, up and down it went as if furiously agitating a can of spray paint.

"Empty yourself," she said, "be rid of suspicion, of doubt. Give in. Be free." And now she roared, "For us, for us. Give it to us!"

Then she jammed two fingers in my mouth. They tasted of sweat and cunt and sage and smoke. "You like that," she said, "Say it. Tell us." And then, perhaps because I couldn't bear the idea of speaking, of hearing my own voice, my own mind, or because I loved the flavor of her fingers, or because her unremitting fist had reached unbearable speed, I did as she asked, gave her what she (they?) wanted: an orgasm of outrageous force which drew up from some yawning void within me, the world whitening as it rose.

And what did they do? What shook me from my euphoric stupor? Not the sweet nothings of my captor, nor the churchy pabulum of Lord Light. No, it was applause. While Crystalline spread my belly with the results of her work, the crowd cheered.

The last thing I wanted in the world was to see. There in my cozy darkness, I was already feeling the familiar sweep of guilt. I had to get home, to my shower, to sleep, to oblivion.

When I found the courage to open my eyes and leave my dark room, when orange light and all those faces, that fire and smoke came rushing in, I saw Plume first—hair barely covering her breasts, wearing an expression of sublime sympathy.

Facing her, my guilt dissolved into the desolate sadness I always felt after sex. Even after an experience so strange, so physical, I felt the same—incapable of existing entirely within my body. As Crystalline held me in her warm arms, I gazed into Plume's inscrutable, confounding eyes. I felt then a disconcerting sense of intimacy which was vastly more unsettling than anything that had transpired here, more than the long march into the woods, the ridiculous rhetoric, the sweltering lodge, the naked beauties, Crystalline's agile maneuvering, her indecent urging. It was that I felt a simple tenderness for these people.

In none of them did I see contempt or mockery or disgust. It's true that slunk down as I was, head resting between my midwife's breasts, in Sebastian Light's face there was a glimmer of righteous pride, the serene expression of a noble victor. But it didn't bother me, surprised as I was by the gentleness of my lovers. Even Siddhartha, who insisted he stood apart from these maniacs, looked at me through the smog, I thought, I was nearly sure, with compassion.

Crystalline held me tightly between her milky thighs while one after the other the Gardeners rose, bent double and, as they passed, touched my head, or the back of my neck. Some of them kissed my cheek, some my forehead, others my lips, as if in benediction, and like that, just as they had poured into the lodge, they dribbled out into the night, sighing in the cool air.

Plume kissed my forehead, her breasts gently bumping my eyebrows, Siddhartha put a hot hand on my shoulder and kissed my ear, Sebastian Light placed his great palm upon my head, said, "Now we are clean," and was gone. Then Crystalline gently released me.

And so I was alone there with the dimming coals and their dying heat, flat out now on the soiled blankets. I traveled from Robert Capo to Charity, to the bullies and hypocrites and their hollow marketing, through all those years of fighting—my stupid, stubborn refusal to bend, all those mule-headed years of climbing, of ignoring my matriarchs. I went then to Lina Klein, whom I loved so purely, who was gone, who said enough was enough, who'd mustered the unfathomable courage to do the very thing she had decided to do. Lina Klein, whom I had never been able to condemn. Who once in the last grubby bar on Ninth Avenue told me, a little drunk, "Don't you ever put your faith in a poetry of blankness and don't you dare pretend you don't know what I mean."

Her white hair was still thick then and cut within an inch of her flawless skull. She wore a white turtleneck, a black leather jacket and black jeans, as if she were still twenty-two out looking for trouble. I didn't really know what she meant, and I wasn't sure if she knew either. She was always reaching back and stealing other people's saws even if they weren't very clever. But now I knew exactly what she meant I swore to myself then, in my shame, naked on those damp blankets, I would never again, no matter what it took, give in.

I crawled out of that lodge of iniquity and immediately felt better with the chill, unpolluted air on my wet skin. Someone had taken my underwear. I got dressed. I got myself together. All the candles in their lanterns had burned out, but I found my way through the trees and onto the pasture path and, fighting a growing sense of shame, into the center of The Spiral.

Ernst Frankel on shame: "The burden of fools."

When he said it, we were standing on the roof of his building at night drinking whiskey, sharing a cigarette and looking out over both bridges all lit up bright with Brooklyn twinkling beyond and it was all too pretty, too perfect for me to think. I nodded and filed it away as more excellent wisdom, another aphorism to live by. Experience is all. Beauty is brutal. Burden of fools. Go anywhere, be anything. A poetry of blankness. Only after the profile was published and I read that scene in print did I realize how little it meant, and I was ashamed.

One early morning Frankel played "Frère Jacques" on my buzzer until I was up and out of bed. When I came down, he was standing on the street in his grey ushanka and a ratty red wool coat. I was bleary and hungover and at first it was difficult to tell where the fur of the hat ended and his beard began. It was very cold, but he didn't want to come up. He wanted to walk.

We stopped for bagels and as we were leaving Russ and Daughters, he kissed the side of my head. Out on Houston, I handed him his coffee and looked for an explanation, but he just nodded and smiled and slung his arm around me and kept it there as we walked.

It all seemed spontaneous and sincere, but we were getting to the end and maybe he just wanted to be sure. It didn't matter. By then I'd have done anything for the man.

That same morning he showed me the building on Hester Street where Jacob Epstein grew up. Frankel admired him, he said. He told me he was proud to live only a few blocks away. He loved Epstein's *Severed Head*. He told me that one day he hoped to display it on the first floor beneath the skylight. That it was locked away at The Met didn't seem to concern him.

"Force of will, force of will," he said. Then he told me a good story about Oscar Wilde's tomb. "It was only Epstein's second commission. The sculpture was *controversial*, vile milquetoast word that it is. Why controversial? The balls were too big. Anyway, they refused to let it pass customs as a piece of art, so it comes through classified as a hunk of rock. Still, up it went but not long after, Epstein goes to Père Lachaise and finds the offending testicles smothered in plaster. Can you imagine that? Fucking puritans. He had to bribe a cop to look the other way while he devandalizes his sculpture. Then before the big unveiling, they covered the nuts with a bronze butterfly. Epstein was furious. Then they bring in an occultist writer who, by the way, later invented some crackpot religion, to pull the tarp off the sculpture. In protest, Epstein refused to show up. A few weeks later, the occultist, wearing the butterfly as a necklace, finds Epstein in a café, leans over and says to him, "Now, sir, your sculpture is as you made it to be."

Frankel laughed as loud as I'd ever heard him laugh.

"It gets better. In the sixties someone stole those poor nuts, chopped them right off. I once heard that for a while, the cemetery caretaker used them as a paperweight. Who knows? They've not been seen since. The mystery remains. Is that not the most wonderful story? The world used to be so much fun, Solomon."

By then we'd chucked the coffee cups, the bagel wrappers. At my door, he drew me in and kissed the side of my head again and whispered, "I'll see you, kid."

Then he turned and lumbered off back down Orchard Street. I watched him go until he disappeared into the throng.

Later, at his studio, I'd hear him tell that same story, practically word for word, to a voluptuous painter who worked in kosher animal blood on the fourth floor.

23

At lunch, in spirit and letter, I obeyed the law of silence. I skipped dinner. I kept my eyes down. I didn't see Sid. I didn't see Crystalline. Instead, I walked the perimeter of the property. From a distance, I watched the artists moving through their days—playing music, picking lemons, washing kale, staking their beans, rolling closed their great studio doors. Sebastian Light was nowhere to found. Plume, too, had made herself scarce. I thought I might do the same. Why stay? Why subject myself to the humiliation of this place? Was there really anything to see here? To say? To write?

Two or three days after the night of The Lodge, I ate my precious pride and went to see Crystalline at her studio. It was after dinner. She was painting when I rolled back the door, but she waved me in and told me to sit at her table. From the back of a low cabinet, she brought out a bottle of Stolichnaya, two glass tumblers and a tin of brownies.

"Why'd you pick me, Crystalline?"

"We are the Bolsheviks of The Garden, Solomon," she said and poured each of us a shot.

"To the revolution then," I said.

"L'chaim."

We both drank and she poured us another.

"You took your time coming to see me."

"Yes, well."

"If it makes you feel any better, we've all been through some version of it."

"Of what?"

"Ritual humiliation."

"What was your version?"

"It's always more or less the same."

"As what happened to me?"

"Oh, did something happen to you, baby?"

I laughed. "This is a regular thing?"

"Yes. More or less."

"What changes?"

"The rhetoric, mostly. And the success," she said, her voice having gained something somber.

"The success?"

"He wants an orgasm. It's the only way it ever stops. But for women, obviously—"

"You can pretend."

"Well, yes, of course, but with Light, I would say perform. The actual orgasm is a secondary requirement. He wants a shuddering body, clenched fists, arched back, all the Hollywood shit. He demands it. He wants it to look just so."

"And everyone goes along? Submits?"

"You did," she said, looking at me with some mockery in her eyes.

"Yes."

"And did you like it?"

"No."

"So why didn't you stop it?"

"I'm not sure."

"Of course, you're sure. You're already naked. It would be impolite, wouldn't it? Awkward to extricate yourself from the party? You don't want to disappoint all those nice people. Least of all your host."

"Is that why you let it happen?"

"What? You think it's different for girls?" She shook her head. "I thought you were a sophisticated city boy."

"Does he say what it's for?"

"What it's *for*. What is it ever for, Sol?"

"I don't know how you do it," I said.

"Keep a straight face?"

"Among other things, yes."

"I'm a woman. I've spent my entire life keeping a straight face in front of men like him."

"Is that true?"

"You know women who haven't?"

"I haven't ever known a Sebastian Light."

"You think he's more unusual than he is."

"Maybe I've just never met anyone so shameless."

"Well then you're either very lucky or not very bright."

"It's the second one," I said. "What do you know about him?"

"Nothing, really."

"Nothing?"

"He seems to inspire loyalty," she said.

"Inspires loyalty how?"

"Those he loves, he treats very well."

"And those he doesn't?"

"They don't last."

"Like Theo."

"Exactly."

"Does he love you?"

"I don't think he feels one way or another about me."

"He didn't mind you contradicting him at the eval."

"He tolerates me, I guess. I know how to please the patron just enough."

"Tell me what else you know about him."

"Oh, the rumors are endless."

"Go on."

"He was in prison. He was a doctor. He's an heir to an oil fortune. He was a preacher. He had his own church. He's a famous Austrian artist. He's from Argentina. He's from Florida."

"That's it?"

"As far as I can remember. I never cared that much. None of those would surprise me, least of all the oil heir."

"You're not curious?"

"I guess I don't think he's all that interesting."

"No?"

"Sometimes I imagine this place as one of those farms for wounded animals. But the animals are artists, and the wound is absence of talent."

I laughed. "Is that what you are?"

"No," she said sharply. Then she stood up and walked to the back wall where she picked up a square canvas. "Did you come to interrogate me or see my work?"

"Both."

I wanted so much for her to be the real thing. I thought, if she spins it around to reveal a pod of cheerful dolphins swimming gaily with a wise old whale, I'm going to go sweat myself to death. I watched her walking toward me, the frame dangling from her fingertips.

She stood so that one of the overhead lights was shining right on the back of the canvas.

For the first time since I'd met her, she seemed unsure.

"If you like it, what will you do?"

"What will I do?"

"Will you write about me?"

"Et tu, Crystalline?"

"Forget I said that," she said, spinning it, replacing her face, holding it up and out as if it were a protest placard.

At first it appeared to be only some kind of experiment in color—gold at the center radiating to a darker and darker green until the edges were a rich black. Then figures appeared as if rising from a haze. They kneeled, ecstatic, naked, looking upwards just above the corona, where a tall man with tar-colored hair stood, palms facing out, smiling toothy and beatific upon his acolytes. Beneath them were brown figures, men and women, naked, prostrate on the green, being crushed beneath a rock wall, their faces twisted in agony. A stern owl spread its wings. Among those acolytes, a naked woman wearing yellow hair and a maniac grin pedaled a bicycle riveted to the wall, while another stood behind her delicately inserting a plumeria stem into the cyclist's anus. Fires burned everywhere—great cities, country villages, a towering gold hotel, oil fields, piles of plastic pill bottles, surgical masks, funeral pyres, garbage barges out to sea, and all their smoke twisting its way into the black edges of the panels where it settled in a greasy residue. A man gleefully cut the throat of another while a laughing boy raised his phone to record it. These small scenes of horror and comedy were everywhere, but all of it had no impact on the central scene, where the golden figures gazed up into the shining eyes of their leader.

I was impressed by the intricacy of it, the combination of rage and control. All of my cynicism, my desire to dismiss and discount and mock, all of it was gone.

"The Coded Garden of Earthly Delights," I said.

She lowered the painting. I watched the muscles tightening below the down and pale skin of her jaw.

"It's wonderful."

She stared at me.

"I mean it," I said.

She propped the canvas against the wall and came back to the table. We both looked at it for a while.

"How do you stand it here?"

"I have nowhere else to go."

"Nowhere? No trust fund?"

"Fuck you. No. I have no trust fund. I don't even have an apartment. Or a studio. I've never even had a show."

I nodded.

"Yes, I could get a job."

"But why would you?"

"Yes. Why would I? You have to eat someone's shit."

"That's for sure," I said.

"At least he's a vegetarian."

I laughed. "He's going to tear you apart for this."

"I'm not sure I'll show it to him."

"That's too bad."

"I have something else for the Biennale."

"I'd like to see it."

"I guess you'll have to stay another week."

"Are you sure you don't want to show me now?"

"You're not going to stay?"

"I don't know."

"Are you going to write about him?"

"Do you want me to?"

"I'd rather you write about me."

"I think you overestimate my power."

"You've got more of it than I do."

"Bullshit," I said. "I could never make something like this. Never."

I stood up and walked to the wall and kneeled before her painting.

"Why not go live somewhere else? Don't you think these people will destroy you? Your work?"

"To do what? Be a waitress, freeze in some shitty studio?"

I stood up and faced her.

"To be in the world."

"Are you lecturing me?"

"No. I'm parroting my grandmother. I'm sorry. I love your

painting. Thank you for the drink and the brownie and for showing me this."

"I'm not like the rest of them."

"That's what Sid says, too."

"About me?"

"About himself."

"I know, I know."

"Isn't he just eating shit to get along? Just like you?"

"It's a matter of degree. Make sure you understand that. It's one thing to get along. It's another to collaborate."

"Collaboration. Serious charges, Crystalline."

"Listen. Just because I play along does not make me a hack, all right?" She leaned back. "Just wait another week. You'll see."

I stood up to go. "What's your real name?"

"Come on, Sol." She laughed. "Why ruin the fun?"

24

In the following days, meals weren't quite so well attended. There were fewer artists out and about, fewer pods of communing beauties, fewer examples of ostentatious bonhomie, in general. The Biennale was coming soon and perhaps they were painting and worrying into the night, taking their meals in their studios, but since the night of The Sweat Lodge, I had the sense that there was real uneasiness in the air, that something had shifted. Of course, whether that shift was ordained, I could not say.

One evening, alone at dinner, I looked up from my plate to find Ridge sitting across from me. I still couldn't quite understand what made him so handsome, and yet there he was, goofy and magnificent and blank. He appeared to have recovered from his ordeal.

"Do you mind if I sit with you, Sol?"

"Of course not," I said.

I waited, but he asked no questions and after too long a silence, I couldn't take it any longer. I said, "Are you happy here, Ridge?"

He smiled that uncanny smile of devotion. "I am very happy. I have been given everything," he said with an eerie, droning enthusiasm.

"Everything?"

"A way to be, to paint, to speak."

"To speak?"

"About art. He has given me a language."

I nodded. "You didn't have one before?"

"I was a child."

I leaned forward and narrowed my eyes. "When did he give you this language exactly?"

He pulled back. "What do you mean?"

"I'll ask you the very same question."

Now it seemed he couldn't wait to get away. He began to eat faster and the minute he'd finished his sweet potatoes, he was up and gone without even a goodbye.

I watched him lope into The Barn to deposit his dirty plate, and I thought, God, I hope the guy is an actor, because if not, he is in some real trouble. Either way, there is just no chance he's an artist. And then I came back to Lina Klein and how what she loved most about art was the very simplest idea: first there is nothing and then there is something. At the heart of it, this is what thrilled and preoccupied her. Countless times, she insisted on that wonder.

"A woman walks into a silent room, Soli. She closes her eyes and hears music. She needs nothing more than a pencil. And then there is something beautiful. That's it. Out of nothing, something."

In a thousand ways over the course of my life, or the course of hers, she said this to me, but aside from when she told me the story of Charlotte Salomon, I don't remember her ever talking about its opposite: out of something, nothing. It just isn't as beautiful. Or maybe it is.

Maybe it is, I was thinking, maybe it is, when Siddhartha appeared, all smiles. Siddhartha who I'd barely seen since The Sweat Lodge.

"Hello, stranger," I said, trying my best to play breezy.

He sat down across from me.

"You okay?"

"Why wouldn't I be?"

"The whole smoke house thing."

"What red-blooded American boy regrets a hand job, Siddhartha?"

He smiled, but I could tell he didn't buy it. He put a cube of pumpkin in his mouth.

"Do you wonder why she chose you?"

"Who?"

"Crystalline. Why of all the people there, it was you."

"One of two things."

"What are those?"

"She was doing his bidding, or she thinks I'll write about her."

"Will you?"

"She's very good."

"At what?"

I smiled. "Painting."

"She showed you her work?"

"You look concerned."

"So, you're going to write about her then?"

"I don't know."

"What about the rest?"

"The rest?"

"Don't be coy."

"What I'm trying to figure out is why so many people keep asking me the same question."

"I'm sorry," he said.

"Why are you sorry?"

He shook his head and looked away. "It would help me to know," he said after a pause, "if you're going to write about him, or her, or anything at all."

"Help you how?"

Again, that look. There was disgust in it, but I couldn't tell at whom it was directed.

"Listen, Sol, forget about it, okay? I'm going to go work. I'll see you tomorrow."

Then he stood up and, as they all did so well, walked away, leaving just a bit of mystery behind.

25

In 2015, two years before her suicide, Lina Klein left me the following message: "She killed him, Soli. Charlotte Salomon. She *killed* her grandfather. They published the letter in France. She mixed poison into an omelet and watched that cruel old fucker die, and all the while she sat there watching, drawing his portrait. What a woman. Call me."

I'd been with Charity at the opening of a clothing store in SoHo. When I went outside and called her back, my grandmother was less excited.

"It may not be true. Just an invention, fiction. It's possible."

I was looking in through the glass at Charity standing beneath a massive photograph of a naked model with a paintbrush between her teeth.

"Are you disappointed?" I asked. "You prefer that she murdered him?"

I watched Charity smile and blow kisses at someone.

"I really hope she did it. But either way, I love her."

"I hope so, too," I said. "I hope my namesake is a cold-blooded killer."

She laughed. "I love you, Solomon rabbit."

"I love you, too" I said. "I wish you were here."

The next time we spoke, she told me about going to Amsterdam with some painter and how she stumbled on the first public exhibition of *Life? or Theater?*

"It was an accident. The man, this artist, who it turns out wasn't much of an artist, he was suffocating me. I went out for a walk. I smoked a joint and got very high. I just happened on it. Just a building in a foreign city. Then I was inside. I had no idea. I stayed until they kicked me out. It was like walking through a door and entering my own mind. As a girl in Berlin she had everything and then, just like that, she had nothing."

Ernst Frankel didn't like Charlotte Salomon. He said she'd stolen it all from Chagall, that if her story wasn't so interesting, no one would have paid attention.

The only time I ever disliked him was when he told me that.

26

The next evening, or maybe the evening after that, I was at home at my little table with an open notebook and a pen in my hand when Siddhartha materialized from behind a palm, striding toward me all slick and clean in loose pants, and a white shirt, sleeves rolled and collar sharp as if threatening his throat. When he saw me, he said, "The journalist at work. What a picture you make."

All the gloom and hesitation appeared to have been erased. He was his brightest self and when he smiled at me, it was a shattering thing that brought so much light and intelligence to his face I had to look away.

"Go for a walk, Soli?"

I said yes too fast and was on my feet before I could think. We headed toward the ridge and as we passed below his house, Sebastian Light was up on his veranda gazing out as if waiting for his sailor to return from sea.

We walked down the hill and into yet another forest path, this one far less traveled. He cut so elegantly through the air and I tried to think of nothing, to listen only to the sounds of our footsteps, and the occasional rush of wind forcing through the densely bound branches.

We entered a tight clearing not ten feet wide and I lost him for a few seconds. The sounds of singing cardinals faded. Then there was Sid again, sitting on the wall, which was so entirely covered in moss and lichen that for a moment in the gauzy light he appeared to levitate.

I don't know if he'd done it for effect, but it was an image of exquisite beauty.

I could feel his eyes on me.

"Do you want to sit with me here, Sol?"

He turned his back to me then and swung his legs over the other side.

I climbed up next to him so that we were side by side, our legs hanging over the edge, both of us now looking into a steep ravine, a deep gash thick with jungle.

"Light brought me here when I first arrived," he said. "It was part of his tour."

"It's strange."

"He told me that these walls appeared out of thin air. That one day there were no walls and then the next day they encircled the land."

I laughed. "Might be news to Sunny."

He gave me a tight smile and said, "It's just a myth."

"It's not very original."

"No, I suppose not."

"My grandmother loved art for that same reason. Out of nothing, something."

"Me, too. I'm really sorry," he said. "I hope you know that I mean it. No matter what happens, no matter what you think, I want you to know that I'm not just saying it."

"Thank you."

"Do you believe me?"

"What do you mean, no matter what happens?"

"Tell me. Do you believe me?"

"Sure," I said. "Let me ask you something, though, Sid. Why do I have the impression that you don't want to talk about Sunny? That you regret sending me down there?"

"I didn't send you down there."

"No?"

"Maybe you have that impression, Sol, because—"

Then he stopped, looked at me and then all at once his arm was around my shoulder and he was kissing me, very slightly tightening his grip, more a suggestion of strength, than a show of it. His lips were dry at first, but quickly they became wet.

I took his face in my hands, but he pulled them away and, gripping my wrists, pushed me back. I worried that my gesture had been too romantic, too gentle, that there had been a level of emotion that he did not want, whatever this was, or whatever he wanted. Soon I was on my back, stretched out along the top of the wall. I opened my eyes in hopes of catching his, of getting some sense of what he thought, what it might mean to him, but I was too late and all I could see above me was the canopy and all that eerie light like fine green powder blown into the air. His mouth was on my neck now. I felt his teeth on my skin, and the cold hardness of the wall against my spine, and his body lowering down, easy, bit by bit and I slowly accepted his weight in increments, his hands crushing my forearms against the stone and there was some pain but it was far off like something you feel while asleep and have an arm twisted in some unnatural way but the sleep is too deep, or the dream too good and you file it away as something you'll return to in a while, when the other things are dealt with first and then finally he gave me his full weight and his mouth by then was on my shoulder and I felt him so solid against me. Whatever pain I felt was so far away and then it was gone entirely. I must have made some sound because he said, "Yes, Sol," as if answering a question, or agreeing with me about something, calm, thoughtful. He wasn't panting or tearing at my clothes, which I was glad for. I liked that he seemed so easy and in control of himself. Of me, too. I would have hated it if he'd been any more violent. Or if he'd been sloppy. Though there was no way he would be sloppy about anything and then for an instant I was thinking that this would be just the trait that would separate us finally, that must have separated him from so many people, so many lovers past, an enduring reserve, an incapacity for abandon. And then I began thinking about his paintings and I had the idea all of a sudden that he must save all his madness for them and how I'd need to see those paintings soon just as I'd needed to see Crystalline's. And I thought, I'm already making excuses for him, explaining away his coldness as the idiosyncrasies of the Great Artist and I hadn't even *seen* his art and even if he *were* a great artist, so what, that's no excuse, he should treat me better. Then I was embarrassed by that whole stream, and I should just give in and how I was exactly like him, and did it really take fucking a man to see myself for what I was? And then as he was opening my shirt, and his lips were on my chest, his arms stretched out and the pressure on my wrists relaxed, I was imagining some faceless person sitting across the room from him saying just the kind of thing Charity had said to me, *you give nothing, you're never vulnerable, you don't let me in*, or any number of other television platitudes and for a moment, just before he took my right nipple between his teeth, I had the strange sensation of making love to myself, or no, more the sensation of what it might be to have been one of my own partners, how it might have been both satisfying and awful, how the pleasure of being taken care of, of being tended to, not by a cruel person, but a remote one, would have been difficult for Charity and those few who'd come before her, maybe not at first, but ultimately, and I was lost in this strange vision, when he bit down, and I was rising to the edge of pain, all of that thinking was slowly being driven away. I pulled my hands free and wove my fingers into his dense black hair and it was a relief to have something to hold on to. Now I no longer felt as if I might fall from the wall or that he could do with me whatever he wanted, but then on the other hand I was a little disappointed because it seemed like an act of cowardice and I wished he'd take me over again, but it was impossible because now he was too far away for me to even touch his hair, he was kissing my knees and I thought, how is this possible? Where has he gone? I missed the pressure of his body and I didn't want such tenderness just as, I guess, he didn't want his face in my hands and so I mustered the courage to open my eyes for an instant and saw that he was now standing on the ground and leaning over me and this I didn't like at all because I immediately felt like a corpse on a slab, or, at least, a patient on an operating table, that I was just laid out there exposed and the whole thing felt so clinical, as if I were being evaluated or prepared for ritual sacrifice rather than being made love to or fucked or whatever we were doing and yet I couldn't bring myself to say anything, and I didn't *want* to say anything, I just wanted him to *know*, I just wanted him to do it, to cover me up again, to hold me down. I wanted to feel his weight, his strength and warmth and I couldn't figure out why I couldn't speak, why I couldn't just say, no, not this, not this, *that*, but then just as I was thinking these things I felt his arm slip beneath my knees, and the other behind my neck and I couldn't believe he was going to do it, but he did, he lifted me from the wall and laid me on the damp earth and then I felt him on top of me and I was very hard again, and so was he and he pressed his mouth right up against my ear and he said, "Okay?" I immediately said yes, without even thinking about it, without knowing what he was asking exactly, and then he was drifting from me and again I wanted to say *no*, would he just stay where he was, but I didn't, I couldn't get myself to say anything as if I was suddenly concerned with being polite, as if I didn't want to offend him. And then all at once he had my cock in his mouth and the pleasure of that feeling blasted everything else away so that I could no longer think and for however much time it lasted I was free of my mind.

Later, he sat with his back to the wall, and I lay with my head in his lap. He was combing my hair with his fingers and neither of us was talking. I'd done nothing for him, made no real gesture toward pleasing him, but he didn't seem to mind at all. I had the sense that it wasn't what he wanted and really the prospect of doing anything other than precisely what we'd done seemed entirely impossible to me. We hadn't spoken for what seemed like a long time and then a brilliant green insect appeared on my knee. We both watched as it made its way down my leg and then over to his. It was mesmerizing, that shocking emerald against his grey pants, the bug plodding away on its journey, and when it came to the hem and stepped gingerly down onto my naked foot before disappearing into the leaves, we both began to laugh.

Then he said, "I hope this doesn't make it into the piece."

I sat up. He was smiling, but something was wrecked, and I could not find a way to say so with any dignity and without sounding like a stock character in a soap opera.

We were both sitting up now. I buttoned my pants and pushed my hair back. He stood, reached his arms over his head in a long feline stretch.

And then we were no longer there in the clearing, but instead were walking toward the edge of the trees. I could see the pasture and its paler, colder light.

It was a pretty night, unusually still, with tall pink clouds dragging along the horizon. I felt foolish and manipulated and rattled and no matter how many times I replayed it, I just couldn't decide what he was, or how I might matter to him, or what he wanted. We weren't talking but we were still traveling together, and I was following his lead, thinking of the underside of his wrist when we came to the high knoll that rose above The Spiral.

Now a low, wide-reaching tree appeared in silhouette. I was nearly sure it hadn't been there the last time I walked this way.

He turned and we began to climb. When we were only a hundred yards from the top, it began to sparkle like a Christmas tree.

I looked at him and said, "What is that?"

His response was to pick up the pace, and as we got closer, it became clear that they weren't string lights, but little fires burning in the branches. By the time we were right there beneath it, I saw that there were hundreds of plastic figures, little green army men, each of which had been hung by wire, and as their bodies melted, small balls of blue fire fell toward the ground.

The tree itself wasn't burning. There was no crackling, no wind, and so the only sound was the hushed whistling of liquid plastic on fire.

I turned to him. "Did you do this?"

He didn't take his eyes off the tree. "I'm an artist, not an arsonist."

"How long have you been saving that line?"

He shook his head but didn't speak.

I turned back then to watch those tiny soldiers burn against the lilac sky. I tried my best to give myself entirely to it, to allow its force to obliterate my instincts, but I lost to curiosity and vanity. Who had made it and how had it been ignited and when and why and for whom and was it sanctioned and how was I being played and by whom and to what end?

Staring up into the branches, I said, "There wasn't even a tree here yesterday."

By the time the last man had dissolved, and all the flames were extinguished, I was thinking that they must have had someone watching me all the time. Not only when I slept, not only when I came and went. The timing was too good. Bits of plastic only burn for so long. I unhooked a hot wire from the tree. The helmeted head of a soldier was fused to it, his body had become nothing but a flimsy dagger. I put it in my pocket and turned to Sid, but, like magic, he was gone and now Plume was striding up the hill.

"Just in the neighborhood again?"

She stood beside me.

"At least this one's beautiful," she said. There was a note of resignation in her voice.

"It's well-timed in any case. Is it your work?"

"I'm not an artist, Mr. Fields."

"Right," I said, laughing. "What *are* you exactly then?"

She opened her mouth as if to say something sharp, quick-witted, but stopped herself.

Instead, she returned to the script: "I hate to press you, but I'd very much like to know whether you've decided."

"You are all so relentless."

"The least you could do is grant him a fair chance."

"A fair chance to do what? Look, you're all very good at intrigue and intimations of mystery, but I'm tired of it. What has he *done*, Plume? What has he *made*? Because what I've seen is just not enough. You want me to believe he's some kind of what? Performance artist? That he doesn't mean any of this? It's all theater? Or that this resort is a really a work of art?"

"You're afraid, aren't you?"

I sighed. "What am I afraid of?"

"Of writing again. Of failing."

"Plume, listen to me. I'm not afraid, I'm *bored*."

She shook her head. "Listen, I really don't want to chase you anymore. There's no time left for that. It's come to the point when you'll have to make a decision. The Biennale is in a few days. But let me say this before I go. You have an opportunity, Mr. Fields. It's your decision, of course. But be honest. You can pretend to be as unimpressed as you want, but you know there's a real story here. One way or another. Maybe it's a tragedy. Maybe it's a comedy. A morality tale. A satire. Revenge. Redemption. *Whatever.* You're the writer. But you know it's there. You *know* it. Either you have the courage to do it, or you're just another coward from New York City."

She sounded like Charity. She sounded like my mother. She sounded like Lina Klein.

27

At the end of 2001 Frankel bought the building on Hester Street just a few blocks west of Seward Park. Since then, he'd taken out the entire second floor, cut a wide shaft through the other four and installed a glass roof so that daylight could fall all the way to the ground where the party was and where he worked on his largest pieces.

Over the months I spent there, I heard stories—from Malice, from Maja, the Polish woman with the straight scar across her left cheek who ran the bar next door, from a Chinese painter who made flowers into monsters—of Frankel's persistence, of untimely evictions, of payoffs to expedite his renovations.

I asked him about it at Judy's one night and he shook his big wolfhound head and looked at me, for the first time, with contempt and disappointment.

"I bought that building not three months after those cocksuckers flew into the towers. How much real estate was being sold back then, Sol? In those days no one wanted to live here. Everyone was terrified. Artists were moving to Hudson, to fucking *Idaho.* Cowards. But I *bought*. I hired builders when no one was building. I *invested* in this city."

"All right," I said. "All right."

I didn't have the courage to point out that he'd paid peanuts, that one might see the purchase as a kind of profiteering, that the place was now worth ten times what he'd paid. And I didn't ask what had become of the tenants.

I told myself I was writing about art, not real estate. Really, it was that I never forgot my debt to the man, which was, I'm sure, how he wanted it. I needed him in ways professional and otherwise. I shouldn't have felt such pride when we left the studio together, his arm around my shoulder, walking at his side as he was greeted every block like a neighborhood mafia don until we crossed Chrystie Street, where suddenly no one noticed. Aside from Lina Klein, I felt more tenderness for him than any person on earth and no matter what he gave me—his cool hand on the back of my head, advice, anecdote, aphorism, theory, history—it wasn't enough. I was greedy, insatiable, and I think half the reason I returned so often had nothing to do with the profile.

I ignored other details, too. Malice would tell me later that it was Frankel who bought her the Rickenbacker, that he bought many extravagant gifts for her and for the other regulars. In return, she said, he expected a "loyal presence." It was an ominous phrase I've never forgotten. I should have quoted her, I should have pushed him on the building, done more digging, but I was afraid of losing him. Both as subject and friend. I didn't think so then, or didn't allow myself to, but he came across as a bit too golden in the end. It would have been better had I been a bit less of a loyal presence myself.

And yet, looking out at Sebastian Light's empty pasture, I missed the days I'd spent there with all those people, all that life, and more than the embarrassment I felt for writing with such adulation, I was ashamed for having disappeared, for having hidden from him like a child.

My grandmother said, "To be close enough to touch a man like that, to have won his affection, and then you walk away. It's pathetic."

She was right, even if she only half-understood my reasons. It was pathetic. I'd been manipulated and I knew. I'd been weak and I couldn't face him. I didn't do the work I should have. I let him slide. I made him perfect.

By the morning of the day before the day of Sebastian Light's Biennale, a hush had fallen over The Coded Garden. No one was in the fields. There was no sound of guitar or laughter as I walked along The Ridge where all the studios appeared to be occupied. I watched Heaven going after a massive canvas with a great deal of sighing and slashing and sweat on the brow. Crystalline's studio was sealed shut. I resisted the temptation to walk around the back and peer in her window. Theo's studio remained empty.

I walked on until I found Siddhartha, who seemed annoyed that I'd interrupted his work. I hadn't seen him since our walk to the wall and now, facing him, I felt exposed in a way I hadn't anticipated.

"What, Sol, you don't wait for an invitation?"

"I took your invitation to be implicit."

"You can stay, but only if you don't talk."

He kicked a chair toward me, and I sat in it so that now I was looking up at him. Most of his body was replaced by the back of the canvas he was working on. I could only see his legs from the knees down, his arms from the elbows out, his forehead and his lovely hair. I could feel the hook of the wire noose jabbing against my thigh, but it didn't bother me. I liked to feel it and I was content to watch him. I liked to see his left hand darting in and out of view. For a moment I was tempted to leap up and come around to see what he had done, but I worried I would find his brush dry, the canvas blank, the whole thing a pantomime.

Then I hoped that it was. It would have taken them such effort, so much choreography. So much vision. It would have been beautiful.

I stared at him for a while, which he didn't seem to mind at all. The image of this man taken over by fabric and wood and silver staples was magnificent. I don't know how long I sat watching, but then it was lost as he stepped out from behind the easel and came toward me.

I wondered how much time I'd have to spend with him before the shock of his beauty would subside. I stood up. He pressed his lips to my cheek.

"I'm sorry," he said, "if I made you feel used."

I removed the soldier's head from my pocket and held it before him. "I thought these were very moving," I said.

"This is from the other night?" He took it from my fingers.

"I don't know how you got them lit at once, but the timing was impeccable."

"What are you talking about? I was right there next to you. How could I have done it?"

"You didn't have to light it for it to be yours."

"Maybe this place is making you a little crazy. I'm a painter. I don't do stunts."

"Let me see your painting, then."

"Tomorrow at The Biennale."

"I wish everyone would stop using that word," I said. "It's ridiculous enough in Miami. It's unbearable here."

He looked for a moment as if he might say something of consequence, but then he only shook his head.

"And I don't feel used," I added. For a moment, I thought I saw a look of pity in his eyes.

I left in search of the grassy knoll. I wanted to be certain I hadn't been drugged, that the burning bush wasn't a hallucination, but a mighty symbol whose meaning was yet unclear to me. Given the speedy disappearance of the cardboard figures, though, I didn't really expect to find anything but some disturbed earth.

Yet the tree still was there, the noosed heads, the daggered torsos. It was surprising, this enduring symbol of disorder. Plume had evidently neglected to bring in the cleanup crew. Another indication that the gardeners were under unusual stress.

I kneeled and laid my hands upon the ground. I felt the edge of the tree well where the grass had been newly cut and damp soil surrounded the trunk. I rolled onto my back and summoned the insipid Englishman. I tried to free myself of myself. I tried to watch my thoughts blow past as leaves across a lawn. But Mind GApp was no match for Lina Klein's eyes.

I tried to see her in the blackness above the tree. Was her decision so complete? Did she really imagine it some last act of art? I tried to conceive of a quality of pain sufficient to generate that kind of courage.

"We are not programmed to imagine pain," she told me once, "we're not even built to remember it. We exaggerate the memories of pleasure, of joy, while diminishing those of suffering. How else could we survive? Why else would I sing you so many pretty songs of the Lower East Side? Those days so full of loneliness and violence and desolation."

I tried harder to imagine what it took to do what she did, and whether her entire life had counted to her as something "quite insanely extraordinary" as it did to me. And that brought me to my mother, who all my life had been telling me that Lina Klein was an egomaniac, a cruel narcissist. Who on the telephone after finding her body said, "Really, I'm not surprised. She never cared about anyone. You were fooled. Don't be too hard on yourself."

I thought of the speed with which my mother's posture had changed, of what had gone from her body, from her eyes. I tried to see my grandmother with some objective mind, or my mother's mind, to see the sociopath she claimed to see. But aside from her occasional impatience, her fixation on my living according to her strict codes of pleasure and art, her denouncement of poor Charity, I found no cruelty in my grandmother. I could summon no memory of malice.

There was Lina Klein frail on the beach in Santa Monica sitting in the blue shade of our tower wearing her black sunglasses, a bright red cotton sweater and a pair of jeans rolled to her calves, green bruises on her shins, while I, wet from the cold winter ocean, ran toward her in the way I may never in my life run toward anyone again, and I wondered if the utter pain that image caused me was anything like what she felt before undressing for the last time, and I became lightheaded, the ground seemed to be pushing upwards against my back, while lifeless language, ugly phrases, insidious jingles, seemed to swirl and dive all around me like swallows in the evening.

PART THREE

The theater must always be a safe and special place.
—DONALD JOHN TRUMP

28

On the evening of The Biennale, the washed-out sky was streaked with scars the color of raw beef and, suspended above The Barn's gaping entrance, burning in blazing blue neon, were looping letters:

La Biennale
Art is Life, Life is Art

More generic tattoo drivel, yet I was moved by the prettiness of the scene. Was I at last giving in? Losing the war? Perhaps I was only feeling nostalgic for this place I knew now I would soon have to leave. I wasn't sure why I'd stayed so long. Nearly a month had passed and still I was here. For what? Crystalline's promised painting? Another walk with Sid? Or, more simply and shamefully, to prove something to Light I couldn't quite name? I was teetering now on the edge—exhausted by the endless babble, and all the never-ending arguments, here and away, about how and where and why to be.

There was Saber plucking away at his guitar, sending soothing notes to his sisters and brothers in arms, while doing nothing to ease his own furrowed brow. There was Crystalline, leaning against a wall of wood, eyes to the ground, her curls especially dark against a white chemise. She smiled when she saw me coming up the path.

There was pacing and panting, sitting and meditating. A neck roll, a downward dog, a cat, a cow.

And then from the blackness, Siddhartha, handsome all in white, standing alone, eyes as nervous as Heaven's.

And then the procession.

A flash of light from above. First, Plume, dressed in black—a sheer dress falling freely from where it fastened at the throat, down to the tops of her fine feet. Her back and shoulders and arms were bare. Hair pulled up and wound into a dense dark pastry pinned atop her head. Her eyes were lined thick with kohl.

Behind her came the man himself. As he moved, his thick hair rippled and shone in the string lights. He wore an excellent black suit. His skin, the color of well toasted Wonder Bread, was amplified by the bright green of his shirt, its collar open and in his lapel, a boutonnière of purple plumeria. No one, not a single one of us, could look away.

They gathered beneath the neon.

Crystalline sidled up beside me.

"*Art*. Such a small word. So unassuming. A single syllable. Not much of an agent for our noble cause. I have often wondered how three meager letters can be associated with such extraordinary company. But then," Sebastian Light sighed, "I must remind myself that small, ugly people have always fed on the fat of the glorious."

It was difficult to see those fearsome sapphire eyes beneath the darkening sky, in the glow of his burning blue platitude, but I was sure he was looking directly at me.

"We will always be treated very unfairly, my friends. Art. Art. Art. The more you say it, the more inadequate, the more offensive it becomes. And yet when I hear that word, more a groan really, I am uplifted. Why? My friends, because it is a truth. I hear it and I think, yes, it is so simple. It is exactly right because what we do here is groan, sigh, lament, moan. Yes, and out of these most basic utterances, in spite of the cruel, the ugly and profane, every now and then, rises a great beauty and that beauty is named Art."

I leaned over and whispered to Crystalline, "My father's name is also Art."

She gambled not even a smile.

He went on, "When there are starving children, when there are suffering animals, when there is so much pain in the world, how can we *justify* what we do here? How? Because we know that beauty, that art, that most human of grunts, will save us all. Say it with me. Art."

"Art," the crowd repeated.

"Now grunt it. Let the word become only a sound. Let it be what it *is*—an expression of pleasure, of pain, of desire, of loin-need. Let it be the very *sound* of orgasm, of birth, the expression of lust and grief, of *life*, of life itself."

"Argh," they said. And "urgh," and "ohhh and "awoo." They went at it. Wailing and keening, moaning and groaning. Even the sinners, the Eves, the Lucifers. Even me. "Nurgh," I cried. And "Hunnmg."

Why not? Why not cave in? Why not join *this* wrong-headed circle just as I had joined them in The Sweat Lodge? Just as I had bent over that lustrous desk and joined Robert Capo's dark arts order. Or Charity's cheerful cult. Why resist? What good was it? What difference could it possibly make? Who *hadn't* lost his mind? Were we not all devouring ourselves? Were we not all of us zealots and self-righteous snobs, all of us frantic and alone? Was my mother not? Had my grandmother not been? Were we not all frightened, furiously digging our bloody nails into one idiotic idea or another, pretending to possess some distinct understanding, some magical wisdom? Before the end of the world, before our wretched little race was cooked to death, before nature, the one true God, destroyed every deluded one of us, in that infinitesimal moment of geological time before oblivion, weren't we all subway preachers, street corner soap-boxers feverishly clinging to our precious convictions? Charlotte Klein, Marxist-cum-

Zionist; her mother, hypocrite hedonist-aphorist; Sebastian Light, guru of goodnes; and me.

"Yes, my compatriots, my brothers and sisters in arms, yes," cried Sebastian Light. "*This* is what we're here for—in our soil, upon our sacred earth—this is why we're here. Cry into the night. Turn your fear, your rage, your pain, your lust, your wild impatience, all your horrors, your trauma, turn it all to beauty, to beauty, to beauty."

The crowd cheered. He raised his hand.

"There are those who still spit that dusty nonsense about truth and beauty. We, my friends, know better. Our job is *uplift. Uplift!* Let us endeavor to *raise* the spirits of those who look upon our paintings. Never be fooled into thinking that this world needs *more* ugliness and less beauty. Art must soothe, its message must be kind, it must, as beauty itself does, shelter and secure us. For contrary to fashion, contrary to those cynical, little people so sure of themselves blathering on in New York, our job is to depict glory, not defeat. Ultimately my friends, art must always, always be aspirational. Let us give the world a sunlit field, a perfect breast, a geometric jaw. Let us provide shelter, let us provide hope. We are warriors of light, my friends, warriors of light."

By this time, I was ready to raise up a pitchfork, storm the Bastille, join the Light brigade. What harm could he be with his disinfected aesthetics, his garden borough, his Williamsburg of the willows? Things could be far worse than living in a protected, pretty place, among pretty, purposeful people, free and generous with their bodies, united around a single futile cause, which was not wealth, nor fame, nor power, but beauty. Oh Charity, were you right all along? Why *not* just be happy? Integrity is an indulgence. Nobody cares about the purity of my soul. I have no greatness to offer. I am no master painter, no Che, no Fidel, no visionary. No, the best I can ever do for this world is hide behind these stone walls and abandon every last one of my toxins in a briny pool at the bottom of Sebastian Light's sacred sweat lodge.

"Let us then, my brave friends, begin what we came here to begin."

Plume stepped forward, cleared her throat, and called out, "Please enter The Barn and stand behind your work. And we mean it in both senses. Do not remove the sheet until you're instructed to do so. And remember, no matter what tonight's outcome, we are on your side. *Benvenuti alla biennale d'arte!*"

Now we entered and all along the periphery, the artists zipped behind their white-draped paintings.

What a choreographer he was. In a matter of seconds, he'd managed to place me alone at the center of his vast gallery.

Sebastian Light took his position on the low stage at the back.

"Solomon," he called. "Where will you stand?"

Question of the ages. Cool and dismissive as I wanted to be, there was no denying the power of his blocking, or the mockery in his odd eyes. The artists wanted their evaluations while he wanted me to squirm. "Where would you like me?"

"Oh Solomon. Forever asking to be directed. Forever searching for a home."

In spite of myself, I was humiliated. I went to stand next to Plume. Now we were three facing the sheets.

Then it began.

Plume and I followed Light forward.

"Heaven, are you ready?" he said.

She looked skinny and depleted, even more than she had in the sweat lodge. She was touching and sad and I wondered how she'd come to be here. A humiliation? A failed career? A bad marriage?

"Pull," Plume said and Heaven yanked to reveal an unremarkable landscape—field, sky, reddened sliver of moon. A lone figure striding across the horizon.

"Hmm," said Sebastian Light, sinking his chin into the heel of his right hand. "Pretty. Dark though. In palette and mood. Technically quite lovely. What is it saying to us? What are we telling the lonely man, Heaven? What are we offering the suffering woman?"

"I don't know," Heaven whispered.

"But you *must* know."

"Okay." She took a breath. "I guess, well, what I'm offering is a glimpse of this place when it is especially beautiful."

"But is that enough. A *glimpse*? Would your lovely painting, and it *is* lovely, be ever more so if your glimpse was more of a cry? A shout? An explosion?" he said.

Then Sebastian Light stepped back and swiveled toward me.

"And what do you think?"

This was a change in the rules of the game. He had always made me an audience member of his immersive theater, but today I was to be a player. I glanced at Heaven, who looked to the floor, and I thought of the fear on her face in The Sweat Lodge.

"It's nice," I said.

"Mr. Fields, I'm certain you can offer more than that."

"What difference does it make what I think?"

"Are you not the art critic from New York City?"

There was acid in his voice now, the mockery more pronounced than ever and now I was nearly sure that his tactics had changed, that he'd made some new calculation.

"I'm not an art critic."

"Semantics, my friends."

He stood back and looked around the room.

"This is, as you all know, Solomon Fields. A man who once wrote award-winning essays about our most famous artists. And he stands before you and says of Heaven's painting, a painting she's been working on for months and months, 'It's nice.'"

I glanced at Crystalline, who held my eyes. There was no sympathy in them, just as there had been none when it was Theo under the gun.

"So, go on then, Mr. Fields, enlighten us. Tell us what you think."

I looked back at the painting. "It's fine," I said.

"*It's nice, it's fine*. Tell us what you *think*. Mr. Fields, we have, for weeks now, been baring our very souls while you sneer at us in private, dismiss us, look on, like any tourist, revealing *nothing*, risking *nothing*. Have some courage now. Sneer in our faces."

I knew he was goading me. I knew, too, that on some level he was right. But fuck it, life or theater, I may as well commit to my part. I'll stop playing the passive observer and inhabit the role of nasty New York snob he's brought me here to play.

Heaven was still looking at the floor.

I said, "It's terrible. On every possible level, it is a terrible, terrible painting. It is utterly meaningless. It is an argument. An advertisement, propaganda. That is what I think."

I did not look at Heaven's face. I was looking only at Sebastian Light who was smiling at me now in such a way that made me believe I had, for the first time since arriving here, given him exactly what he wanted. I was ashamed to have been so cruel. And for what? Devotion to the *truth*? The name of *art*? What would I have lost by mustering a little theater of my own? What would it have taken to be kind, to have proven Light wrong, to have said, This is nice, that is pretty, well done, you have a great career ahead of you. But he had dragged me down with him into the muck, the way they always did, these craven, pious men, and I had stooped to meanness in honor of my own ridiculous piety.

Sebastian Light turned to the others. "You see, my friends, *this* is the truth. This is what you get from your New York art critics. Look at Heaven's painting. Do you see meaninglessness? Do you see something terrible? No, of course not. But *they* do. We are at odds, my friends. We are at odds."

At last, I looked to Heaven. She appeared more broken than ever. There was such sadness and desolation in her expression. And I, pretending to be some absolute arbiter flown in from the great center of taste and style, had cut her down for no reason other than my own weaknesses and failures. Lina Klein might have been proud of me, might have said, Good for you, Soli, let there be no question, let no one undeserving of the name call herself an artist. But she'd have been wrong.

The tension was high now in The Barn. I could not work out why I was still there, following this guy around his room, but on and on we went, each of us in search of an ending. Sebastian Light did not look at me.

Next was a boy named Sylvan, who was to my eye practically indistinguishable from Saber—long blond hair loose around his shoulders, expression especially conciliatory.

"Pull," commanded Plume.

A crimson canvas, a black storm at the top, a white figure at the bottom holding above him a yellow basket from which golden rays of light escaped skyward.

"Ah, Sylvan, now here is something. An excellent painting. Such power. Such hope. It's very moving the way your man there is facing the storm, offering up his brightness, saying, I will not be broken. *This* is what I am. Gorgeous. Gorgeous."

When I first started going to Frankel's studio, I watched him sit with a young artist who'd been hanging around hoping for some attention. He gave the kid so much time and spoke to him with such focus that I assumed he was talented, but when I asked about it, Frankel said, "Not at all."

I laughed at that and he chastised me. "It's not funny. It's very sad, really, Sol. Don't ever make the mistake of confusing contempt for taste."

I brought myself back in time to hear Sebastian Light say, "Of course, our friend from New York will certainly disagree."

"No," I said with as much sincerity as I could muster. "I like it."

He scowled at me. I had not been loyal to my role. I had not followed the script.

He turned back to the crowd and said, "This, again, my friends, is what you will find in New York. This mockery, this cheap humor. I am glad you can all see what it looks like. What it sounds like. There he is. A member of the foul cabal. Look at him. Listen to him claiming to know what the *truth* is. Listen to him mock us, our values. Memorize what you see. We have offered him everything. We have shown him our *work*, our *ways*, our *land*."

Plume raised her hand, a subtle gesture as if she might interrupt him, perhaps to point out that he had misinterpreted what I'd said. But she stopped herself and now, looking increasingly worried, watched as he began to rage. I thought, *This* is the unvarnished version. This is the real man.

"This land we have *slaved* over. And what do we get in return? We get New York. And the irony? He, too, came here as a refugee from that inferno. He too arrived broken of spirit, soul hanging by a thread, determined to escape the emptiness of that city, those people, their bitter ideas. But he is them. They are him. And he cannot escape his arrogance. *Their* arrogance. He is a member of a people, a tiny fraction of this nation's population, and yet they are so sure of their exceptional nature, so certain of their *righteousness*, as if an absolute definition can ever be known, as if they alone possess it. Have no doubt, it is a *conspiracy*. How is it that so few people have so much power? How is it that in a nation, in an entire *world* of artists, a speck of an island thousands of miles away from here has come to determine what *is* and is *not* art? This is why we are here. Why I have created our garden, why I have put my blood into this soil, why I have raised up this wasteland, this *swamp* into a glorious homeland. In *this* way we are revolutionaries."

Now his brow shone slightly. Maybe the speech had been prepared and rehearsed, but its passion, its vehemence struck me as entirely true. Instead of awe, it seemed to inspire embarrassment amongst the artists. Saber coughed into his hand. Heaven kicked her toe against the floor.

Plume had begun to gently pinch the skin on the back of her neck. It seemed that with every minute we spent in this charade, the cracks in her smooth coating became more and more pronounced.

While he stood glaring at me, panting, I said nothing. No one did. I held his gaze and waited until he returned to Sylvan and the Golden Basket.

He said, "It's a great painting, my friend. You should be proud."

Sylvan gave him a smile and looked away. I was sure that no one in the audience, not even its creator, believed it. The question, the only one I was still trying to answer, was whether Light did. There was something off in his eyes now, the crackling of an unstable current.

Then he came to Sid. Again, I prayed for him be good, to be anything but one of these people.

Several strands of hair had become matted against Plume's forehead, and twice I saw her raise her right hand to her neck as if to touch a cross that wasn't there. "Pull," she called.

The canvas had been divided into six vertical rectangles. Portraits: three men and three women, all of whom gazed just slightly upward. In the backgrounds, the blur of crowds. Each of the men wore expressions of calm, whereas the women all looked on in despair. Each set of eyes expressed either pleasure or displeasure, peace, or disenchantment. At the bottom of each panel, in small, clean black script, he'd painted the word *masterwork*.

Even if it wasn't quite as arresting or original as I'd hoped, his painting made me love him. I liked those six faces, the depth of their expressions, their sorrow and wonder. He was not a fraud.

"Hm," said Sebastian Light, and I thought, Say one cruel word and I will cut your throat.

"What are these masterworks they're looking at?"

"I'll leave that to the viewer," Siddhartha said.

"Clever. But a little lazy, no?"

Sid said nothing.

"These faces, the three happy ones, they're very nice. But I have to ask you, what good is the sadness in the others?"

"I'll leave that to the viewer," he mumbled, as if he were so exhausted, he could barely get the words out.

"Laziness again. You have the technical skill. Undoubtedly. But do you have enough courage for the purity of joy?"

He shrugged.

"Answer me," Light said.

"I'd prefer not to."

"Am I to understand that, after all this time, you've chosen to reject us?"

"I'm not rejecting anything. I'm just painting."

"I thought you were coming around," Sebastian Light said, "but clearly, you've been tempted away." He turned to the rest of the crowd. "A word of warning, my friends. They are seductive, these ideas. Siddhartha has let himself be convinced of the worn-out lie that violence, ambiguity," he paused, "that *self-destruction* can be art. But he is wrong, and we must pray that he returns to us soon."

He spun away from Sid's painting and crossed the room.

"Perhaps we'll find some relief with you, Gem," he said in a stage whisper.

Snap went the sheet and there we were confronted with a sky of blue, a young woman with long red hair, hovering above a blackened earth from which large, claw-like hands reached ominously at her ankles. In gothic script, *anger*, *violence*, *trauma*, *pain* were tattooed upon her outstretched arms. Above her was a floating garden whose roots snaked down the edges of the canvas and wound themselves into that burnt earth. It was, save for the comically obvious arms, the unnecessary tattoos, surprisingly inoffensive.

"Oh, Gem" Sebastian Light said, "come to me." Like an adoring, grateful child, she came, and there before us and the gods of art, our priest took that child into his arms. This was, I had to guess, the expression of a perfect 10. Praise be unto you, Gem, for you have pleased our king, and when the raja raised his face from her hair, he said, "My friends, sometimes you make me so happy."

Then, high on fealty, empowered and emboldened by the presence of proper propaganda, he turned to Ridge.

"Pull," said Plume and with a flick he unveiled a washed-out background of blue, two disembodied eyes peering down through white clouds upon a plain of yellow where a long, ecstatic woman lay prone, arms and legs spread wide, red hair in a symmetrical fan behind her. In metallic red block letters, "on earth as it is in heaven."

It was as if The Garden were a slogan storehouse at a bad tattoo parlor. Still, without the text, I thought, it really wasn't an awful painting. I was glad to know old Ridge had some talent.

There was the requisite praise from Light, but it was clear that the evening performance hadn't been quite what he'd hoped. His voice was thin and dry. He looked tired and frustrated. Plume hovered anxiously at his elbow, as though she feared he might collapse.

Now, finally, after kissing Ridge's forehead, Light turned to Crystalline.

When he spoke her name, some tension returned to The Barn.

"Are you ready?"

She nodded.

"Are you certain?"

"Yes," she said, drawing her shoulders back, and, paying no attention to Plume, she pulled.

What had I hoped for? Some fiery painting of violence and satire. Panting acolytes salivating at the crotch of the king. Gem as grotesque goose, gullet overflowing with uncooked quinoa. Plume devouring her fatty liver. More, a thousand noosed gingerbread men, a tree of melting soldiers aflame, her signature on a Garden rebellion. Mystery solved.

Instead it was a self-portrait. Crystalline looking straight out at us, her pale skin incandescent, a white light falling from her right side, her left cheek shadowed, both of her eyes clear, serene and unshakeable. Her hair, nearly indistinguishable from the darkness behind her.

The vibrancy and surprise of the image was so arresting that it took several full seconds for me to see the rest of the painting, to hear the gasps.

She was entirely naked, her hair drawn back from her shoulders, nipples slightly upturned, and several inches below them, her hands held a silver platter and resting there, on a bed of moldering hundred-dollar bills, was the severed head of Sebastian Light, his thick hair pooling around her right wrist, his eyelids wide open, framing two blue eyes. Yet they were not lifeless. There was a tenderness, a gentleness to the uncanny expression. It was chilling and endearing, and, more than anything, terribly sad.

People were moving around me, but I did not want to look away. There was so much intelligence and power in her face. And in contrast to the slackening skin stretched over the severed head of our ruined John the Baptist, the image became so vibrant that it was nearly frightening. I could barely breathe. I moved between her expression and his, back and forth, back and forth, until I felt sharp and vital and clear.

I don't know how much time passed before I was able to break away from Crystalline's painting. But when I did, I thought, There is no way he'll survive this. It'll kill him. Only then did I look from the painting to the painter herself.

She met my eyes and all I wanted was to go to her, to kiss her, to thank her, but before I could move, Sebastian Light said, "No."

He was breathing hard through his mouth.

"No," he said again. Then he raised his voice. "You have forgotten your position. You are a *guest* here. *Crystalline.* This is *my* land."

Plume touched his elbow, and he spun on her. "Don't!" he yelled, staring at her with fury. "You—" But he did not go on.

Then he turned from Plume and stepped toward Crystalline. Now I was behind him and what I saw was dizzyingly strange: the back of his head, Crystalline beside her portrait of herself, Sebastian Light's head again, this time on a platter.

I slipped to the side. All the other artists had crowded around me. Everyone was facing the painting now. For a second, I felt the earth moving us all through space and then Crystalline raised her chin just slightly, which brought the two faces into perfect symmetry.

I wished for Lina Klein.

He stepped ever closer to the canvas. I'd stopped noticing his height, but now in his distemper, he appeared enormous.

I watched his fingers take up the sheet from the floor.

"Cover it," he said.

She did not blink. "No."

"Cover the painting."

"No."

"I'll ask once more," he said, a bit of spittle landing on the simulacrum of Crystalline's nose. I feared his saliva would run the paint.

She seemed to me entirely sanguine.

Looking straight into Sebastian Light's eyes, she said, "I did not paint it to hurt you."

His eyes were blazing and unsteady. He took deliberate breaths. Now and then he darted his ruddy tongue.

He let the sheet fall to the ground, which seemed for a moment a sign of surrender. He lowered his voice then and said, "You have tracked filth into a pristine place."

He hung his head and I thought, this is it, he'll go, and he did turn, and he did walk toward the door. One slow step after another and I was sure that all of us were praying he'd keep going, walk out into the night and leave us to our exquisite portrait, but he stopped and still facing the door, reached into his pocket. Then he whirled and came back and in an instant was at the easel again, this time with a box cutter in his hand.

In three ominous clicks he extended the blade and held it to the painted throat.

"I should destroy it," he said looking not at Crystalline, but around the room.

I was sure I saw something berserk quavering in his eyes. I watched the point linger close to the canvas and imagined blood pouring from the wound, down her long alabaster neck, between her breasts, over Sebastian Light's sad, peaceful face falling through space to pool on the worn boards of The Barn.

It was so quiet now that when he punctured it, the soft pop came like a shot and all of us gasped.

Only Crystalline made no sound. She stood defiant as he cut a small smiling arc just above her collarbone.

To my true surprise, no blood fell. I was very dizzy.

Then he was backing out of the room with Plume at his flank and the box cutter still in his hand, saying "For true art, my friends, I am willing to die, but for true art, I am also willing to kill."

And then, exeunt, they were gone.

What a show.

I looked away from the great black void into which our villains had vanished. Crystalline was crouched now behind her canvas, inspecting the damage, and through the slit in her throat, I could see slices of her eyes.

I thought I might pass out. I sat on the stage.

All the artists were moving faster now, whispering like witnesses after the shock of a crime. I looked for Siddhartha, but still I could not find him in the melee. The din was rising. No one was leaving, no one was outraged, no one was preparing to storm the hill. They were chattering and chattering. The noise grew louder. I hung my head between my knees and concentrated, trying to listen to them, to catch some break in character, some definitive answer, but I found their language impossible to comprehend. It all sounded like garbled laugh tracks, and pop lyrics and tag lines. I looked up and tried to read their lips, but no matter how intently I watched them I could not make out a word.

Then I thought, Lina Klein must have been planning it. But for how long? Months? Years?

And was it something like the way Frankel claimed to live with a sculpture for so long before he sculpted it?

Was there a way to make this comparison with any honesty at all?

Was it possible to believe that she ended her life in the spirit with which she tried so hard to live it?

I wanted to ask Siddhartha what he thought of my desperate theories of art and suicide. Whatever he was, for whatever reason, I trusted that he alone would tell me the truth. Again, I scanned the room looking for him, but he was nowhere. I had the impression that there was a lull, as if they'd run out of script and were treading water until the next cue, which was slow to come but did, finally, in the form of a commotion and the artists rushed outside in its direction.

I stood up to follow, but then I thought, Let's see what happens if I don't give them their audience. Soon they were all gone, and I was alone in the empty gallery. I went to the portrait and ran my thumb along the cut.

I didn't like to admit it, but what he'd done had added something good. There was precision in it. Such nice geometry. I loved the painting more now and I wanted to take it home. I wanted to buy it and hang it above the fireplace on Orchard Street so that Lina Klein could sit with me on the sagging green velvet couch and look up at the slit throat and those two expressions, the one of tenderness and power, the other of total depletion and peace.

There was a cry then from outside. I turned toward the massive open doorway and the cube of black night within it. I didn't want to give in. I'd wait until one of them came for me. But none did. I've always been far too interested in the way things end, so I left the portrait on its easel, which caused me no small amount of pain. I went through into the cool air and immediately I could see a fire just a few hundred feet from the jacaranda.

I joined the crowd, which was gathered around a large canvas burning on an easel.

Speaking to no one, I said, "Whose is it?"

"It's blank," Siddhartha said, arriving out of the ether.

I felt both separated from and very much a part of the world.

"Where have you been?" I asked him, but he didn't answer me.

We watched as the legs of the easel gave way and the whole structure collapsed on itself. It lost its defining form, and then it might as well have been a campfire we were all gathered around to keep ourselves warm.

From the darkness, someone said, "I don't understand. Is this part of it?"

I began to laugh.

I saw my mother at the kitchen table holding onto a cup of coffee. I missed her and understood now that I couldn't leave her alone in our dismal apartment with my grandmother's bleeding ghost. I'd have to go home soon and try to revive her furies.

I loved the self-portrait. So far, that was my favorite. It was better than Sid's *Masterworks*. Better than the inane sermons, or The Sweat Lodge, the gingerbread men, or those flaring soldiers. I focused on the waning light now.

"Sid," I said, "listen, I'd really like to know if you're on the take."

I had to look over at him to makes sure he was still standing beside me.

After a long silence, he said, "What difference does it make?"

I tried, but it was a question I could not answer, so I walked away, and he did nothing to stop me. I walked along The Ridge, past The Library. And as always, I made my way to The Spiral where I found Plume sitting at its center, smoking a cigarette.

"Things must be very bad, Plume."

She opened and closed a silver lighter. "One a year," she said.

"You don't have to explain it to me." I sat down beside her. "Quite a night."

She shook her head. Even in the gentle light, she looked broken.

"Tell me," I said, "all that stuff with the tree, the soldiers. Was that you?"

"I'm not an artist."

"You said that before, but it's not much of an answer."

She glanced up at me and then let her head fall. "He's not a bad man, you know."

"No?"

"He saved my life."

"How?"

"The same way he has saved yours."

"I have to say, I'm about out of patience for all that."

She sighed. "All right. I was young. I was unhappy. Very unhappy. I met him. He invited me out here. He gave me a home. That's all there is to tell. Have you really been bored here, Sol?"

"No."

"You were joking when you said that?"

"Sure."

"I don't want to argue with you anymore." She sounded so tired.

"Are you sure you're okay, Plume?"

"I just want to give him what he wants."

"Very few people get to be artists," I said sounding like Lina Klein. "It's just the way it is."

She shrugged and said, "You know, I think I'd be dead, Sol. Without him coming along when he did. I really think I'd be dead."

"Tell me that story."

"It isn't the point."

"All right," I said. "Get some sleep. And in the morning tell your man I'd like an audience."

"Why?" She looked at me, more wary and exposed than I'd ever seen her.

"I'm going to do what you asked. I'm going to give him a fair shot."

She drew a breath almost as if to object and then she only said, "Thank you, Sol."

"Crystalline's painting is brilliant. You know that, right?"

She took a long drag, blew the smoke through her nose. "Yes."

"I'm glad. And after I see him, I'm leaving. However it goes, whatever he decides, I'm leaving. Maybe you can give me a ride to the airport."

She nodded and then once again, she seemed to me just another other press secretary bound to an angry king.

"And I'll need my phone back," I said, before making an exit of my own.

29

Lina Klein took me to Hot Dog on a Stick, a restaurant she claimed was her favorite in the city because she liked places that did a single thing very well. The year is unclear. I was old enough to see some of her flaws, but, as she would say, too young to believe that time had anything to do with me.

It was cool out and she wore her tan raincoat with the sleeves rolled up to reveal its tartan lining. We'd been to see a show of portraits by a young Korean painter at a gallery in Santa Monica.

We dumped our napkins and sticks and mustard-smeared trays into a trash can and walked under the pier where she took my arm with both hands and held herself against me, a gesture which always made me feel as if I were a more powerful person than I was. We came out from the dark to see the tops of the low mountains rising toward the evening sun.

"Listen to me, Solomon." She held me tighter as if I really might protect her. "I love you more than anyone on earth. More than your mother. More than *anyone*. Do you understand that?"

It chilled me, the way she clutched my arm, her voice tinny and strange. This was so long ago. I was a child. Had her plans stretched so far back? For her last performance I wanted so much to call art.

"Never pretend you don't know what someone is capable of."

I'm nearly certain this was the closest she ever came to warning me.

"I wish you'd stop giving me advice," I said. "You could just talk to me. Or you could just shut up entirely."

"When did you get so wise?"

"I'm not wise."

For a while she didn't speak, and it was nice like that, just the two of us walking together.

Then she said, "If you live long enough, Solomon, you get tired of speaking."

"You've clearly not lived long enough," I said.

She laughed and pinched my arm. "It's what I love about art, you know. It doesn't need a single word."

"I know."

"I want you to be very happy."

"I'll try my best."

"Promise."

"I promise that if ever I have children, I will never, ever give them advice," I said.

She turned us off the bike path to cross the wide beach through the wind toward the retreating ocean. When we could see the sun reflecting in the wet sand beneath our feet, she said, "Your father used to come down here on days just like this to dig for clams. Before they were poisonous. Or before we knew they were. I liked him, you know."

"I liked him, too," I said.

"Good. Sol, it's better not to condemn people."

"But you condemn people all the time."

"Yes," she said, "I really do, don't I? Soli, listen—"

"If you give me one more piece of advice today, I'll throw you in the ocean."

"That wouldn't be so bad," she said, "but fine. No more advice. No more language at all. I'll say one more thing and we won't speak again until tomorrow, okay?"

"Deal."

But I cannot remember what that last thing was.

30

The morning after The Biennale I woke late. For the first time since I'd arrived, there was no breakfast, no note. I was very hungry, but when I got to The Barn it was locked.

A few of the artists were milling around. Saber was perched on the picnic table, his bare feet on the bench. He gave me a sad smile and said, "No food, bro."

"Has this happened before?"

"Not since I've been here."

"Have you seen Crystalline?"

"Haven't seen her all day."

She was in her studio sitting at the table drinking a cup of tea. To my relief, the painting was there, too.

I said, "I wanted to see it again."

"But not me?"

"You, too."

For a long time, we sat together looking at the canvas, not speaking at all. It had not changed in the daylight. Like the previous evening, it made me miss Lina Klein. I had obeyed her. I had found an artist.

"I've seen a lot of paintings," I said after a while, "but I'm not a critic. I don't know very much. I'm not that smart, but this is *really* something unusual."

"Thank you."

"It's been a very long time since I've been so moved, so surprised by a piece of art."

"You don't think it's too much of a copy?"

"A copy of what?"

She smiled at me. "The celebrated art critic doesn't know his history."

I laughed. "I'm not a critic. And I just told you I'm not very smart."

"It's Salome."

"I figured," I said. "But the only two paintings of her I can think of are the Klimt and the Caravaggio."

"Maybe if you were better educated, you'd be less impressed."

"Ain't that always the way."

She smiled at me. "It's in Nantes. Jean Benner."

"I've never been."

"I was there once with a guy I didn't like very much. We got into a terrible fight. It was the first time a man had ever hit me. It was winter. Late in the day. Cold, but no rain. I went into a café, stood at the back at the bar and got a little drunk and felt very sorry for myself."

As she was speaking, I kept my eyes on the painting.

"I felt ridiculous." Crystalline laughed. "Like some pathetic woman from a bad French film. Leaning against a bar with my swelling cheek and my eyes all red drowning my sorrows. It was the first time I'd ever done that."

"Done what?"

"Went to a bar alone. Got drunk alone. Afterwards I went out and stumbled on the museum. I hadn't meant to go. It was one of those lucky things. It seemed as if I'd been delivered there. First to the museum and then to the painting. I'd never even heard of Benner. I stood there for a long time. I want to say hours, but it probably wasn't that long. When I looked up at her face it gave me such a sense of power. I was calm and strong."

I turned from the painting to look at her. It felt like a trick.

Even if there was no way at all for her to have known about Lina Klein discovering Charlotte Salomon in Amsterdam in almost precisely the same way. For all his best efforts, I thought, really, this is the only magical thing to have happened since I arrived in The Coded Garden. I looked back at the painting. I wanted to tell her about my grandmother in her own European winter, but I thought I'd lose control of myself.

"I never even went back to the hotel. I just left the museum and got on a train and went to Paris."

"That's a good story," I said.

"You okay, Sol?"

"Are you angry? About what he did to your painting?"

She looked at the slit in her throat. "No. I like it."

"Me, too," I said.

She smiled. In the silence, however long it lasted, there was something there between us, a kindness, a moment of correspondence.

"So, have you figured out what you'll do?"

"You mean will I write about this place?"

She nodded.

"I don't know," I said. "I haven't decided. Maybe I'll write about you instead."

"As you like."

"Well, there's some refreshing indifference. What will you do with the painting?"

"I don't know."

"I'd like to buy it from you."

There was a change in her face then, something I couldn't read.

"How much?"

I shook my head. "I don't know. Think about it. You tell me."

"Okay."

"I don't mean to offend you."

"No, of course not. I'm flattered," she said, though I didn't believe her.

I stood up. "Whatever you decide. I think it's exquisite."

"Do you think if I sell it to you, I'll have to add his name alongside mine?"

"Please don't," I said. "No matter what you do with it."

She looked down and dipped her right ring finger into my tea. Then she held out her hand.

"My name is Eva."

We shook. "So much better than Crystalline," I said.

"Eva Solomon, in fact."

I shook my head. "Come on."

"It's true. When we get married, you'll be Solomon Solomon."

I laughed and got myself out into the afternoon air and out of the presence of her painting.

I hoped to see more clearly, but still I was lightheaded from hunger and time and a world that refused to settle into a single thing.

The doors of The Barn remained closed, but many of the artists were there now, sitting in a circle on the lawn beneath the jacaranda and in the middle, spread out on a red blanket, were bags of chips, and gummy bears, M&Ms and packages of cookies. Ridge offered me an Oreo. I took it and sat with him.

"I didn't know you people ate this stuff."

"Nobody's that pure."

"Where are you from, Ridge?"

"Tallahassee."

"Have you been here long?"

"Couple of months."

"Do you know where you'll go when you leave here?"

"Not sure. Probably head to Bali."

He offered me another Oreo. I thanked him and went back

to my cottage to try to write for a while. It was the first conventional conversation I'd had since landing.

By the time I looked up from my notes it was evening, and I was sick with hunger.

I figured there had to be dinner, at least, but when I got back to The Barn, the doors were still locked and the picnic had grown to include fruits and vegetables mixed in with their contraband, which had doubled in quantity. There was a bottle of bourbon, a giant bag of Cheetos. Dozens of silver-wrapped chocolate kisses were scattered over a picnic table.

Astonishingly, they were kind to me. Even Heaven offered me a slice of avocado and a couple of Funyons. It was relaxed and convivial, and I was happy to sit with them. Mostly, they seemed like kids abandoned at camp without their counselor. There was a lot of talk about what might happen next, where Light and Plume had gone. Even Eva showed up after a while, carrying her bottle of vodka. She sat with me and Saber who had just started to play "Sweet Baby James." Citrus/Duckling was telling Gem that she might go stay with some friends in Mallorca. Someone over my shoulder was talking about moving to Montauk.

Eva slid the bottle across the table through the sea of silver kisses as if to remind me that she was here and, by extension, just a few hundred yards away, her painting, too.

"Where's Siddhartha?"

"Forget him. He's a coward, Sol."

She was drunker than I'd thought.

"Why do you say that?"

"All kinds of reasons. But above all?"

I nodded.

"Above all because he'd rather be polite than great."

"Maybe he doesn't have a choice."

She threw a Cheeto at me. "Don't buy that bullshit. He's

here, isn't he? You think he dragged himself through the slums of Delhi to get to our little paradise? Please."

I laughed. "Well, I'm going to find him."

"*Vaya con diablos.*"

"Eva," I said, "my grandmother would have loved you."

Sid was sitting at his studio table with a cup of tea looking out the window.

I sat in the empty chair. His hands were clean. There was a vacancy about him now. The sparkling sharpness of his eyes had gone.

"You're not hungry?"

He took a long time to respond and then only shook his head slowly, keeping his eyes fixed on a point beyond the glass, middle distant above the pasture hill. Then he said, "Sol, what did you mean the other night?"

"When?"

"When you asked if I was on the take."

Now there was something defiant in his expression.

"You know."

"No," he said.

"Does he pay you?"

"Does who pay me?"

I laughed, but Sid only shook his head and tightened his lips, as if I were irritating him.

"Sebastian Light. Does he pay you?"

"Why would he pay me?"

"That's the best question of all."

"Did you come here to interview me, Sol?"

"I guess I did."

"Is it common for journalists to fuck their subjects?"

I laughed.

"Go ahead, then," he said looking back out the window.

"What did you think of Crystalline's painting?"

"I thought it was easy. I thought it was disrespectful. I thought it was cheap."

"I see."

"I know you loved it. You think she's the second coming of whatever."

"You seem a little strange, Sid."

"I'm just tired."

I reached across the table and laid my hand on his wrist.

"I'm sorry, Sol."

"Why are you sorry?"

"I think you must know."

"You won't tell me?"

He shook his head.

"Sid, tell me this then, was it your painting? I mean, did you make it? The *Masterworks*?"

"Yes."

"I hope so," I said. "I liked it."

"You think someone else painted it?"

I shrugged.

"It's mine, okay? I painted it."

"All right," I said. "All right."

"And?"

"And what?"

"You know what. What do you think of it?"

"I told you, I liked it."

"Tell me the truth. Is it a good painting?"

"I think so. I really do."

"Never mind. Never mind." He shook his head as if disgusted or disappointed with himself. "Is it true you're going to write about him? That you might write about her, too?"

I let go of his hand. "Where did you hear that?"

"What made you decide?"

"I *haven't* decided."

"Listen, I know you believe in all that art-is-everything

shit. That we should die on its altar. I do, too. But I also believe that it's possible to be both."

"Both?"

"Yes. To be pure and committed while at the same time being respectful of those who support you."

"Sure," I said. "You're probably right. Anyway, I'm not an artist."

"No. You're not. Which is why it's so easy for you to cling to your little fantasies."

"Take care of yourself, Siddhartha," I said.

I never saw him again.

31

All morning, I sat at my desk looking at my notes, trying to work out some way in, but around noon I was so hungry, I went up to The Barn. The doors were still locked. There were empty candy wrappers, plastic bags and bits of foil blown across the grass. There were dead leaves on the paths. On my way to the gate, I passed a pigeon pecking at a dead tree rat. Soon I was free.

Along the highway, I passed the hole in the jungle and thought of going out to Siddhartha's secret cliff edge, but there was nothing more to learn there.

All the while, until I walked into Sunny's, I could not shake Eva's Salome.

Sunny was up on a ladder, his head swallowed by the drop ceiling. A red toolbox was open on the bar.

"It's Sol again," I said. "From up the hill. Am I bothering you?"

He ducked and peered down at me through a rain of dust. "We're not open yet."

"I was hoping to talk to you for a few minutes."

He sighed, came down and washed his hands at the sink. When my stomach growled, he shook his head. "Come on, sit."

I watched him cook my burger and when he was done, he brought it and two beers over to the table by the plate-glass window where we sat facing each other.

"What can I do for you?"

"I want to ask you about Sebastian Light," I said, beginning to eat.

"Go on."

"How old were you when your mother sold the land?"

"Thirty years younger than I am now. Give or take."

"Was it legal?"

"You've decided to write about him, then?"

"If I can figure out what the story is exactly."

"And you want to quote me?"

"I won't if you don't want me to."

"I don't care either way."

"I'm still not sure if I'll do it."

"Why not?"

"I don't know what's out there. I've done no research. He's confiscated my phone."

"Why?"

"Something about technology being antithetical to art. Who knows?"

"Well, even if you had your phone, you wouldn't find much."

"Why not?"

"I never had any luck. Not that I tried all that hard."

"But you've looked?"

"Every now and then over the years."

"What do you know?"

"Just what I told you, that one day he showed up here with a lot of money."

"And?"

"And he used it to buy the land."

"That's it?"

"That's it."

"You never had anything to do with him again?"

"No."

"He never paid you to do anything for him?"

"Like what?"

"I don't know," I said. "I'm just trying—"

"To what?"

"Get a sense of the guy. Beyond the property."

"Well that's all I know about him. He came here. He paid my mother. She paid the debts she owed to some other people who came here with money. And then he had his—whatever it is he's made up there."

"You've never been inside?"

He looked through the glass to the street.

"You've never seen it?"

"No."

"You're not curious?"

He looked back at me. "Curiosity is not what I feel."

"What do you feel?"

"Tell me, why do you want to write about him exactly?"

"I think he might be interesting."

"Do you write about everyone you think might be interesting?"

"I haven't done this for a long time."

"When you did."

"No. Of course not. You have to choose."

"And how do you choose?"

"I don't know if it's as simple as that."

"Why not?"

"It's instinct and circumstance and timing. Sometimes you need the money. But sometimes it's some other thing."

"What other thing?"

I shrugged.

He looked away and said, "He's not that interesting."

"No?"

"You want to write about a rich man with a pretty garden?"

"He does some interesting things in that garden."

"Does he?"

"Do you like art?

"Some."

"But you're not an artist yourself, Sunny?"

"No."

"And he's never paid you to do anything for him?"

"You just asked me that. What do you think? That I'm his employee?"

"It's possible."

"Like some kind of gardener?"

"No."

"What then?"

"I don't know. I thought maybe you were in on it."

"In on what?"

I shook my head. "I don't know. I'm sorry. It's been a very strange few weeks."

"Listen. I own a bar full of bad equipment I'm not very good at fixing. I have two teenage daughters I'm not very good at raising. This guy you find so interesting with his fake name and his money doesn't mean shit to me."

"So you'd *never* work for him?"

He bristled. "I can't afford to turn down good money. You probably can."

"I'm not trying to offend you."

"Yeah? You come down here saying you want to talk to me, and all your questions are about Sebastian Light. You don't ask about what people like him do to this place."

"I *would* like to know about all of that."

"No. You wouldn't. Because it's the same old story and that same old story doesn't sell."

"I think—"

"*What* do you think exactly? You go to your paper or your magazine or whatever it is, and you say, Hey, I've got two options, pick one. Local people lose their land—again!—to a rich motherfucker from somewhere else. Or: billionaire creates tropical paradise for painters. You want to tell me that your guy in New York is going to say, Yeah, give me the first one? Bullshit."

He took our empty glasses behind the bar.

"I really didn't mean to offend you," I said, getting up.

"Stop saying that. You *can't* offend me. I just don't think he's as interesting as you do, that's it, all right?"

"All right."

"Let me ask you something." He leaned over the bar. "What does it matter?"

"What does what matter?"

"Whatever he does up there."

"I have no good answer. And you're right, they'll take his story over yours."

"I know I'm right," he said and climbed back up the ladder.

I put a twenty on the bar. "For the food and the beer."

"I don't want your money," he said, his voice muffled by the ceiling panels. I moved to leave and just before I reached the door, he said, "You know, it's not true. I did work for him once."

I stopped. There was the quick whine of a drill. "A long time ago. A few years after my mother sold. The guy starts digging just as the wet season starts. My mom always said, Reason never stops the rich. They get as far as a pit for the foundation before the rain comes. The backhoe was already gone. I went up there to dig some trenches. She wanted me to do it. In those days, my mom thought if we were nice, he'd let us keep our garden."

"She was wrong?"

"She was wrong."

I watched his boots shift on the ladder. I thought he might come back down or keep on talking, but after a while I heard the drill again.

Now as I walked along the highway, I was embarrassed by my half-formed fantasies of Sunny as outsider artist scaling the castle walls at night. I was ashamed, too, by what he'd said. He was right. I was, it turned out, the worst kind of tourist, the worst kind of journalist: bound to my own preoccupations, blind to worlds beyond my walls, consumed by the same old stories.

I entered the darkness of the eucalyptus canopy and tried to appraise the cast: Siddhartha, maple-syrup cipher; Eva, wild-haired rebel painter unwilling to bend to the whims of the ruling class; my father, absent Arthur, who went out for a ride and never came back; Lina Klein, of the overdone blade-and-bathtub suicide, aphoristic orphan of the Shoah preaching straight from her beloved Song of Solomon: for love is strong as death/passion fierce as the grave; Charlotte Klein, midlife adolescent, all these years lived and still raging against her mother; and me, who was worse than me? Just as Sunny said. As Plume pointed out all those days ago. Another walking cliché.

I came to the gate. For the first time since arriving at that crackpot colony, in the bright daylight, at last I could read the words stamped below *The Coded Garden*. They read, *Beauty Will Set You Free*.

I began to laugh a foreign laughter of a forgotten time: uncontrolled, impossible to contain, incomprehensible in its force and meaning. I pressed the blue-lit button and sat on the ground with my back against Sebastian Light's iron curtain. I was a maniac alone, struggling to breathe, tears in my eyes, and then I caught a vision: of an unkempt man wet with sweat, likely middle-aged, possibly days from death (who knows?), slumped against rusting metal, yelping and wheezing in the wind. I clutched my belly, actually clutched my belly like a cartoon, and fell to the side, because no matter what I did, no matter where I went, the God of Cliché would find me.

The women Klein would be appalled. Yet another testament to my vanity. Charlotte, at least in the guises of her former selves, would have said, You see what happens when you join an ashram instead of doing something for the *world*? You sit on the side of the road like a deranged vagrant laughing at horror. You neglect your history, your people. If I am not for myself, Solomon, who will be for me? And if I am only for myself, what am I? And if not now, when?

And even Lina, never one for my mother's make of moralizing, would have been saddened. At the very least, Solomon rabbit, you should recognize the references.

I could hear footsteps on the other side of the wall now. I righted myself, stood up and was looking at daylight coming through those words when the door opened.

Plume stepped aside to let me enter.

"Is it intentional?"

She closed the door behind me, and we began to walk.

"Is what intentional?"

"Your slogan there on the gate."

"What about it."

"You've replaced *work* with *beauty*."

"I don't understand."

I really didn't know why I should have bothered. Except for the story. To see how things end. Maybe that was reason enough. Or the only reason ever.

I said, "*Arbeit Macht Frei.*"

"What is that?"

"German."

By now we'd come to my cottage. I watched her face with all the focus I had left, using all my powers, and still I saw nothing but blankness.

"It was above the gates of Auschwitz," I said. "'*Work* sets you free,' not beauty."

She made a soft grunt of recognition.

"It's not intentional," she said.

I laughed.

"But would it offend you if it were, Sol?"

"Would it offend me?"

"I can't imagine it would," she said, "defender of dark art that you are. Warrior of freedom at all costs." It seemed to take her real effort to return to this old persona, Garden wisdomatic, cool dispenser of saws.

"You put on an extraordinary show here," I said, shaking my head.

"Please answer my question."

"Would it offend me?"

"Yes. You're a Jew, right?"

"I am."

"So then?"

"No," I said, "it would not offend me."

She looked exhausted and harried.

"I'm certain it's only coincidence."

"The coincidences here are excellent."

She reached into her pocket. "You asked for this," she said and handed me a burnished black slab, which I didn't immediately recognize.

I thanked her and for a moment we watched the sunlight stretching across the bright lawn.

"Have you enjoyed your time here?"

"I have. Best show I've seen in years."

She glanced at me "You'll never understand, will you?"

"Probably not."

"It's not a show."

"That's really a shame, because if it's not a show—"

"What?"

"Then there's *really* not much to write, is there?"

We looked out on the grass which was beginning to buckle in the rising wind.

She stepped off the porch, a pretty woman in a purple sheath with a fresh afternoon coming to life behind her.

"Mr. Fields, you have devoted yourself to such a terrible church."

"Well, really, it's a temple."

She ignored my joke. "If it were up to me, I'd drive you out of here now."

"You mean with a pitchfork?"

"I mean in an SUV."

"But the man wants his fame," I said. "So."

"So. He'll see you at six-thirty this evening," she said and walked on until she was consumed by the far shade.

32

I showered in the plumeria air and for all those minutes beneath his intoxicating water I could not find a convincing argument to leave. Give them what they want. Maybe you are only a deluded paranoiac driven by grief to fantasies of elaborate conspiracies. Calm down. Concede. Paint the man as he wants to be painted, however that may be. Join them. Stay. Be the court reporter, chronicler of the king. What do you lose? A terrible church? Futile faith? Vain notions of integrity inherited from depressive elders?

Charity once told me, parroting her own mother, "Our bills are paid with cash not integrity." And I said, "You're fucking right about that," which she didn't think was very funny. But who could argue? She came from no more money than I did. It's just that there were no ladies Klein tipping poison into her ear.

Pretend you're undercover. Pretend you're an investigator. Pretend you're writing a book. Pretend you'll blow the whole thing wide open. Or don't pretend at all. Give in, give up the fighting, fall into your perfect bed and close your eyes. Relax your jaw, feel the tension melt away, separate yourself from your thoughts (they're just thoughts), watch them float off as if upon a gentle stream. Let the smoke and feather rock you to sleep. Listen to the bamboo, exhale red, breathe in blue.

Instead, I wrapped myself in a Garden robe, chewed at my thumbnail and waited.

I knew what Lina Klein would tell me, but for all her certainty, look at her now. And I knew what my mother would tell me. Or would have once. Look at her.

Ernst Frankel was still out there. Maybe. But otherwise, I couldn't think of a single friend left from my years in Inglewood or Intersections, college, or Orchard Street, or of anyone from the days of Pale and Charity, to whom I might ask my questions.

You are alone, I thought, but that's what you get by clinging to absolutes, by setting all roads behind you on fire.

By twenty past six, the last of the sun was casting his white house pink. I promised myself I would talk to him without contempt. I would look at him just as Lina Klein had trained me to look: "Imagine away the skin, Soli. No one is a single thing. No one. There is *nearly* always more to the man. And *always* more to the woman. The poles of heroism and villainy are fantasies of children. Don't be distracted. Our war, as I have told you a thousand times, is always, always with orthodoxy."

Whatever he was, I would arrive with an expansive mind. I swore I would not do to him what he had done to me.

I came around to the front door, removed my shoes and called his name.

I hadn't been to his house since I'd first arrived. I hadn't seen him since he'd drawn his little blade.

There he was now, a long, striding silhouette. As he came closer, I could see he was dressed in black jeans and a black shirt, utterly without flourish. No cravat, scarf or boutonnière, no sign of disorder or disarray. He was a handsome old man on his way to an opening.

We shook hands as if he'd never come undone (maybe he hadn't) and then he led me outside where a small café table and two thick-cushioned, bentwood armchairs had been arranged. On the table were two champagne flutes, a blue bowl of purple radishes, a white bowl of shelled peanuts and to the side, in a standing, sweating, silver bucket of ice, a bottle wrapped in white linen.

"Are you going to propose?"

"Clever," he said, as we took our seats. "No, I don't think we'd make each other very happy." It was the first time Sebastian Light had dared a joke.

"Oh, I don't know," I said. "You're very handsome."

"Well, marriage or not, we do have something to celebrate."

"What is that?"

He drew the bottle from the bucket and expertly removed the foil, wire and, with a subtle pneumatic sigh, the cork.

"We are here together at last," he said, pouring the champagne, "having come to an understanding."

"Which is what?"

"You have agreed to write about us, have you not?"

"No promises."

"I see," he said and raised his glass. "Well, I have faith."

We touched the flutes together and drank while we watched in silence as the sun blazed on the horizon before disappearing. His timing was faultless. It had always been.

"Shall we begin then, Sol?"

"All right. Do you mind if I record this?"

"Not at all."

I laid my phone on the table.

"You see, Mr. Fields?" He pointed at my screen. "It's only a simulacrum of a button."

"And that bothers you?"

"I'm old. Do you know how old I am?"

"You asked me once before. Twenty-five?"

"Right. Funny boy. Soon I'll be eighty."

"You look nothing like it," I said.

"All it takes is a little attention to the body."

"And a great deal of money."

"I've been alive much longer than I've had money."

"How did you make your money?"

He smiled. "Oh, you can do better than that."

"You won't answer?"

"I would rather talk about The Garden. About art. About what we have made."

"All right," I said, "How were you able to buy this land?"

"The land wasn't expensive. It was nothing when I came here."

"According to the man whose family once owned it, that's not at all true."

"There was a clapboard shack if that's what you mean. It was a mess. Abandoned cars. Weeds. Junk everywhere."

"But people lived here, which is very different from your story."

"And I paid them. I do hope, Solomon, that you're not going to start lecturing me about the righteousness of taking other peoples' lands."

I was not going to be dragged down twice.

"I have no intention of lecturing you," I said. "Where did that money come from?"

"It was money I had saved."

"Saved from what?"

"Why are you so fixated on these things?"

"You brought me here to write about you."

"I did."

"And what did you expect I might write?"

"You misunderstand. You confuse the plural for the singular. I'm not interested in stories about myself, Sol. I want to see this place, our art, our lives, our beliefs, receive their due. We have created something great. That is what is essential. We have made something from nothing."

"Do you have children? Are you married? Have you ever been married?"

"I have no interest in telling you about myself. I want what we have made to be enough."

"I admire that," I said sincerely, "though I don't know an editor in the world who would allow these questions unanswered."

"So, you won't do it then?"

"What is it you want exactly?"

"For you to write about us the way you wrote about Ernst Frankel."

"But Frankel is a single person. I discussed his biography at length. He told me everything. And I must have spoken to fifty people about the man."

Again a smile. "You believe he told you everything?"

"I understand you knew him."

"Let's say I knew what he was. Perhaps better than you did."

This shook me for several reasons, but above all because he'd turned on a pin and suddenly, devoid of theater, spoken with dead confidence and in a tone I'd never before heard from him.

I said, "I wrote about his childhood, his parents, his lovers, his studio, all of it. But in any case, to do this, I'll need to know how you came to arrive here. Where your money comes from. Where *you* come from. How you grew up. Where. What you mean and what you don't. When you're joking and when you're not. What you intend as art and what you don't."

"I've told you: it is all art."

"But what do you *mean* by that?"

"It doesn't seem complicated. Everything we do here, every single thing, is art."

"Then all of this is performance?"

"I didn't say that."

"You didn't not say it."

"An impeccable row of lettuces is a kind of performance, is it not?"

"It amazes me that you can say things like that with a straight face. After a while though, murkiness gets to be a little boring, don't you think?"

"I'm being perfectly clear. Perhaps it is your mind which refuses to allow the light through."

I laughed. "A good example. When you speak like this, are you sincere?"

"What do you think?"

"I truly don't know. Your story is far more interesting if you're not."

"You people are so hungry for irony, but you know what is truly avant-garde, Mr. Fields?"

"Tell me."

"Sincerity."

"So, you're saying you are entirely sincere?"

"Let me ask you, without knowing these things you insist on knowing, could you write your story?"

"It would be very difficult."

"But it could be done."

"I suppose. I'd have to find the answers elsewhere. But why is it that you won't answer my questions?"

"I am that I am. I am this and this is me," he said, gesturing to his kingdom, "from its stones to its traditions. I will answer all of *those* questions."

"As God said to Moses."

He smiled.

"How much of what I have seen here was done for my benefit?"

"What do you mean?"

"You say you want me to write about your art, but again, it is not clear to me what that is."

"We seem to be spinning in circles. Did you have this problem with Mr. Frankel?"

I laughed. "No, but—"

"But?"

"He had fifty some odd years of work behind him. And he's one of the great artists of the century."

"So you say."

"So a great *many* people say."

"A not so great many."

"You're questioning his greatness?"

"Not at all. I admire his work immensely. What I question is the greatness of the many."

"You're suspicious of the critics."

"Do you blame me?"

"Not at all. They're mostly awful."

At this he beamed and topped up our glasses. "You see," he said, "we're not so far apart after all." He snapped a radish in half with his front teeth. The sky was reddening, the wind was rising.

"Tell me, Sol, have you ever painted? Tried to make art of your own?"

"Never," I said.

"Why not?"

"I have too much respect for talent."

"Talent is a myth."

"Is it?"

"Yes. When you people say talent, what you mean is opportunity."

"You keep saying, *you people.* Who do you mean?"

"New Yorkers. The media. The elites. The elect few making decisions about who gets attention, what is and is not of quality, what is beauty and what is not."

He set his eyes on me then. They grew radiant and frightening. He had shifted modes again. No longer was he the generous host or impassioned preacher. He was something else, something hazier, more obscure.

"You've been here a while now. Tell me, what work of ours do you find most compelling?"

"As I keep saying, it's still unclear to me what is and is not meant to be art."

"If you expect me to be honest with you then you must be honest with me. It is Crystalline and Siddhartha. You think their paintings are real and pure and full of life and power and passion and daring and blah, blah, blah."

"Yes, I liked their paintings most of all."

Another slight smirk. There was no sign of the rage and madness he'd displayed the night he cut and ran.

"You seemed quite upset by Crystalline's portrait," I said.

"I was."

"Why?"

"Would you like to see your head on a platter?"

I laughed. "I wouldn't mind."

"But *you* haven't spent your life making a haven for artists. You haven't given your time, your money, your blood so that young painters might have a safe home away from the cynical cabal."

"That's true. I haven't. Speaking of cabals, I note you've borrowed your slogan from the gates of Auschwitz."

He smiled. "We turned something ugly into something beautiful. I hope you're not offended?"

"No," I said. "But it does seem a curious choice."

"All choices are curious."

I was beginning to reach the limits of my compassionate mind.

"Are you an anti-Semite, Mr. Light?"

"Of course not. Ask anyone, nobody loves the Jewish people more than I do."

I smiled. I thought, He will look you in the eye and insist that what you see you do not see. It was another provocation, another trap. Do not allow him the pleasure. I said, "All of them?"

He waited, but I gave him nothing and after a long moment

of his ostentatiously regarding his thumbnail, he said, "So many jokes, Solomon Fields. Let's return to the question of choices. When it comes to art, yes, I believe all are curious. You want so desperately to organize and arrange and categorize and *understand* everything. Why are you so determined to separate the white beans from the black, the screws from the bolts?"

"Let's come back to Crystalline's painting. You were very angry."

"I don't think it's too much to ask for a little courtesy."

"Why do you keep her here then? She insults you, despises your philosophies, your aesthetics, doesn't respect the other painters."

"She's very skilled. I believe we can teach her the rest."

"Is skill different than talent?"

"Certainly."

"How so?"

"One is learned, the other is innate."

"You don't believe in innate talent?"

"I do not. Everything can be learned."

"See, this is what I mean. Are you serious or do you have some point to make?"

"You ask all the wrong questions."

"Yes, so I hear. All right, let me ask you this, do you regret defacing her painting?"

"It's no surprise that you should want to focus all your attention there."

"It is far and away the best thing I've seen here. Or anywhere, for a very long time."

He looked so wounded, I said immediately, "But I have seen other work here that I like."

"Such as?"

"The heads. The hand in The Spiral."

He nodded.

"Are those yours?"

"Would you be surprised if I told you they were?"

"I think my supply of surprise might be spent."

"I'm pleased to know that you like them."

"I do," I said. "Particularly the hand."

He sighed as if he'd just tasted something good.

"But they don't quite hew to the local aesthetic."

"How so?"

"They're a bit sad, no?"

"Perhaps you see them that way because you are yourself a melancholy boy."

"Maybe. When did you make those sculptures?"

"Years ago."

"Do you still sculpt?"

"No."

"Why did you stop?"

"Why did you stop writing?"

"The ugliest reasons of all."

"Which are they?"

"Cowardice and money."

"A person has to live."

"I *was* living."

"Just not well enough?"

"It was a lot of money."

"I understand," he said, and in this I did not doubt him.

For a long moment we sat together, sipping our champagne, not speaking. The alcohol and the vista and the evening air were all making me too calm. For a while, nothing happened and then, far down below, moving from The Barn I could see a black procession.

"What's happening there?"

"Saber is giving a concert this evening in The Spiral."

It was another nice, carefully composed image: all those people twisting toward the center and its six-fingered hand.

"So, things are returning to normal? Will they be fed tonight?"

"From time to time, I find that it is necessary to remind our artists of what we give them."

"For example, when they don't display their loyalty?"

"I won't apologize for expecting loyalty."

"Will you apologize for being cruel?"

"Cruel? How have I been *cruel,* exactly? I do nothing but give to them."

"Do you think Heaven wanted to participate in your ritual the other night?"

"She had every opportunity to leave. She chose to stay."

"The way Sunny's mother chose to sell you her land?"

"That is precisely right, Mr. Fields."

"As simple as that?"

"Yes. As you have seen, more than once, our guests are free to come and go as they please."

"And the way you speak to Siddhartha? To Crystalline? Cutting her painting? Expelling Theo? You don't see any of this as cruelty?"

"Mr. Fields, at a certain point, people must always suffer for their beliefs."

I laughed.

"You laugh because you don't understand what we have done here. What we are willing to do. What has been sacrificed in the name of change. This is a benevolent dictatorship. The rules are complete, but the doors are always open."

"Do you ever get bored of yourself, Mr. Light?"

"Oh," he said, as if entirely surprised by the idea. "Never. Never once in my entire life."

I nodded. "That's remarkable. I don't think I've ever known anyone who could say that."

"How sad."

I changed tack. "Plume tells me that your time in New York didn't go well."

This didn't please him. "Plume is not always her best self."

"What is your relationship to Plume?"

"She is many things to me."

"I see. Is she correct about your time in New York?"

"It did not go well."

"Would you tell me about it? About your time with Frankel?"

"Again, I do not understand why."

"If you want to see your face in one of the magazines or newspapers you seem to so revile, you'll need to play along."

"I think I've made my feelings about New York clear. But because you are so desperate for simple answers to complex questions, I will say this: because it is a place that pretends to celebrate art and beauty, while only celebrating money and fame."

"A little simplistic."

"If you say so."

"New York is many things, no? Eight million people, eight hundred languages. The world you describe is a splinter of it."

"And yet it's a splinter with so much power."

"When did you change your name?"

"Who told you I changed my name?"

"Do you intend to answer any of my questions?"

"Your questions are reductive."

"Do you still paint?

"I do."

"Would you allow me to see your work?"

He smiled at the horizon. "Oh, yes, of course."

"When?"

"Soon, soon. Though you have already seen so much of it."

He was so dull. I had to fight to keep going. I didn't know why, but it seemed to me then as if by stopping, by giving up, I would forfeit; I would fail; I would lose something vital of myself.

"Where do you keep your paintings?"

"There," he said, pointing to the chain of studios. "The first along The Ridge. The first we built. Hundreds of canvases. A lifetime of work."

Now at the horizon there was only a fading stain of red, otherwise, the sky was becoming its old incandescent blue and in it a few bright stars appeared.

Sebastian Light stood up, pointed above us to the west and said, "Venus." Then he went inside for a moment and returned carrying a folded blanket whose color I couldn't see. He shook it open and spread it around my shoulders.

"You seem cold, Sol."

I hadn't been, but the warmth and weight of it was soothing, and his gentle gesture felt better than it should have. I was afraid to speak and so I didn't thank him.

He took his seat again, and said, "I understand, Sol, that your grandmother killed herself."

He had surprised me, and he knew it. Such a simple sentence, each word meaning only what it did. Incontrovertible, unyielding, solid. I kept my mouth shut. Whatever his intentions, I was grateful to him for saying it. Even if now I was certain about Siddhartha, it didn't feel a betrayal, really. More, it was like the shock of house lights coming up at the end of a sad play. And maybe this revelation meant Sebastian Light was a genius. Or a lunatic.

Or maybe it only meant that his artists must sell out their lovers in exchange for patronage.

"Yes," I said, "she did kill herself."

He didn't offer his condolences. He didn't say anything. I knew he'd meant it as an attack, but I was thankful for the kindness of sparing me another empty assembly of words. For the wine and the blanket. The perfumed air and this view over his darkening world.

I was supremely comfortable then, my body dense and heavy. I had slunk so low in my chair that now everything I saw before me was framed in a vertical rectangle formed by two balusters and two rails. The faint burn of the horizon line was at the top. There to the bottom right, the barn in its yellow light, and toward the center, his narrow archipelago of studios where Eva's painting rested on its easel and where, supposedly, somewhere was stored his lifetime's trove of canvases.

A royal palm bent beyond the frame to the left while ribbons of footlights twisted and rolled in all directions. He shifted slightly in his chair. I glanced up at his fine jaw, which he engaged as if to speak but mercifully did not.

I saw Lina Klein looking down at me from her Orchard Street bedroom window, teetering a glass of red wine in her right hand, laughing, threatening to pour it on me as I stood squinting at her from the sidewalk. I thought of my mother on her knees scrubbing the bathtub, her exhausted eyes, and all at once, my adrenaline began to run. I felt a fast rise of anger and then something vibrant and close to the skin. An old sensation I hadn't felt since my first years in New York.

I said, "My grandmother was like you in some ways."

"How so?"

"She was a terrible mother in service of an absurd ideal, but without talent she really had very little to show for it in the end. She was damaged and selfish, and her daughter suffered for it."

"Are you trying to insult me?"

"No," I said.

"Then what?"

"I came up here with every intention of giving you a chance. But what I realize now, Mr. Light, is that I cannot do more for you than what Eva has already done."

"And what has she done?"

"Made you a person."

"That painting? She made me a monster."

"Not at all. She was very gentle."

He stared off into the darkness for a long time.

"And so what does that mean?

"That I'm not going to write about you."

"Of course you are," he said.

I shook my head.

"Why did you come up here then?"

"I thought I could do it. I was wrong."

His voice turned dry and meager again. "Do you not see that what we have made here is rare? Don't you see that what we are doing is *good*? That it is *art*?"

"No," I said. "I don't see it as either."

"You have to."

"I don't."

"Listen to me, Sol, write something. I don't care what it is but write something."

Bit by bit, he seemed to be abandoning his controlled, domineering self for something more like the wild-eyed man backing out of The Barn. I watched now as he ramped up and, for the last time, I tried to work out if any of it was earnest.

"I mean it, Sol. Make me out to be a lunatic, an autocratic madman, a monster. Put my head on a platter like your little friend did. I don't *care*. But you have to write about me. We've come too far. You have no choice."

It was a slip of the pronoun. At last he'd said what he meant.

"I'm sorry," I said. "It isn't a matter of choice. I just don't think I have the skill."

"The *skill*?"

"I don't know how to do it. I don't know how to write about you without being cruel. Without making you a fool. I'm sorry."

"*Be* cruel, then."

"Listen, Mr. Light," I said, "if you tell me right now that all of those terrible paintings, your ridiculous lectures and slogans, the cliches, the cant, the aphorisms, the jargon, the self-righteous nonsense, *all* of it is performance, an elaborate installation, then I will write about you, but otherwise, I can only paint you an idiot and I won't to do that. I'm sorry, I wish I had the kind of talent Eva does, but I just don't."

For what seemed like a very long time, he didn't make a sound, and I watched him, waiting, hoping for some grand revelation. Was I right? Was he no more than a sad, wealthy, wounded, woefully sincere old man who had nothing left to offer?

"But," I said. "I'm very grateful for your hospitality."

"I see." He said the words softly. "And that's your final decision?"

"It is."

Then after a long moment, he asked me very quietly, "Do you know *Death of the Doll House*?"

"What is that?"

"I thought you'd be smarter, Sol."

"You and me both."

"Heather Benning. Canadian. She replaced the side of an abandoned farmhouse with plexiglass, made the whole thing just so, all the rooms exposed to the public."

"I don't know her work," I said.

Very delicately then he placed his glass on the table and closed his eyes and kept them shut for a good five seconds. When he opened them, he said, "Eventually the foundations began to fail, the structure was unsound. So, she burned it to the ground."

Then he took a deep breath, exhaled with an unnerving little moan and raised his right hand. I flinched. I thought he would hit me. But he didn't. He kept it raised at forty-five degrees between the horizon and Venus before finally letting it fall gently to his knee.

Nearly a minute passed without action.

And then, through the frame, as if on canvas, or television, I saw a flame.

There, at the bottom right corner. The whole front wall of The Barn was, in a single, violent shot, obscured by fire. I glanced sideways at him. His eyes were on the burning, lips parted as if in wonder, as if he himself were surprised.

I took the railing in my hands and pulled myself up so that I was standing, leaning forward toward the fire.

The whole structure was now nearly consumed, roaring and cracking.

"What is happening?"

He stood at my side. "You wanted it darker," he said. "You wanted chaos."

Whatever he'd used as an accelerant was working well. I could just begin to feel the heat. The wind whipped the fire to burn with greater ferocity. A massive beam collapsed and crashed and sent sparks splashing outwards. And then all at once the outline of The Barn was utterly gone. Now it was only flame.

I said, "This can't be real. You can't be serious."

Then the studios went up. At the base of each, a small burst and then another rush, the same rhythm all the way as if being played along a keyboard, until the last down the line, the one he said was his, exploded as if it had been packed with gunpowder. I gasped then as they all joined together in a single ridge of red and yellow, tearing at the sky.

I thought, He must have warned her. It has to be a trick. She would have saved the painting. At the least he would have warned them.

Light's face was bright orange. "Now you'll write it," he said gently, pleasantly, as if making small talk in church.

"Have you burned her painting?"

He laughed and, nearly in the same instant, The Library exploded.

In that surge of flame, I could see figures come racing from The Spiral. They all appeared as silhouettes. The firelight cast their shadows across the lawn. They were moving so frantically and so constantly it seemed there were hundreds of them flashing and cutting here and there until they began to pool and gather in the jacaranda's stretching shade.

Against the flames, the sky appeared to be pure black, unadulterated by stars or satellites, planes or planets. Sebastian Light gripped the back of my neck and dug his fingers into my flesh. He pressed his mouth to my ear and said, "You have no choice now. You have to write it."

I said, "Have you lost your fucking mind? What have you done?"

I saw one of the black figures separate from the group and streak toward the house.

I couldn't get myself to break free of him. He wouldn't let go of me. The wind shifted and now smoke was everywhere, its smell oppressive, suffocating. My eyes were burning. I was having trouble breathing.

He pressed his hard forehead against my skull and moved his lips against my ear. "Answer me," he whispered. "What will you write?"

I kept trying to blink away the stinging smoke and ignore his mouth. I wanted to see it to the end, but the smoke was making it more and more difficult. I thought I could hear people yelling down below, but it seemed impossible given how loud the collapsing buildings were. It looked exactly like every fire I'd ever watched on television.

He said, "You have no choice now. You have no choice."

I tightened my grip on the railing. I couldn't speak.

And then Plume was there at our backs, screaming, "What the fuck have you done? What the fuck have you done?"

I tried to turn to see her face, but he was powerful and unrelenting. He had me in a strange vise, using his height and his head and his arm and his thick fingers to keep me facing forward. I wanted to see if she was part of it still, if there was some logic here, some last theatrics, but I could only get a brief glimpse of her pounding on him, her fists like little plastic hammers, her eyes wild and furious. He paid no attention to her. He had managed to return my head to his burning garden. His fingers dug in deeper and all the while he was speaking in his madman's whisper: "Keep looking, Sol, just keep looking. This is what you wanted. Now you have no choice. You have to write it."

Plume was sobbing on the floor now, but he didn't seem to notice her.

I said, "Did you burn her painting?"

He refused to answer me, but it was obvious that it was gone and when I fully understood this, I gave up talking altogether and watched as the jacaranda dissolved into the stinking, yellow-tinged gray. Then the sky became indistinguishable from the ground and soon all I could see was a massive bank of golden smoke.

33

In my first winter in the city, I went to The Met to see Alice Neel's *Elenka*. Lina Klein said, "Look until you are woozy. Stand there until you can see *me*. She is how I would like to be. Will you remember me that way, Solomon?" I did as she asked. I looked until they coalesced, until Elenka's long, regal nose became Lina Klein's, until the fight in her eyes became my grandmother's, until I was lightheaded and had to get outside. And then a strange thing happened on the train home: my eyes were closed, and I was looking at that image of a face which flamed with intelligence and daring, left hand raised, fingers curling, caught between affectation and fist, surrender and war. Then someone sat next to me, and I stopped looking at Elenka to see a woman at my side. They were about the same age and she, too, had vibrant, disturbing eyes. The stranger took my hand away from my neck and replaced it with hers. She said, "It's all right. I'm harmless. Let me do it. Close your eyes again."

It wasn't in my nature to give in so easily, but often then New York refused me my nature, and so all the way from 86th Street to Union Square she massaged my neck. When she stopped, I turned to her and she said, "You'll be fine." Then she gathered her things and stepped through the doors.

I touched my pockets. I still had my wallet. She hadn't tried to fuck me or take anything from me or sell me anything or turn me to Scientology. I would never know what she wanted.

I came home and stood before my grandmother's tall living

room window with a slice of pizza in my hand looking down through the orange light of Orchard Street and swore oaths of devotion. I was brightly alive, grateful to the museum and to the painting. I loved New York and the inexplicable woman and the trains full of lunatics and depressives, strivers and frauds, amateurs and prodigies, painters, musicians, poets, filmmakers, murderers, fascists, sadists, lovers, geniuses and fools.

That was in 2004, in a time of rare confluences of youth and happiness, when the pleasure and relief I felt from the company of a painting, or the presence of a stranger, was enough to keep me burning, before I began to wonder whether I was a person at all.

After Sebastian Light torched his garden, after he threw me out of his plantation house and locked the doors, after the cops and the fire department came and went, after I kicked through the ashes of Eva's studio, after I found her sitting on the knoll, sanguine, homeless, face slashed with ash, after we walked together to the highway, after we hitched a ride and shared the bed of a red Toyota Tacoma with an Australian Shepherd named Hercules, after she gave me her phone number and I gave her money for a plane ticket home to Tucson, I flew to Los Angeles to sit with my mother again at our sparkling swap meet table.

The first thing she said was, "You smell like smoke," which made me laugh.

"What's so funny, Soli?"

I didn't know, but I couldn't stop and even she wasn't tough enough to stop herself and then there we were giggling together for no reason either of us could have explained.

Eventually we got it together and were able to catch our breaths and wipe our eyes and drink our coffee.

"You seem better," I said.

"I was fine to begin with," she said, but without the stupid, stubborn rage of her earlier iterations. She said it with a little knowing, a little self-deprecation and I felt such a rush of love that I had to get up and go look out the window.

"What are you doing back here?"

I turned around to look at her face.

"I've come to revive your furies."

"What the fuck does that mean?"

I shrugged and returned to the table. "I don't know. It's just a phrase. Something I wrote while I was away."

"About me?"

"Yes."

"I don't need *reviving*, Solomon."

"Good."

"Where have you been all this time anyway?"

"Fuck if I know, Mom."

"You went to an ashram, didn't you?"

"It's possible."

She smiled. "And now what?"

"New York."

"Better than an ashram."

"I hope so."

That night my mother roasted a chicken, while I cubed and fried potatoes. Later I found a dusty bottle of Manischewitz under the kitchen sink behind the Clorox and poured us two glasses before she could complain.

"Where did this come from?" I asked.

"I'm sure it was your grandmother's. Come on," she said and walked out of the kitchen. When I found her, she was sitting in the empty bathtub with the bottle between her knees, looking up at me.

And then there we were, fully dressed, facing each other in the dry, cold tub right where Lina Klein had stopped her life. We touched glasses and drank the terrible wine.

After a while, I said, "Do you forgive her?"
"I think that depends on whether *you* forgive her."
"Why?"
"If you did," she said, "it would be easier for me."
For my mother, this was a remarkably tender thing to say.
"I forgive her then."
She poured us each another glass.
"All right."
"All right what, Mom?"
"Then I forgive her, too."
I didn't believe her. I said, "You know what I was thinking about on the plane?"
"Tell me."
She was already a little drunk.
"I was ten, maybe eleven years old. I'd lost another fight the day before and I didn't want to go to school. For some reason you said, Okay."
She smiled. "Not like me."
"No. It was not like you. But you picked up the phone and called in sick for us both. We spent the whole day watching reruns of *The Twilight Zone* and eating popcorn with garlic salt and grape popsicles from Safeway, pretending to have sore throats."
"I remember," she said, reaching down to squeeze my ankle with her free hand. "The next day you went back to school and got your ass kicked again."
"Yeah."
"You turned out all right in the end though."
"God, look at us. I sure hope this isn't the end."
"One never knows," she said and closed her eyes.

I hadn't been inside the Orchard Street apartment since I'd abandoned it for Chelsea and Charity and Pale. All those years and God knows how many tenants of various durations, yet it seemed to me the same. She'd resisted all the real-estate people who'd advocated for fewer "personal effects," for newer, more fashionable furniture. She'd taken her clothes and left everything else, even the art. She told me that anyone willing to spend so much money on rent would be too stupid to notice what might be stolen. This never struck me as sound reasoning, but she'd gambled and as far as I could tell, it was all still there, even the small Epstein dove on the mantle, even the Frankel Christ on the dresser. The green velvet couch in the living room looked no worse for wear. The two mediocre Lina Klein portraits were still above the bed and, in the hall bathroom, above the toilet, was the framed photograph from the *Times* of Frankel with his big arm around my shoulders. One of these days, I'd have to go back to Hester Street and face him, but it was something I still didn't have the courage for.

After I let some air in and filled the fridge and unpacked, it was all so much the same that in those first months home I often forgot that Lina Klein was no longer alive. Often I would come home from an opening or a party or a play and reach into my pocket to call her in California, to tell her that I'd returned to advocate for this city as she loved it, as I believed it to be when I was young, as somewhere it must still exist, for its wild corners, its dead-end alleys, its tunnels, its windowless basements, its abandoned water towers, places untouched by the world of Pale, where nothing is for money.

Just as I did thirteen years ago, I began with bits and pieces. Five hundred words here, a thousand there. Mostly no one had heard of me, but everyone was desperate for *content.* After seven months, I went to see the asshole editor.

"No one's ever heard of Eva Solomon," he said. "You have to give me more than a talented painter."

"It's not merely talent. It's something else," I said.

"You need more."

I held out for nearly a month, but finally I broke and went back and sold him the whole story: Sebastian Light, The Coded Garden, The Biennale, the box cutter, the fire, the lost painting.

"But she's central," I said. "She has to be the point."

"Write it and we'll see what the point is."

I went to see Charity at her apartment. Everything appeared utterly the same—the television on the wall, the grey Italian couch, upon which she sat very straight with her legs crossed, the view over the galleries divided into a perfect grid by her polished factory windows.

I said, "I'm sorry for having disappeared like that. There's no good excuse for it. No matter what happened. I really am sorry."

She looked at me as if we'd only just met.

"You've always been a bit of a coward, Sol."

I nodded.

"Still," she said, "I am sorry about your grandmother."

"Thank you. The apartment looks good."

"You never liked living here."

I didn't want to lie to anyone ever again.

She shook her head. "Did you find your life of purity?"

I smiled, but her expression remained impassive.

"It was cruel to leave the way I did."

"Yes" she said and stood up. "There's a box of your stuff in the closet. Your peacoat is on the hook."

I followed her to the entryway and once she had handed me my things and I was standing in the hall, she said, "You know you're no different than anyone else, right?"

"Yes."

"You don't," she said, and closed the door.

When I had the asshole editor's guarantee, I called Eva in Tucson.

"Are you still an artist, Eva Solomon?"

"I'm still painting if that's what you mean."

"Good. I'm going to write about you."

"Come on. Why?"

"Because you're great."

"What if you're the only one who thinks so?"

"Then you're very lucky. I've got ten thousand words to make you famous."

"I don't want to be famous." She sounded giddy.

"Then hang up and stay in the desert."

"Otherwise?"

"Otherwise, meet me in Nantes in ten days."

"Are you serious?"

"Yes."

"What are we doing there?"

"We're going to go and look at Benner together."

"You know I can't afford that, Solomon Solomon."

"I'll take care of it," I said. "Will you come?"

"Of course, I'll come."

In all my memories of New York City, I am separated from its people. Even in those magnificent moments of the early years, in recollections glossed by the distance of time, even if there were others present, no matter the glamour, the romance of novelty and prospect, still, all of it is unshared. I am always removed. But I swear that I will no longer stand at the edge of things, half-committed, peering in on lit rooms, a frightened child spying from the dark.

There are artists here with so much less than I have, artists who refuse to bend, who would rather starve than give in to the algorithms. I have a small fortress. I have some gold. I could help build hospitals. I could feed the hungry. I could return west to look after my mother. I could join Hamas or the IDF. But I won't do any of those things. Instead, I choose to fight for Lina Klein's legacy, for a world of lawless art and illogical passions. Instead, I have come home to this minuscule island to fight our futile war.

"Find a beautiful ship, bind yourself to it, sail and sail and sail and when the time comes, Solomon, bail water until you drown."

Hers was often terrible advice, but I have liked to follow it anyway.

Acknowledgements

This novel, in general, owes much to the writing of John Berger. More specifically, his portrait of Ernst Neizvestny, *Art and Revolution* informed the creation of Ernst Frankel.

Plume's quip on page 86, "Every passion borders on the chaotic," is taken from Walter Benjamin's "Unpacking My Library: A Speech on Collecting" (trans. Harry Zohn). The line in full reads: "Every passion borders on the chaotic, but the collector's passion borders on the chaos of memories."

I am grateful to the John Simon Guggenheim Memorial Foundation, whose support of my work, extraordinary in both its surprise and generosity, was instrumental in allowing me to write *The Long Corner.*

Many thanks also to The Corporation of Yaddo, Colombe Schneck, Antoine Flochel and the Can Cab Literary Residence, Joe Blair, Deb Blair, Michael Reynolds, Eric Simonoff, Scott Sayare, Leslie Maksik and Jon Maksik.

Without Madhuri Vijay's extraordinary intelligence, passion and vision, this book would be significantly worse than it is. Or, like so many other things, simply would not be at all.